Sinful

Secrets

A novel
by
M'Hogany

Dedication

October 6, 2013 was such a drastic change in my life. On that Sunday afternoon, my namesake, twin, and grandmother was called home to Glory. As my heart remains shattered in millions of pieces, I reflect on the final words she spoke to me *"I'm Proud Of The Woman You've Become"* and I thank GOD for allowing me not just 28 years with her, but 7 months, day in and day out of just quality time with her. Pouring back into her what she poured into me when I felt like I was defeated. This literal journey is dedicated to the memory of a phenomenal woman that will be deeply missed by many. Minister of Music,
First Lady Mary Ann Beal-Kelly

I Am Her, She Is Me, We Are One
M'Hogany

Acknowledgments

First and foremost I want to give reverence to my father in heaven that sees fit for me to yet experience another day, despite my shortcomings, I thank you. You are God and God alone and I'm humbled just to be called your child. To my parents, thank you for being involuntarily transparent with my siblings and I and letting us see the real you as we discovered the real us. My sister, thank you for learning how to get along with me (lol). Thank you for challenging, pushing, and questioning my personality as a child. You get on my nerves sometimes (as I do yours) but I wouldn't have it any other way. Lici, wait, I wasn't listening. (Inside joke) thanks for the work you have done and will do. EXECUTIVE ASSISTANT! My Brother, Boy, thank you for being that ear for me when I am fearful of not having anyone to talk to. You and shon grew WITH me and not just claimed me. My babies, Nyra-Doo (my pretty girl), D-Jr, Pooh-Pooh, Katelynn (mini-me), Mari (my tinky), and Deythan (my stinka man) words can't express how much I love you little people. From the day each and every one of you were born, I felt as if life got more interesting and I made it m business to be the best auntie your little minds could create. My other set of special babies, Jacquanda, Jainah, Bear, Lisi, Romelle, Jesselyn, and Amber. Some of you refer to me as th favorite cousin. We may not be as close in age as most cousins, but know I hear you. I listen to you. I relate to you. I will never stop you from being you and experiencing life for yourself...................within reason. I may be big cousin and the fun one, but I WILL DIG IN DAT A$$ IF NEED BE! Luv Ya! To my aunts and uncles remaining and the memories of the ones that have passed, thank you for being the examples of adults that aren't afraid to go through something and OWN IT. Special shout out to Uncle Eddie, MY Photographer. I'm ready when you ready! My Houston family, glad to say I have two homes. I love you guys sooooooooooooo much, I'd come down there on a regular! But see, the way gas prices are setup...

  My support system outside the bloodline, Greg. My Ace Boon! We're the only two people I know that can go to the fair broke with only $20 to our name and still walk out with arms full of stuff! Also, everything is so much fun with you around, even ranking on random people in Walmart. You'll turn a sad situation into a gut holding oops I just pissed myself moment. I'm sure we'll hit up D&B many more times! You gotta win me some more stuff lol. P-Wee, my boy, what can I say. You've been there for a lot and you've done the best thing possible...you never gave up on me nor judged me. Thank you! My other husband ;-) (I'll give em back Baba!). Charles, aka Chah-less. We've always been close since high school and I've never bit my tongue with you. You've really come through for me during this process, even though you don't think you have. The many MANY times I wanted to quit, you "talked me down off the ledge" per say. You listened. You gave me your undivided attention. Thank you. Sam, Samsung, the little sister I never wanted but got stuck with. Thank you. In spite of the situations you don't like, thank you for allowing me to experience them. Thank you for being that shoe that freely kicks my ass too. You can do that cause you're my Sam. Mrs. Thomas (she knows who she is lol) from our long nights as teens up playing games on king.com until 4 in the morning to our spats and you being more hurt than me when I was the one in the situation. If that isn't a best-friend then hell, I don't know what is. (Even though you have a million and one of them lol)

    My FB all-stars. Ebony Smith and Nisha Lanae. We've become such close friends over such a short amount of time. Ebony, you were the first to send flowers to my grandparents' house upon hearing of my grandmother's passing. You moved me to tears hunny and for that, I'm more than grateful. Nisha, I know I get on your nerves with my banter and second-guessing, but you entertain me nonetheless. My boo Dyphia Blount, HEY DYE BOO! The first to support me financially with my gofundme campaign. To have Ms. Dyphia Blount look at me as *competition* oh hunny you KNOW I was on some cloud number! Thank you pud for the always encouraging support. My sisters Dani in the Chi and Steph in Cali! Over 10 years and we still haven't been in each other's presence but you still love me as if we lived around the corner from each other. Love you ladies. Everybody's main man, Treasure Blue! Ok, so we're not pahtnas that chop it up on the phone every day, but your openness and will to help the new authors such as myself is just overwhelming and heavily appreciated. Rocky Rose, thank you mama for the opportunity to pick your brain. Bringing things to my attention that you experienced as a new author good and bad. Not to mention not telling me to go to hell when things got personal. Ms. Sabrina Eubanks, such a vet in the game. Thank you for keeping your doors open for me to come and not just talk about lit, but about life! Tracie Holmes, thank you for the opportunity to be a contributor to the Literary

Lounge Magazine and for letting me bug you. You were one of the firsts to support me and give kind words.

To those that comment, request, inquire, and support from afar on this journey thank you for taking a chance on my complex mind and me. We apprcciate you lol.

To *punkin*. There hasn't been a word created to express my feelings. I would be doing you as a person an injustice, so I won't make the attempt. I don't regret anything, but know what I say it true, sincere, and real. *Olive Juice*

To those that purchased this book, thank you. To those that liked my fb page, thank you. My editor, Joy Thank You! Everyone that I worked with on this, THANK YOU! To those that talked about me as a child and STILL talk about me as an adult because of my *CHOCOLATE SKIN*............THANK YOU! I hope you enjoy the read and open your mind to the characters livelihood. If I missed anyone, please charge it to my head and not my heart! Or better yet (Insert Name Here)

Some may sound familiar, and some will make you wonder. Everyone has a Sinful Secret, only time will tell when it gets revealed...................
Ways to contact me:
www.facebook.com/mhogany
www.twitter.com/author_mbeal
Instagram: @songbyrd8403

Sinful Secrets   *M'Hogany*

Chapter 1
Symone

"Symone Renae Johnson," the announcer read as I walked across the stage to receive my MBA in psychology. A rush of liberation and accomplishment consumed me. The smile I wore attested to that. I was on a natural high. The excruciatingly high price of student loans I'd accrued over the years couldn't ruin the moment.

"I'm so proud of you baby-girl," my father said embracing me with a hug.

"Thanks Daddy," I beamed. Nothing was gonna bring me down, at least not that day.

"Now that you're done with school, you have time to focus on landing that husband and producing us some grandbabies," my mother interjected.

Welp, that did it. "Mama, can you lay off for just one day please I mean ONE DAY!" I pleaded. It was the same ole song with her and I wasn't going to entertain it on MY DAY.

Throwing up her hands in surrender she said, "Ok ok..."

6 Months Later

I'd opened up my own practice in Dallas, TX and I was super excited. The clientele that I'd established while away at UT Austin has had no problem migrating towards my newly rooted home.

Knock Knock

"Hey hey busy lady!" a male voice crept in my office.

"Ray!" I excitedly yelled nearly knocking the plaques off the wall that I had just hung. "How have you been?" I asked while we shared a friendly embrace.

"You know me, just making it do what it do!" Raymond had never been good at talking in slang and keeping a straight face so something had to be going on.

"Ray, hun, what's going on? And don't lie to me either, cause we both know that you suck at it," I demanded while closing my office door.

"Damn Symone, how do you do that every time?"

"Don't deflect Ray, sit, spill, now go," I instructed while I returned to place my accreditation on the walls.

"Well, you know I just had a daughter…"

"Yesss! Oh my she's gorgeous Ray."

"Thanks, but…" he started.

"But what?"

"I got laid off from my job 2 weeks ago, and she's getting bigger and bigger by the day."

"Oh hun I'm sorry to hear that," I stopped to console my friend.

Sitting on the desk facing the strong man breaking from the seam, he took his hands away from his face and started to panic. "I mean I have a mortgage, bills, diapers, 4 other kids, student loans..." As he kept going, he became more jittery.

"Ray...Ray...RAY!" I flagged. "Pause! Flag on the play! First, breathe! Bring it back hun."

"Symone, I need a job badly. You know I can't go

without work for too long. I'm not built for this," he stated with a look of desperation plastered on his face.

"Ok, let's see what we can do," I stated while going to my desk and logging into my system to figure something out and see what I could do for him. "What was your last job?" I asked without taking my eyes off the monitor.

"Construction."

"Construction?"

"Hey I know, but it paid the bills Symone."

"No no, didn't we BOTH go to school as psych majors?"

"Yeah we did, so what."

"And you DID finish right?"

"Yeah I did, but I don't see what that has to..."

I logged off my system and headed back to my accolades.

"What are you doing, why did you stop?" he asked in a frenzy.

"Calm down. You, Dr. Watkins will now be working here. So case closed."

"Seriously Symone, don't play with me like that."

"Who's playing Ray? You are a qualified therapist with the degree to prove it, yet you've been working in construction. Look, don't argue with me on this. Just take it."

"Symone I..."

"There's an office across the hall that's empty and you can setup there. I have clients that I haven't been able to get to because well, what do you specialize in again?"

"Children and family therapy."

"That's even better. I have couples with children

and teens, but since you specialize in that, I'll send them your way. That way you'll build your clientele."

"Seriously Symone, I swear I could kiss you right now!"

"Uh since we're colleagues now, um that sexual harassment clause does come into play sir! So back back, gimme 50 feet..." I said following with a slight dance.

"You know what, I'll roast you and that old ass song later," he said with a laugh as he turned to go across the hall to the vacant office.

"Good cause we've got work to do and people to help!" I shouted.

Chapter 2
Home Sweet Home
Symone

"Symone, can you come down here please," my dad beckoned from downstairs.

"Here I come Daddy," I said while putting on my pea coat and grabbing my hairbrush, I head downstairs to see both of my awaiting parents. "Daddy you called me? What's going on is everything ok?" I asked slightly out of breath from the stairs.

"Were you going somewhere?" my father asked.

"Meeting up with Ra'Chelle and Raymond for a little bit."

"here," my mother said while placing a plate of sausage, grits, biscuits, scrambled eggs with melted cheese and a glass of apple juice. Before I dug into my favorites, I sat down and looked at both of my parents.

"What's going on?"

"Nothing baby-girl, just have breakfast," my father insisted picking up a sausage convincing me to indulge in the breakfast my mother prepared. As I sat down and began to satisfy the inner hunger demon, I failed to notice my parents quietly nudging each other as if they were confused as to who was going to go first.

"Um, Symone, baby girl..."

"Yes Daddy?" I asked placing sugar in my grits.

"Well, um, your mother and I have uh something to

talk to you about," he struggled to get out. "We... um...our concern is...well you see..." he staggered. You'd think a well-known pastor who speaks in front of thousands on a regular could format his words for his daughter better.

"What your father is TRYING to say is we're a little worried about you hunny," my mother interjected past my father.

"Lord, here we go with this again," I mumbled before I took a sip of apple juice.

"Sweetie, are you dating anyone?" she just bluntly asked.

"What in the world?" I managed to get out while choking on the juice. "Ma, where is this coming from? Is this..."

"Symone, your mother, and I are concerned about your future baby girl. We know you are a hard working woman but we're concerned that you spend more time on others relationships and none on starting your own. Your sisters are married with children and..."

"DADDY! Has she gotten to you too? I'd expect this from Mama, but not you," I yelped while grabbing my purse and keys and storming out.

As I got into my car, cranked up and put it in gear, I sped from my parents residence. "I can't believe they ambushed me like that," I mumbled gripping the steering wheel. My stomach was doing knots at my parents trying to damn near marry me off to be like my sisters.

My oldest sister, Briel, is married with three children and is an elementary school teacher. My younger sister, Madison, is also married with two children and expecting her third in 4 months. With five going on six grandchildren, you'd think my parents would be satisfied with being grandparents.

Chapter 3
Corner Bistro
Symone

"You're late," Ra'Chelle said looking at her watch.

"I'm sorry I'm sorry," I apologized while twirling my hair into a bun.

"For nearly 12 years, I've seen you running more to gatherings or meetings," she spewed.

"I'm surprised you didn't run track," Ray added while stuffing half a stack of pancakes into his mouth.

"I got cornered by my parents," I briefly touched on while giving the menu a once over.

"Same ole speech?" Ra'Chelle asked before drinking her mimosa.

"Oh my goodness yes. And this time she recruited my daddy in it."

"Not the pastor! You're daddy's girl though."

"It had to be my mom's idea because Daddy was stumbling all over his words left and right."

"Your dad never stumbles, so he HAD to be nervous," Ray added with his mouth full.

"Do you HAVE home training? Never mind, I forgot bats hang where they shit."

"You know what you," he started but was cut short by the waiter.

"Are you ready to order ma'am?"

Thank GOD, he came when he did. I can't take

these two right now!

"Yes, three buttermilk pancakes, ham, grits, apple juice, and a large side of fruit please."

"Yes ma'am. I'll return with your apple juice shortly," he smiled as he took my menu and left the table.

"Well damn, hungry much?" Ra'Chelle commented.

"Girl I couldn't eat breakfast this morning following that damn conversation."

"What was the topic today?" Ray asked still stuffing his face.

"The age ole *Symone we just want you to be happy and you're not getting any younger to have children* story. How I'm soooooo engulfed in my work I should be looking to settle down and pop out little crumb snatchers yada yada yada."

"You know what, I kinda agree with your parents on this one. When was the last time you actually went on a date Symone? I mean I know helping people view life in various ways is exciting, although I will never understand how, but boo you gotta look out for you."

"Chelle, I know I just don't have the time, patience, and energy to waste on teaching a man what I feel he should know," I proclaimed as I started to dig into the food the waiter brought during Chelle's mini speech.

"As much as I hate to say it, I'm gonna have to agree with the walrus over here," Ray stated. "What do you do in your spare time? Nearly every time I see or talk to you, you're either working on a client's file or headlining a seminar, workshop, hell SOMETHING!"

"Not you two! I already have enough going on from my parents; I don't need the added inputs from my best friends."

"I mean, what about music? Have you just COMPLETELY given up on that?"

"We're not talking about that."

"Why not? The sea lion has a point," Ray jabbed again. "Singing puts you in another world. Anyone that knows you can see that. What's keeping you from doing that in your downtime?"

"You guys know damn well my father would nearly have a stroke if he heard me singing anything other than gospel!" I replied while occupying myself with my calendar on my phone. My receptionist messaged me that my noon appointment canceled.

Snatching my phone out of my grasp Chelle said, "Dammit Symone! It's not about your parents or what they want you to do, but it's about what makes YOU happy! Hell they should be humbly blessed to have a damn daughter that can blow!"

"And you know she's a pro at blowin'," Ray retorted.

"You know what I'm bout sick and tired of your shit you walking disease!" she started in on him then returned her attention towards me. "Tonight I'm meeting with my A&R exec to speak on some business. I'll pick you up around 6."

"I normally don't do this, and I know I'll regret this...Ugh, I think I'm about to throw up in my mouth a little, but...Chelle might be onto something. Maybe whatever she has to discuss can spark something in you with the exec. Don't worry about your parents," he said.

"Don't have a choice now do I?"

"HELL NO! So either you can make it easy on yourself, or…"

"Ok ok ok, I'll meet you there. Just send me the address."

"Oh no you don't miss lady, knowing you you'll get caught up in something that'll have you missing the meeting. I'm picking you up."

"No, seriously, I'll meet you there."

"Give me one good reason why you don't want her to pick you up Symone?"

"Well if you MUST know I have a meeting to get to before I head back to my parents' house."

"About that, YOU NEED YO' OWN SHIT GIRL!"

"Well damn Chelle, I don't think the people in the damn UKRAINE heard you!"

"I'm saying, you've been back home way too long to still be living at mom and dad's house."

"That's what the meeting is for. I am meeting with my realtor and I close on my house tomorrow."

"**TOMORROW?**" they both yelled in unison.

I hung my head in shear embarrassment. How did I manage to have such ghetto ass friends? "Yes tomorrow."

"When the hell were you gonna tell us heffa?" Chelle barked.

"Hell, **AFTER** I closed!" I mocked.

"Look at you then, I guess you are actually doing something productive."

Looking at the time on my phone, I see I need to leave in order to make it to the closing in time "I'll text you when I'm in route Chelle."

"Mmmmmhhhmm, you better!"

Chapter 4
Room for One
Symone

"Alright Ms. Johnson, the seller has agreed to all of your requests and if you will you can sign here, here, and here. And now, here are your keys to your new home. You've made a great choice in this new development area. I wish you nothing but the very best," my realtor said and smiled.

"Thank you so much, this is long overdue!" I smiled as I took the keys to my new home.

"Is there a Mr. Johnson that will enjoy this lovely space with you?"

I don't know whether he was flirting or just being nosy, but I laughed it off and responded, "When he comes, I'll let you know," and we both shared in a light laugh.

"Take good care, hopefully I'll see you around," he reiterated while slowly shaking my hand. Ok. Yeah. He was indeed flirting. He was cute, but I wasn't ready to get back into a situation.

I'm headed to the place now, where are you? You better not be late... is what the text said following the address to the location. Shockingly I was only a few minutes away so it didn't take me long to get there.

"It's about time you got here!" Chelle exclaimed when I arrived.

"My realtor's office was just 10 minutes around the

corner, calm down."

"Well, I'm glad you made it and didn't give me no wack ass excuse as to..."

"As to what?"

"Never mind because I feel like I need to lay on this table and just pour out my most inner issues DR. JOHNSON," she whined.

"Chelle, don't start ok. I just left a very important meeting and…"

"Ra'Chelle?" a masculine voice bellowed up behind us.

I took a seat and answered the messages in my phone. I didn't need to really be there, so I just turned into a fly on the wall not interested in their conversation.

"Cornell, hey. I see you found it. No problems huh?" she stated while embracing the man whom I was guessing was the A&R exec.

"Not much of a problem," he replied before sitting at the table we were at.

"This is my girlfriend Symone," she said nudging me under the table and giving me the evil eye.

Without giving him a second glance, I extended my hand and said, "Hi."

"Cornell, Symone. SYMONE, Cornell," Chelle formally introduced through gritted teeth.

"Nice to meet you," he stated with a slight smile.

"Sit sit, let's get to business," she started.

"Of course you know we're looking for new talent with style and skills," he said slowly starting the conversation. "They're down my throat about finding a new artist that's not so easily animated or auto-tuned."

"Lord knows this auto-tune business is sweeping the music scene and frankly I'm tired of it," she chimed in.

"So I need someone with vocal talent that's gonna not only shock the big guys, but have that IT about them."

"I'm sorry to interrupt, I'm gonna have to take this, excuse me," I stated answering my phone and walking off. "This is Dr. Johnson..."

"Ok, I was waiting for her to get out of range, but the reason I brought you two here is because I wanted you to hear her sing," Chelle leaned in to say.

"Her?" Cornell pointed.

"Trust me, when she's in her musical element, the girl is FIRE. Look, I know this isn't a formal audition or anything so before you say no just listen to her sing."

Looking skeptical, he said, "I can't promise anything Ra'Chelle. This is my job on the line here so I only have time for seriously dedicated artists."

Returning to the table I said, "I'm sorry, Chelle I have to go in to the office, and handle some issues that came up. Cornell is it? Nice to meet you," I said before kissing Chelle on the cheek. "I'll call you later."

"Sure you will," she said rolling her eyes.

Walking to get into my car, I called my receptionist. "Ashleigh, I'm headed there now."

Chapter 5
Cornell

I approached the venue where Ra'Chelle had me meet her. "Ra'Chelle?"

"Cornell, hey glad you made it. This is my friend Symone, Symone this is Cornell."

"Hi nice to meet you," I said extending my hand.

"Hi," she dryly responded.

What the hell? This chick didn't even look up from her phone to speak properly. Where did Ra'Chelle find this snobby broad, I thought as I sat down.

"So getting straight to business because I know you are a man of valuable time, what is the status with the heads of the label?"

"I'm being hounded about finding talent that will launch the label more to a solid platform. Nearly everything I'm being presented is either auto-tuned or easily duplicated with lack of depth."

"That's the truth, this industry is over ran with microwave dance songs that all sound the same and they expect to shoot up within seconds and be given a fat payout."

"I'm sorry I have to take this, excuse me," the rude woman, Symone, said before she got up to take her call. Before I dismissed her rude ass, I caught a glimpse of her soft smoky hazel eyes hidden behind her Gucci glasses and her wavy hair slicked back into a neat bun. A strong chill ran from my chest to the tip of my dick causing me to shift in my seat.

"Cornell!" Chelle stated bringing me back from my gaze.

"Oh, yeah, right. Um, where was I?"

"The head honchos, their demands…"

"This industry is gasping for fresh talent to breathe life into it with substance so-"

"Sorry Chelle, I have to run to the office and take care of urgent business," Symone rudely interrupted once again. This time she made eye contact with me and she could have had me out of my draws looking at me with those eyes. "Cornell right? Nice to meet you," she said before she left.

The bulge in my pants grew more and this time I swear I started leaking pre-cum. "What the hell is with this woman," I whispered to myself as she walked out of the venue.

"What was that?" Chelle asked.

"Oh uh nothing, so not trying to be rude but…."

"Why did I have Symone here?"

"You saw it coming?"

"Symone has this voice that will captivate any human. She can sing the national anthem and make a grown man cry."

"Really, now I wish I could've heard her."

Just then, my phone vibrated. *Where are you* the text read on my phone.

In a meeting. I'll call you once I leave, I responded while getting up to depart the venue with Ra'Chelle.

"Let me get some things in order and I promise you that you won't be disappointed."

"I can't afford to be disappointed Ra'Chelle."

"Well then I guess when I call, you need to come runnin'."

"I can't promise that'll happen."

"Miss out on this once in a lifetime opportunity and you won't be promised a check either. Tootles," she smirked with a ratchet hair toss of her weave.

Shaking my head as I headed towards my car I thought about her point. I can't afford to strike out with these execs, but I was still curious as to why she was so passionate about the music business. Only time will tell.

Chapter 6
Humble Abode
Symone

"This is a be-you-tea-full house Auntie Mone," my 4-year-old niece Miyah said with a wide grin on her face.

Shocked at her attempt to talk like us 'grown folk' I tickled her saying, "Who taught you to say beautiful?"

"Stop Auntie!" she laughed curling up on the floor.

Regaining my composure and glancing around the gorgeous space, I had to actually admit that at four, she was absolutely right. It was 5,000 square feet, with five bedrooms, three bathrooms, a media room, finished basement, office, gourmet kitchen accented with black granite countertops and standalone island, two living areas, and a three-car garage. It was the fruits of my labor and I was completely blessed with the space.

Snap Snap

"Symone," my mother stated with a few snaps in my face, "hunny, we're waiting on this grand tour."

"Oh, right, sorry," I smiled.

We walked past my father and brothers-in-law who were assembling my furniture and placing everything in its assigned place.

"C'mon Auntie Mone!"

"Slow down Miyah, auntie doesn't want you to hurt yourself going up the stairs. Ma, can you make it up?"

"Chile, I carried you and your sisters and I'm still standing, a little stairs won't hurt me. And I'm still running from your father!"

"Ma, I didn't need to know that," I stated as we reached the top of the winding staircase and approached the first set of rooms. "So this room here on the left is mainly the guest room. These two rooms here," I pointed across the hall, "are the rooms for the kiddos when they come spend the night."

Miyah ran into the rooms checking for her seal of approval one after the other. Both were adorned with shelves that held blocks of the letters from the alphabets, chests with toys for both girls and the boys, little outfits for church and play clothes, and both had neutral painted walls.

"What do you think Amiyah?" my mom asked.

"I like 'em, which one is my room?"

"You have to share this with your sister and other cousins and the boys have the next room."

"Why I always gotta share with them?" she pouted.

"Because you don't have nobody's job miss lady," my mother said. "Now let's go see the rest of auntie's house."

"This room, I'm not quite sure what to do with, but I'm sure it will come to me over time."

As if I gave her free range my mom said, "Symone, this would be a great nursery. With a powder blue paint on the wall, this would be gorgeous. It's not too far from the master I'm sure, what do you think Amiyah?"

"I not a boy Nana! I'm a girl and I don't like blue in my room!" she snapped while placing her hands on her hips, more like her imagination.

"This room isn't for you chile, it's for Aunt Symone's baby."

"Uh, Nana, Auntie Mone ain't got no baby!"

"Auntie doesn't have a baby Miyah," I corrected.

"Auntie, where yo baby at?"

Laughing I mumbled, "Lord jeefus my mother has recruited my poor little niece." Then I spoke so she could hear me, "Miyah, when God says it's time, he'll bless me with a little cousin for you to play with."

"But he can't send you a baby wit no husband. You need a husband first!"

"I guess you heard that," my mother chuckled under her breath.

"Go play with the toys in the girl's room little midget!" I said before she ran out in fear I would tickle her again.

"Out of the mouth of babes Symone," my mother started.

"And this is the master suite," I deflected moving past my mother's attempts to start that conversation again. "Through this set of double doors is the master bathroom. The marble floors are temperature adjusted so on cold nights they can be heated and on hot days they can be cool. Centered and elevated garden bathtub with built in waterproof pillow. There are speakers built in to play music as well as broadcast the phone conversations throughout the house courtesy of Bose. And here is a walk around walk in closet with standalone island to hold accessories and various other things, dark mahogany shelves for shoes, little knick-knacks or whatever. I'm sure Ra'Chelle will add her touches or give ideas."

"This is really a beautiful house Symone, but…"

"But what Ma?"

"Don't you think it's too big for only you?"

"Ma…"

"Symone, your father and I are so proud of the woman you've become."

"Ma, not today okay?"

"Dammit Symone, sit down! Now I've had enough of this foolishness with you and I'm not having it. SIT DOWN!"

Sitting down and shaking my head I said, "Ma, respectfully I understand."

"No you don't get to talk until I'm done."

"Here we go…"

"What was that?" she snapped with that *don't make me knock the hell outta you* look. "Now your father has supported you, your goals, and your dreams since you were a little girl. We supported all you girls. You always seemed to sit back more than your sisters and stay to yourself. I tried and tried to get you to open up to me and you've made things difficult for me to do so since you were little."

"Ma what do you want from me? I don't understand."

"Symone I want you to be happy!"

"I am happy!"

"I know you see your sisters and their children and husbands. I want that for you…"

"Ma! I love my sisters and their spouses and I'm crazy for these kids, but I'm not in a rush to be where they are! If God intends for me to be married and blesses me with children, that's great, but if he doesn't see fit than I'm fine with that."

I was so tired of this 'talk' with my mother and

wanted it to die and never return. All I heard was *Symone when are you gonna have some babies? Symone when are you gonna start your own family? You not dating anyone Symone? You don't want to be married?* Blah blah blah...

"Don't you dare speak like that Symone!" my mother spat with fear and pain in her eyes that started to well up with tears. The thought of me possibly not having a family of my own seemed to tear my mother to shreds. Sitting on the ottoman in front of my king size constellation bed she said, "Symone, there has always been something special about you since you were born. I know every parent says that to their child, but from the moment your father held you and looked into those soft hazel eyes he said to me with tears in his eyes *Yvette, this one here is destined for greatness* and I thought he was just saying that because of the moment."

"But Ma, I have accomplished so much. I'm well known in over 12 states, my practice is thriving after relocating back home, I've moved into my first home that I custom designed, and I'm more than happy."

"Hunny it's your heart that I'm concerned about. What's all this with no one to share it with? What legacy will you leave behind?"

"Ma, if it happens it will happen. Until then, I'm not team wifey. Daddy raised his girls to be dependent on no man, or anyone for that matter."

"Symone," my mother sat next to me on the bed and stroked the strands of hair from my face, "have you every just stopped, looked, and wondered why your nieces and nephews all go crazy when you appear? Why you can soothe a baby that's in no way related to you? Why children have always flocked to you? There is a natural nurture about you that only a mother possesses. Being a mother is one marvelous goal you are meant to experience firsthand. It's been your glow from birth."

As much as I loved my mother and her concern, she was making it seem as if my freakin' uterus was lined with gold or something.

"Here you are, hey Mrs. Johnson!"

YES! Saved by Ra'Chelle! Giving my mother a hug, I mouthed "thank you" clasping my hands in prayer motion.

"Hey hunny, how are you?"

"Oh you know me Mama Yvette I'm fabulous as usual," she said grinning with her hand on her hip. "I hope I'm not interrupting you two, if I am I can come back later," she said giving me a devilish grin.

Ok that was payback from the meeting, but she would just have to pay me back another way. Sitting there talking to my mother about my love life or lack thereof was done! "No! You're not intruding, I mean, I was giving Mama a tour of the house and just catching up, but we're good." I gave her a *get me outta this shit* face.

"I get the hint, I'll leave you girls," Mama said kissing me on the cheek. "But we are not done Symone."

"Of course we aren't," I sarcastically responded as she kissed Chelle on the way out.

Before my mother could reach the door in ran my niece. "Auntie Mone, we finna go."

"We are about to go Miyah."

"Auntie…"

"Say it Miyah."

"We are about to go auntie."

I knew she was only four, but start 'em early. We all left my bedroom and convened back downstairs as everyone said their goodbyes and offered their congratulations on the house. After closing and locking the door, I headed to the living room to make sure my furniture was in place where I wanted it to be.

"Symone this is gorgeous girl! I see you doing it big boo!" Chelle chimed from in the kitchen. I plopped on the couch to just unwind. "Where are the glasses?"

"In the cabinet next to the wine storage."

"WINE STORAGE? Aww shiznit bytch!"

"Really Chelle?" Coming into the living area, she had two champagne flutes, bottle of champagne, and pitcher of orange juice; she had made us mimosas.

"So, when's the house warming?"

"I gotta get settled first Chelle."

"No house warming, sleep over, freak nick, nothing. You gotta break this place in right boo!"

"OH NO MA'AM! I've been to a Chelle party before!"

"What the hell is that supposed to mean?"

"You know damn well what that means! I damn near got pregnant after one of your damn parties!"

"Oh…"

"Yeah trick OH."

"You gotta admit though, Terry was FIONE!"

"He was though wasn't he? But hell his ass was super fertile!"

"That ain't bad!"

"Ain't bad? The negro had six kids by five different

women and I was NOT about to be baby mama number seven!"

"Tell me the D wasn't good though?"

Looking down at my mimosa I said, "Ok, I see why his ass has six baby mamas cause his head game was on point and you wouldn't be thinking about protection with his face all in it. Oh Lord, and when he swung that third leg out, you'd be lucky if you didn't pass out!"

"Well, since you won't let me throw you a house warming, at least let me take you out to dinner."

"What? You treating?"

"Shut up tramp!"

"Ok, I'll take you up on that. It would feel good to go and let my hair down for the night." Quickly placing her drink on the coffee table, she began to grab her shoes and belongings "What?" I asked confused.

"Girl I'm trying to hurry up and leave before yo ass renege on me!"

"Whatever…"

"Shyt I'm serious, you know yo ass is quick to switch like a damn chameleon."

"Where are we going ma'am?"

"Nice little jazz club. Nothing to over the top or too ratchet."

"What, you actually know places that aren't ghetto and ratchet? Call the mayor!"

"Bitch boo! Yo ass grew up across the street from me in the HOOD! Don't let them bourgeois people make you forget from where you came from!"

"Anyway, what time?"

"Eight."

"Fine, I'll be ready."

"Make sure you're ready to go OUT. It's NOT a work event!"

"Ha ha, I know how to dress outside of work!"

"Oh hunny, is that what you tell yourself...smooches," she said flicking her hair and strutting to her car.

Shaking my head and closing my door I said, "Shit, now what am I gonna wear..."

****

Chelle

Picking up my phone, I made a call.

"I had a feeling it was you Ra'Chelle."

"Remember when I told you to be ready when I called?"

"That fast?"

"Tonight...8:30...Sankofa...Be there."

"Um ok, but...."

"BE THERE. No excuses. Act now with no regrets, or regret it later. I'll send you the address. TOOTLES!"

Click

"Alright Miss Symone, you have no idea what I have in store for you, but buckle up hunny!" I said to myself.

Chapter 7
Sankofa
Symone

"This is nice Chelle. I have to hand it to you; I never thought you would've even known any places like this existed in Dallas!"

"Some things have changed since you've been off to school my friend."

"Apparently so."

"And then again, some things haven't changed SINCE we were in school I see."

"What are you talking about?"

"You did, eh, ok with the outfit, but this hair Symone. Really?"

"What's wrong with my hair?"

"Here," Chelle gave me her clutch to hold. "Hold still."

I stood there embarrassed as she removed my hair from its tightly tucked bun and it fell in waves to my mid back. Fluffing my hair out she said, "Oh wait," then she popped two buttons on my blouse open and pulled my skirt up just a little bit more. "There, now I won't mind saying I'm with you," she said grabbing her clutch back.

"You shallow broad," I chuckled.

"I have a reputation to uphold dahling, fashion sleeps for no one. Let's go," she said and we headed to our table.

It was a really dimly lit setting with candles illuminating the room from each table. I picked up the menu and we both placed our orders and drinks.

"Now I know good and well you are not on your phone woman! Here you fuss at me about being on my phone handling business and you're over there just pecking away," I said.

"Ok ok ok, I'm done. Phone down!"

Our drinks came and I took a sip of my chocolate martini and Chelle drunk her Crown and Coke. There was a live band up on stage playing cover songs.

"Who is this band?" I asked.

"That's Beauty and The Beats."

"They are really really good!"

"Them girls are bad!"

Buzz buzz

Chelle checked her phone again.

"Do I have to snatch that thing from you?"

"I swear I'm done; now we can get the party crackin'!" Chelle isn't too much of a phone person because of her over the top personality, so for her to be engulfed in her phone was odd for me.

"Mmmhhmmm, you up to somethin'," I said with a side eye. "What are you up to?"

"Who ME? I'm not up to nothing!" she said sipping her drink.

"If this is a setup I swear! Did you talk to my mother? Am I being punked?"

"Calm down antsy Andy! Mama Yvette doesn't know anything and no this isn't a damn setup so chill out! Trust me."

"Heffa I wouldn't trust yo' tail with my houseplant!"

"Cause that muthafucka would be dead before it left yo' house."

The waiter returned with Chelle's order, steak, roasted potatoes with the house wine and mine was grilled tilapia and shrimp with mashed potatoes and a glass of sauvignon blanc.

"They really are about it in here."

"Now who's acting ghetto," Chelle smiled.

"How come I never knew about this place and I've lived here all my life?"

"Well, if you scaled back from your busy schedule you WOULD know about places like this! They've been in business for years! If you would just tell your problem ridden clients that you have a life too, then you might just know places like this."

"You know what, I'm gonna let you have that today. I love my job, but tonight I'm work free. Phone is off as a matter of a fact. No emails. No calendar updates. No worries."

"Mmmmhhhmmm, the night is still young."

"Whatever, where is the restroom?"

"Around that corner at the end of the hall."

"Ok, I'll be back," I said getting up to leave the table.

Chelle

While Symone left the table, I pulled out my phone and sent the address to Sankofa. I also waved the waiter down. "Can you go give this to the young man with the clip board over there please, thank you," I said.

I'll be there in 20minutes, came a text.

Symone

As I sat back down at the table, I saw that devilish grin plastered on Chelle's face once again. "What?" she asked.

"Don't *what* me with that look. You've been up to something since I've been gone, what did you do?"

"Why do you think I'm always up to something?"

"Trick because I know you!"

"Look, I'm not up to anything that you need to worry about ok, so just relax."

Just then, the house lights dimmed and a round of applause began.

"Come On! Keep it going keep it going! Welcome ladies and gents to Sankofa! To the first timers, welcome and we hope you become regulars. To our returning guests, y'all ain't guests no more so fuck y'all. Just kidding, y'all know what's about to go down! Y'all ready for tonight?" the DJ asked.

The crowd went crazy cheering and then the DJ continued. "Alright here's how we do this, we have a clipboard over here for anyone that wants to come bless the mic tonight. You can do whatever you want, as long as there's no sex on stage. And if that's your talent, I'm the only co-star in this muthafucka...unless you a nigga..." The crowd laughed.

Did this heffa bring me to an open mic night? I swear I could kill her; then again, I'm jumping the gun. I sat and sipped my martini. Just the DJ's speech caught my attention.

Sinful Secrets   *M'Hogany*

"Ok our first artist is a newbie so I need you guys to show 'em some love. Understand that getting up on this stage in front of every one isn't easy so make sure you show them some love good, bad, or indifferent. With that being said, give it up for our first act Symone."

What the hell! I thought.

"Is Symone in the house?"

"Whooooo Hoooo!" Chelle screamed.

"Well shit she already came with a cheering squad of one. Y'all give it up for Symone, show her some love!"

I looked at Chelle with the *I'm gonna kill you* glare.

Smiling and clapping she said, "You better go on. Your audience awaits."

Nervously making my way towards the stage, I contemplate what song I was going to sing. I wasn't prepared for this. I was more so thinking how I was going to strangle Chelle to the point of satisfaction without chancing murder.

After helping me on the stage the DJ asked me, "Ms. Symone, before you grace us with whatever talent you have, is this your first time performing in front of a live audience?"

"Well no."

"Ok, so you're a natural?"

"I wouldn't quite say a natural, just not a newbie."

"Y'all give it up for Ms. Symone."

I glance at the head keyboardist for Beauty and The Beats, and she whispered, "we'll follow you."

I closed my eyes, said a quick prayer, and started. "If I had one wish boy...I'd wish you next to me...and it could be in summer, fall, or spring boy...cause you make my heart sing…"

Oblivious to the crowd clapping, grooving, jamming, and cheering, I checked out of reality and was overcome by the music.

Chelle

"Hey lady," I heard from behind me.

"It's about time you showed up, you damn near missed it," I said without removing my eyes from the stage.

"How'd you know it was me?"

"Cornell, please, I smelled you when you approached the table," I said still fixated on Symone's performance. "Sit down cause I don't like folk behind me.

As he took a seat he asked, "Isn't that?"

"Yes it is..."

If you only knew...what you really do ain't never had no one that does it quite like you do...

"Whoa, you weren't lying. Girl has some major talent going on. Why didn't you say anything before?" he asked.

"It wasn't time. You have to play Symone right. This is where she belongs. You see the passion she has on that stage? Sexy and sultry. Playing to the crowd. This is what the execs need."

"My my my. Ladies and gentlemen one more time for Symone. I'd hate to be the one to come behind that, then again from here the view from behind isn't that bad," the DJ said.

Symone

Laughing at the MC as he helped me down the

steps, I was focused on getting back to my table to wring the neck of my soon to be deceased bestie. In route, I had to keep a smile plastered on my face from the high fives and accolades from my brief performance.

Once I sat down, I stated through a smile and clenched teeth, "I knew you were up to something and once there are no witnesses I am going to kill you."

"Oh please, admit it, YOU LOVED IT! Especially when you closed your eyes and let the music take over."

I couldn't help but give in and agree, "Ok, so I did. But still."

"But nothing Symone. This is what you should be doing! So don't act all upset and mad at me for pushing you to do what lives within your veins!"

"I'll give you a reprieve tonight, but no more surprises!"

Unaware of his attendance I was surprised to hear, "Beautiful voice Ms. Symone."

I turned to see a smooth brown-skinned gentleman engulfed in Unforgivable by Sean John. Speaking again he said, "Ra'Chelle told me you had a beautiful voice, but after hearing for myself, it's nothing past angelic".

Cutting my eyes back at Chelle I said, "Oh did she now." Looking back at him I asked, "Cornell is it right?"

"Correct," he stated.

"Um, excuse me you guys. I have to go to the little ladies room," Chelle just so coincidently retreated with a devilish grin. I swear I'm going to do some harm to that girl.

"May I sit?" he asked.

"Sure go ahead." As he pulled the chair out, I

noticed his wedding band glisten from the table's lit candle. "If I may be honest, I'm surprised that you even remembered my name."

"Why would you say that?" I frowned sipping my newly refilled martini.

"Well the first time we met you seemed so off to yourself face buried in your phone," he said with clasped hands on the table.

"Well I'm a busy woman. Besides, you and Chelle didn't really need me there to listen to business plans so I kept busy with mine own business."

"Well, she told me that you have a great voice."

"Chelle has a hard time keeping her mouth shut," I mumbled before sipping

"And I must say she is absolutely correct. I may have come in on the end of your performance, but it was flawless."

"I could've done better, but for something off the fly, it'll have to suffice."

"A true artist I see."

"Excuse me?"

"A true artist is always their worst critic. Never seeing their last performance as being great, but looking at how to make their next performance better than the last," he smirked sitting back.

As I put my glass down on the table, I leaned forward and said sternly "Cornell, whatever your last name is."

"Wallace, Cornell Wallace."

"Well, Mr. Cornell Wallace, what do you want?"

Before Cornell could respond, he looked at his

Sinful Secrets — M'Hogany

phone and returned his gaze to me. "I'm sorry about that, busy man. You understand right?" he stated. I sat back in my chair and he continued. "Particularly, I'm very much interested in helping you take that voice of yours further than you could ever imagine. I'm looking to restore music to its rightful origin with raw real talent and I believe you indeed have that."

Once again, I heard ***buzz buzz*** from his pocket. After looking at his phone and sending a few messages, he returned his phone to his pocket. I can only imagine that was the little lady at home seeing where her hubby was at this hour. Pulling out a card from his pocket, he flipped it over, wrote something on it, and slid it in my direction. "I'm sorry to leave so early, but here's my card. If you choose to take your voice to new heights, don't hesitate to give me a call. Have a good night Ms. Symone." He got up and left with his cologne lingering in the air.

Cornell

While Symone was on stage, I stepped away from Ra'Chelle's table to record the angelic voice I was witnessing. After she finished and made her way towards the table, I gave them a moment before I appeared, so I lingered at the bar. *Who is that? She is awesome! I know somebody needs to sign that girl fast.* Patrons were conversing at the bar. *See that's what this industry is missing. That smut and garbage that's being played on the radio now would be shut down with talent like that. That's real raw uncut talent.* I couldn't agree anymore with everyone at the bar, but I had to make my move quickly and not run her off.

Approaching the table, I greeted them. "Ra'Chelle...Symone."

"Cornell...right?" Symone asked.

"Correct. Ra'Chelle said you had a beautiful voice, but after hearing you, beautiful doesn't seem to give justice."

"Oh she did," she said shooting darts with her eyes at Ra'Chelle, causing her to instantly excuse herself. While sitting down, I noticed how she didn't have her glasses on and how her hair was down. Not only was she talented, but she was gorgeous. I mean just breath taking. Not only did I think she was beautiful, but so did my soldier in my pants. "Cornell, is it? What in particular do you want with me?"

To bend you over while pulling that hair and make you hit high notes while plunging in that sweet chocolate pussy ran across my mind. "I want the opportunity to take you and your voice to new highs. You have the talent that this industry is seeking and missing."

While I was making my case, my phone buzzed with another text. *Where are you?*

Dammit not now, I thought. *I'm handling business, I'll be home soon*, I responded.

"Sorry about that, but as I was saying, you have a gift that solidifies you in the realm of greats."

Buzz buzz

What is soon? interrupted the new text. *I'm getting ready to get in the car I'll call you in a second,* I responded frustratingly. Trying to make a good and lasting impression, I grabbed one of my business cards, wrote my personal office line on the back, and slid it in her direction. "I'm sorry to have to leave so early, but here's my card. Please give thought to showing the world your talent and let me know. Have a good night," I said before leaving.

As I headed towards my car, I replayed the video of Symone singing and her voice awoke the beast in my pants. "Calm down," I said in his direction. "I can't let another person get hold of her and that voice, that's something special there."

Before I could place my car in gear, the Bluetooth rang in the car and *Wifey* displayed on the dashboard.

"Yes Sherrone?"

"Where are you?"

"What's wrong?"

"Nothing's wrong."

"So what's up with the constant messaging today?"

"Nothing is wrong; I just wanted to know where you were."

"Let me get this straight, I had to cut my meeting short with a potential artist because you wanted to know where I was? Please tell me that's not what you did. I know that's not what you did."

"Well..."

"You know what, I'll be there soon. Goodbye Sherrone."

Symone
Shockingly when Cornell exited, Chelle returned skinnin' and grinnin'. "So how did it go?"

"Oh heffa you know damn well how it went!"

"Me? I have no idea what you are talking about?" she stated with a hand on her chest giving a BS look of innocence.

"Oh cut the crap Chelle! You talked me into coming out only to set me up to sing at an open mic session, AND you called this man here to listen! You are one sneaky trick!"

"Ok fine! But you know what, I am NOT gonna apologize for it, hell I'd do it all over again. Symone, I love you like a sister and I've seen you bust your ASS for other people and their FUCKED UP RELATIONSHIPS. I know what music means to you and apparently sneakin' to get shit done like this seems to be the only way to get you to focus on SYMONE RENAE JOHNSON! I saw my girl up there. I saw my bestie up there! I saw a STAR up there!"

Well damn. I've never seen Chelle this emotional. She was damn near in tears! Now I felt bad. Was this what I've reduced my friends to? Honestly, I felt untouchable on that stage like it was where I belonged. "Ok, ok don't get all emotional on me. I appreciate your push I really do, and honestly I need it, but can you give a sista a damn heads up next time!"

"No guarantees, but you know I have your best interest at heart though!" she said while touching up her face in her compact.

"I swear woman," I laughed.

"What? You know I have to keep a beat face hunny!"

Chapter 8
Put It All On the Table
Symone

"Dr. Johnson, he doesn't talk to me anymore. I feel like he's distancing himself from me. We never go anywhere. I just don't know what to do!" my client hysterically cried during our first session.

Taking notes, I turned towards her husband "Richard, hearing these things from your wife, how does that make you feel? What comes to mind? What are your thoughts on that?"

"Well, Dr. Johnson, my wife claims I am distancing myself from her and saying I'm don't talk to her but she failed to mention that she's NOT WORKING! Being that she is not working, all of the weight falls on me. She sits at home watching these none working money spending gold-diggers trying to fake the funk, while I go out and bust my ass to support her expensive lifestyle! She isn't contributing to nothing but my damn headache! So yes, I am tired and irritable. No, I don't want to go places hell because I'm trying to collect sleep that's lost during the week of me working! I barely have time to EAT let alone talk to my wife about who had a fight with whom, who threw a glass on whom, who's cheating with whom, what so and so said," he vented with veins protruding out of his neck and forehead.

"Ok I see we're getting somewhere. Now, Sylvia,

Sinful Secrets   M'Hogany

why are you unemployed? Not judging just a question, maybe it'll do Richard some good to hear from you why you aren't working."

"Dr. Johnson, I don't work because it's his responsibility to take of me as my husband," she said with crossed arms and legs.

What the hell I thought.

"When we married, he knew I was high maintenance and required to be kept. It's his place as my husband to fulfill my wants as well as meet my needs!"

"You see this?" Richard said with wide eyes.

"Now, hold on Richard," I interjected. "Sylvia, how long have you been unemployed?" I asked while notating.

"For almost 2 years."

"Ok, 2 years is indeed quite a while."

"Yes it is," Richard mumbled.

"Richard."

"Sorry Dr. Johnson."

"I wanted to stay home after having my surgery."

"That I'm STILL paying for."

"Richard!"

"Dr. Johnson, I'm sorry, but my wife is NOT paying attention to everything I'm doing. She just sees me bringing in money for her to spend. Then she turns and complains for me to be home at a snap of her fingers to fuel her ego. I leave work to go home and hell STILL FUCKING WORK! She acts as if I'm her little errand boy like she can't tend to her own business BEFORE I GET HOME!"

"Sylvia, does Richard have a point?"

Before Sylvia responded, which was taking her a while to; I annotated how outspoken Richard has become thus far. Richard is a client that's more hush hush and keeps everything inside, but he's become very vocal today.

"Dr. Johnson, I shouldn't have to work with a husband. Yes, he works and takes care of home, but that's his responsibility as my husband. I shouldn't have to go out and do the things he can do as my husband. When it's all said and done, I want Richard to not only work, but come home to tend to me."

Clearly, this woman was off her rocker. This man not only seems to love her, but she's failing to recognize the actions she's expecting her husband to condone.

"Sylvia, what I'm hearing is more concern for ME and less concern for US. What Richard seems to be saying is that he's being pushed to his breaking point and you're failing to acknowledge what he does and feels has to do to meet your standards."

I turn my attention to her frazzled husband. "Richard I understand your frustration, but letting it build and holding it in not addressing it is not healthy for your psyche nor your marriage." Placing my glasses on the stand next to my chair, I address the couple. "Richard, Sylvia, I believe there's more to this than just occupational issues. With your cooperation, we will get to the heart of everything and salvage what is necessary. I am not a 'smooth over' therapist, more of a straight shooter. My #1 rule is that you have to be HONEST and open with me about EVERYTHING." concluding our session I said, "Before we make strides in a couple's session, I'd like to meet with each of you separately to make communicating a bit more relaxing. My receptionist Ashleigh will schedule whomever feels welcome coming in first."

I had a feeling that Sylvia would be best being that she feels the need to stay at home. What else is there for her to do anyway? "In the meantime, I have a small activity I want you two to do together. Sit together and make a list of things that you both need done be it around the house or outside of it and sort out TOGETHER, with minimal arguing, what you can do on your own Sylvia while Richard is at work, and what you both NEED to be done together. We will discuss this in each separate session. Until then, you two behave," I said with a smile shaking each hand and directing them down the hall towards my receptionist's desk.

"Thank you Dr. Johnson. We know you can give us insight and we value your opinion. That's why you're the best in the business," Sylvia said returning the smile and walking out with Richard.

Heading back to my desk, I pulled out the couple's binder to make annotations and changes creating separate sections for each personal session.

Knock knock

I looked up to see Ray peering in the doorway "hey, come on in," I welcomed.

He walked in Stacy Adams suited from head to toe. "Hey you have a minute?"

"Actually I have about 45 minutes, what's on your mind? Looking sharp I see!" I smiled as I leaned back in my desk chair while he sat on the couch that was just previously occupied by my most recent clients

"A little birdie said you had quite the weekend at Open Mic," he smirked. "Oh don't worry about lil ole Ray; I enjoy being the last to know. Would you like to go out

Sinful Secrets   M'Hogany

Ray? Me? Sure! I'm just your best friend from high school!' Ray mocked.

"Ray it wasn't even like that."

"Hey hey, you don't have to explain ya'self. I understand," he said starting to fake pout.

"Oh give it a rest," I laughed. "That heffa pulled a slick move on me. I was just looking to go out and relax with good food and good music. I didn't expect to be put on stage to be nobody's entertainment."

"So, you didn't enjoy it?"

Hesitating I slowly said, "I didn't say that."

"Lord woman," he said while shaking his head. "I'm glad that you at least got out, but more importantly glad you let your voice be heard outside the church walls. In other news, when's the house warming celebration?"

"What is up with you and Chelle wanting me to have this house party?" I asked sorting through files on my desk.

"It's a celebration woman! Your own space. Celebrating independence. Getting gifts. I know you women like to get gifts. Hell that and show off damn near everything you own."

"Uh, do you remember who I am?" I asked stopping my sorting. "I don't care who sees what I have or not. I don't work for notoriety. I'm not that shallow."

"I know I know, I still find it weird. You'd think I would be used to that by now knowing you for years."

"I'm not your typical female and I'm very happy with that!"

"Dr. Watkins, your next client is in route," Ashleigh's voice echoed through the speakers in the office space.

"Welp, I guess my time is up here. Friday. Party. I'll bring the DJ and liquor," he said quickly exiting.

"But I said…"

"See ya Friday!" he yelled not even letting me get a word in. He knew I would attest the idea like mad crazy, that's why he left out without letting me get a word in edgewise!

"Guess I'll have to call a damn caterer." 15 minutes after securing a caterer for a light setup to accommodate about 20 to 30 people my intercom buzzer goes off. "Yes Ashleigh."

"Dr. Johnson your next appointment is here, shall I send them back?"

Pulling the Smith file from my cabinet I said, "Yes, walk them back." I went to the door and welcomed my clients. "Racquel...James...how are you? Please, come in and have a seat." Turning to close the door I said, "Thank you Ashleigh."

"Sure Dr. Johnson," she smiles headed back towards the front.

"So, let's see where we left off. Racquel, let's start with you. Tell me in your words what has changed in the past week since our last session?" I started as I sat down and prepared my notepad.

"Well Dr. Johnson, I found out James here hasn't been completely truthful, hell his ass hasn't been FAITHFUL!"

Well okay then! Didn't see THAT coming! "James, is this true?" I asked. If it was indeed true, I had to give it to Racquel. She was too calm to know that for sure.

"Dr. Johnson it's...."

"Muthafucka you got caught SCREWING THE BITCH IN MY FUCKING HOUSE! TELL HER THAT JAMES!"

Oh, damn! This is about to be one of THOSE sessions I don't see ending too well.

"Who was the bitch James, WHO WAS SHE?"

Before I could regain control of the conversation that was going to hell FAST, James blurted, "YOUR SISTER! I WAS FUCKING YOUR SISTER!"

OH SHIT! I thought to myself with stunned eyes, as did Racquel. While she was shocked and stunned at her husband's outburst, I reached over and mashed the intercom. "Um, Ashleigh, hold my calls please."

Chapter 9
Dust Settled
Symone

"Knock Knock," Ray said peeking into my office door. "Is the coast clear?" he asked jokingly.

"All is well on the home front," I responded while updating my files.

"I heard you had a feisty session earlier," he said while plopping down on the couch.

"Oh that's an understatement! That was just brutal!" I remarked placing my head on my desk following a deep sigh.

"I mean what was that all about?" he asked.

"You know good and well I can't disclose that," I said leaning back in my chair.

"c'mon, it was going down in here and you know it!" he begged.

"I'm not gonna entertain that or you sir! But I WILL say it was very very VERY DRAINING! I just want to go home and block this out!"

"Last session for the day?"

"After that 3 hour session, IT IS TODAY! You?"

"Woman, I was done for the day halfway into your WWE session over here!" he chuckled while I packed up my laptop and briefcase to prepare for my next day's work. "So any updates on the party planning?"

"Right now, that's the last thing on my mind," I said

closing my office door and walking down the hallway to exit the building. "I just want to go home and put this day behind me with a nice glass of wine and a hot bath."

"Oh how that would be nice. Go home. Peace. Quiet. Nice nap. Ugh, how I miss thee. Instead, dirty diapers. Homework. Boys fighting over whose turn it is to play the game. Cooking dinner. Hell, I'd be lucky if I eat my damn self!"

"Aww, the many joys of fatherhood!" I sarcastically stated.

"Ha ha, you got jokes. I'll remember that when it's your turn little miss World's Greatest Auntie! That time will happen and I'm gonna jump all on your case!"

"Oh no sir, see I can send them little boogers home to their RIGHTFUL owners! Auntie loves ya, but I don't have to keep ya!" we joked as we approached our vehicles.

"See, you got jokes! Watch, you gonna slip up one day and have a little crumb snatcha of your own and you can't give that little munchkin back!" he laughed while unlocking his 2010 olive green Eddie Bauer Ford Expedition.

"Hold your breath on that one papa bear. Besides, I love my black beauty right here!" I smirked while tapping the hood of my 2013 black Infinity G37 coupe. I'm allergic to extra seats!"

"How I miss two seaters," he said dropping his head laughing.

"I can't deal with these gas prices in a gas guzzler. Why in the world is gas going the opposite way ANYWAY?"

"Uh Miss Lady, you do know that I have a gas

Sinful Secrets   M'Hogany

guzzler?"

"Well I guess it's great that I pay you well then!"

While heading home I received a phone call from Chelle. "Hello," I answered while using the hands free Bluetooth.

"Hey boo, whatcha up to?"

"Girl heading home. Had a pretty interesting day!"

"That's what you get dealing with cray cray people! But anyway, Friday, this party that you finally decided to put together."

"You know what, for you and Ray to not really like each other, y'all are dead set on me having this gathering."

"Girl ain't nobody trying to get all buddy buddy with that damn gremlin, I just know for some damn reason, you'll listen to that troll before you'll listen to me," she said while popping gum.

"And there it is."

"Girl I'm not gonna waste my time talking about no damn booga-wolf, what can I bring?"

"Oh no ma'am! I love you, but uh, this is my house mama and we're gonna do this the right way!"

"So you mean it's a bourgeois party?"

"No it's not a bourgeois party! This is not like our high school house parties NOR your freaknik parties!" I said turning into my driveway.

"You know good and well you loved my parties! Hell, you need to quit being so uptight and let your hair down. You might be able to dust off some of them cobwebs from down unda. I bet you haven't had any meat in your taco since Toney ANYWAY!"

"You know what," I tried not to laugh.

"I know it's true, but anyway I need to head back on set but trust I will have some input in this party. And you will get laid by the time it's over! TOOTLES!"

I swear this girl is touched I thought as I headed inside the house. I take off my 4 1/2 inch peep toe heels and let out a deep sigh as I looked at my well-manicured yet swollen toes that looked like plump Vienna sausages. *Mama...Mama you know I love you* sang from my bag informing that none other than my mother was calling and something told me she didn't want a single thing.

"Hey Mama."

"Hey hunny, I was just checking in on you seeing how things are. Did you just make it home?"

"Yes Mama. I'm fine, just a little tired."

"So what are your plans for the rest of the day?"

"Nothing."

"Nothing? No date?"

"Mama, I just want to relax at home and do nothing."

"Well, ok."

I was uneasy at her quick give. "Mama, what's wrong?" I asked. This woman never gives in that easily.

"Well…"

"Well what Mama?" Now I was getting a bit nervous.

"Well, I talked to Sis. Wilson today and she let me know that her son just made it home. You remember Michael right?"

Did I! Same Michael who went to prison for selling and doing drugs! Not only did he do and sell drugs, but also his ass did it AT THE CHURCH! My daddy's church at that! "Oh yes ma'am, I remember him!"

"Well like I said, he just got home a few days ago and I sort of…"

"Mama what did you do?" I asked while I poured a glass of Chardonnay and took a sip

"We were just talking about how you two should, you know, catch up sometime."

Damn near spitting out my wine I said, "Mama, please tell me you did not get together with Sister Wilson, and set me and her jailbird of a son up."

"Symone, you watch your mouth young lady!"

I hung my head in my kitchen and damn near broke my glass on the counter-top. "Mother, it's been a long day. I do not want to have this conversation. I'm hanging up now, love you," I said before I disconnected the call. "I swear that woman is a piece of work. This dating trip she is on is getting on my last nerves."

Ring ring

"Dammit!" I said before I answered the phone. "WHAT!"

"Um, Ms. Johnson? This is Robbie with All Good's catering you reserved for this Friday. Did I catch you at a bad time?"

Embarrassed that I snapped the way I did I said, "Oh I'm sorry. This is Ms. Johnson. It's been a pretty hectic day, my apologies."

"Oh no need, I understand completely. I'm just calling to confirm the menu and time arrangements for Friday. How many guests are you expecting again?" he asked as I pulled out my planner.

"Yes, the dinner party menu is what we talked about, as far as guests, I am expecting between 20 to 30. If you could manage, 6 o'clock is great."

"6 o'clock it is. And Ms. Johnson?"

"Yes?"

"Smile, you sound too pretty to be stressed," the young gentleman said before the call disconnected.

"Ugh, no more today! Calgon, I'm coming!"

-On Set-

Ra'Chelle

"Alright, this belt with the Jimmy Choos and those thin bangles. No necklace with those earrings since her hair will be swept up and she'll have a plunging neckline," I told my new intern before I heard, "busy bee." While turning around I asked, "Cornell, what brings you to the set boss man?"

"Left another meeting. Had to leave from listening to demo after demo after demo," he started as he sat in the trailer where I was doing my styling creations.

"So you decided to bug the hell outta me."

"Basically. So how's it going?"

"Glad this is the last shot of the damn day! These broads are working the last nerve I have standing! Oh, before I forget, I need to leave by noon on Friday for Symone's party."

"I'm sure we can swing that out. Symone, your singing friend right?"

"Singing friend? Boy don't act all brand new! Anyway, she's having a house warming and you know I have to bless it with my presence and style!"

"Cool, cool. Well, just run the styles by RiRi's camp and let me know what other clients you have on the books next and the timelines for them."

"Speaking of timelines, what are you doing Friday? You're more than welcome to come through?" I asked while lining up the next four outfits to be ran out for the next shots.

"I don't know, the misses might not want to do much, but I'll run it by her," he said while adjusting his tie in the mirror.

"Well, let me know. Now, get outta my space! I can't work with you marveling at yourself in my work area."

"Don't hate cause I make this dressing room look good!"

"Negro please, you don't pay me enough to lie. Get on!"

Chapter 10
Business as Usual
Cornell

"Hello? Cornell Wallace speaking, how may I help you?" I said answering my cell.

"Hey babe, where are you?" the female voice spoke through the receiver.

"Hey, just leaving a set headed back to the office. I've got another long meeting with the execs in about an hour," I spoke while starting up my silver limited edition Aston Martin.

"The girls are coming over on Friday so…"

"So, I'm on my own basically?"

"I mean, you can hang out here with us girls if you'd like. I'm sure they wouldn't mind my hubby hanging around," she said.

"Oh, no, I will not be around for that session! I just got invited to an event for that night anyway. Well I just made it back to the office. I'll call you when I'm in route home."

"Ok, love you."

"Love you too," I said hanging up. Before I got out of my car, I sent *If the offer is still available, I'll be rolling solo on Friday.* A part of me was slightly excited to see Symone again.

"Mr. Wallace, just the man I wanted to see," the CEO said to me as I approached the building.

"Mr. Princeton, yes, what can I do for you sir?"

"The best man for the job. You've done marvelous works for this company and have brought us in millions of dollars helping us to become one of the highest rated and competed labels out. And it's all thanks to you," he said as we walked down the corridor towards the main conference room.

"Well thank you sir, but I can't take credit."

"No, no, no it's all you my man. And, here is our potential new artist," he said as I entered the room.

And again, there was yet another gold chain wearing, pants sagging, grill having, draws showing, illiterate portraying, one hit wonder wanna be that I'm supposed to whip into shape and create millions with.

"Sup bro, you ready for me?" the arrogant alleged talent commented with a smirk as if I should be grateful he was there.

Here we go with this shit again.

Party Time

"Well Mrs. Smith, I must say that we've achieved quite a bit since our last session. Let's continue to work on our communication as well as anger and we can move in a more positive motion." As I annotated her progress in her file, I noticed a change in her posture and demeanor. "Mrs. Smith, is there something more you'd care to share?"

"Dr. Johnson, if I must say, thank you for your patience with me and my husband. I'm not sure how my marriage will turn out but…"

"Mrs. Smith, let me stop you there," I interrupted. "We're here to focus on you right now. We will focus on your husband in his own session. We will address your marriage as a whole later. The focus right now is to address you and what and where we can strengthen you so that you can be stronger in your marriage. I can't speak on what your husband and I will specifically be talking about, but know that's my mission and goal here for the both of you." I grabbed her jittery hand. "We'll get through this hurdle together. You're not alone here."

"Thank you Dr. Johnson. You truly are the best," she said wiping her trickling tears while smiling. I escorted her to the front area where she could set her next appointment.

Once back in my office, my notifications on my cell were going haywire! "OH SHIT!" I hastily murmured while gathering my belongings not noticing Ray walk into my office.

"Whoa, slow down speedy Gonzalez!" he said with hands in his pockets.

"Not now Ray, I'm swamped. I didn't expect that last session to go over as long as it did. I've gotta make it home to greet the florists and caterers. Make sure tables are setup properly. Find something to wear. Fix my hair. Make sure the house is presentable."

"Damn woman, BREATHE! I'm wrapping up in about the next 2 hours and I'll be over to help you keep your head above water. Relax. It'll be fine," he said walking me to my car.

"I don't know why I let you two talk me into doing this in the first place," I mumbled, "This is just too much for me."

"Would you just relax and go home."

I started my car and half way down the street, the phone rings, and Chelle pops up on my dash. "Hello," I frantically answered.

"Hey I'm at your house where are you?"

"I just left work headed there; no one's there yet are they?"

"No, not that I know of. You ok suga?"

"I'm so damn ready for this day to be over."

"Here you go with this shit woman."

"Look, this was all brought on by you and Ray."

"Chile, if you don't stop worrying and bring yo' bourgeois ass home! Hell, yo' ass needs a few shots! Loosen the hell up!" she said with attitude. "See this is why I said you should let me plan this."

"Chelle, we are not going through this today! I'm turning down the street. Hell the way I was driving, I'm surprised Grand Prairie PD didn't pull me over!" I said while getting out of the car damn near stumbling on the gravel in my 5-inch black and purple stilettoes.

"Cute shoes, boo! I see I've rubbed off a little bit!" she said snapping in a circle with one hand on her hip. We walked in and I immediately removed my shoes and scanned my neutral colored living space. "What's your problem chile?"

"I'm trying to enjoy my beautifully decorated and CALM home before it is infiltrated with people I probably don't know who will do GOD KNOWS WHAT to my house!" I pouted.

"Oh jeez girl, c'mon. We gotta get you ready for tonight."

"What you mean ready, I am ready."

"What are you talking about?"

"I was gonna just wear this tonight. I think I did pretty well," I said smoothing over my calf length black skirt with satin deep purple blouse under my black vest.

"You're joking right?"

"Why, what's wrong with it?"

"Oh GOD, she's serious. You really think that's gonna fly."

"Che...." before I could finish my remark, the doorbell rang.

"You handle that and I'm gonna go to your room and perform a miracle on your wardrobe," she said as I went to the door.

"Got the damn nerve to say she gonna look like that at her party, WHAT THE HELL IS HER PROBLEM..." Chelle mumbled as she headed upstairs towards my master "Done lost her damn mind..."

"Hello, we have a delivery for a Ms. Johnson."

"Yes, please come in," I said opening the door for the men to bring in the tables.

"Where would you like us to set these up Miss?"

"Oh, right. Um follow me and you all can setup..."

Ding-dong

My doorbell chimed again. "*Dammit*, um, ok, in that empty space over there," I said pointing to where my formal dining table was supposed to be, "should be fine. Is it enough space for you?"

"Yes ma'am, this is more than enough space for us to setup," the young man smiled as I scurried to the door

Ding-dong

"I'm coming I'm coming."

"Order of 3 dozen long stemmed white roses, 2 short dozen white roses, 8 white vanilla candles, and 8 decorative candle holders for Ms. Johnson."

"Yes, please come in," I said moving aside for the florists to come in and setup as well.

"Ms. Johnson how would you like your arrangement?" the petite white woman asked.

"Oh, um you can put..."

"I'll handle it," commented Chelle from God knows where.

"But I-"

"But nothing, I got this."

"Chelle…."

Ding-dong

"You might want to get that," she said as she sashayed to my living area.

Opening the door I was greeted with, "Ms. Johnson?"

"Yes."

"All Good Catering."

"Please, come in. You can place the food in the kitchen on the island."

Before I could close my door I heard, "Hey hey now, keep it open!" I turned to see Ray coming in with speakers in both arms.

"Now, how were you going to ring the doorbell with both of them in hand?"

"I just woulda beat the door down."

"And I would got that up out your paycheck."

An hour later the food has been laid out: stuffed bacon wrapped jalapenos, seven layer dip, char-grilled shish-ka-bobs, assorted fruits, and cheese. Various assortments of wines both red and white. The tables were accented with the white roses in crystal vases, while the light aroma of white vanilla swarmed the rest of the house. Ray was setting up the music and speakers with the DJ who had a mixture of ole school, neo soul, and today's valid R&B selections. People were starting to arrive and give compliments on my home.

As I picked a few grapes from the fruit tray, Chelle grabs me by my arm. "What's your issue woman? Go upstairs and get dressed. I didn't put together a fabulous outfit for you to be down here looking common!"

"Wait," I said swallowing, "you put together something for me to wear?"

"Bitch, what you think I was doing upstairs? Go on, I got this down here."

****

Ra'Chelle
Mama Knows Best

"Well hello Mr. and Mrs. Johnson," I said opening the door for Symone's parents.

"Hello Ra'Chelle dear," Mrs. Johnson said hugging me as well as Pastor Johnson. "My goodness Symon, this is gorgeous," she gushed.

"Yes it is," pastor said taking her jacket.

"Um, would you two like a glass of wine or something?"

"Hunny, you know the pastor and I don't drink. We'll take a glass of water though."

"Yes ma'am," I said before leaning to pastor's ear. "Jesus turned water into wine pastor."

"I know, so pour me some white Zinfandel in a cup baby-girl."

"Yes sir," I whispered quietly with a smile.

"Ra'Chelle you remember Michael don't you? Ra'Chelle? Ra'Chelle? Hunny?"

"Oh, yes ma'am I remember. How have you been?" I nervously asked.

"I've been good, thank you."

"Uh, Ra'Chelle, where's Symone?"

"Oh, she's upstairs in her room getting dressed."

"I'll go check on her. Ra'Chelle hunny can you make sure you only put three cubes of ice and a slice of lime in my water please dear. Nothing more," she said before she began to tackle the staircase.

"Yes ma'am," I said before quickly turning towards the kitchen. *Lime? Why not just get a damn spritzer? Hell it's just water!* As I nervously made my escape, I bumped into someone. "Oh excuse me, I didn't see."

"No, it's my fau...Ra'Chelle?"

"Cornell! Whew, thank GOD it's you!" I said pulling him into the kitchen with me.

"You okay? You look frazzled," he asked while I poured a glass of Pinot.

"I'm fine," I lied swallowing a half-poured glass and starting to pour another.

"Ra'Chelle," he said jarring me out of my daze.

"What?" I asked as I stared in the direction of the Pastor and Michael. *I can't believe he's here and acting like everything is all good,* I thought to myself.

"You ok?" he asked once again.

"Why?"

"You drinking wine like it's water."

"I'm a big girl and can hold my own," I said not breaking my stare. "Wait, is your wife here? I thought you two were coming together?" I finally looked away now pouring more drinks.

"Yeah, about that. It's a girls evening and I didn't want to be surrounded with all those women, so I took you up on your invitation."

Handing him a glass of cranberry juice and grey goose on the rocks I said, "Well, I'm glad you made it."

****

Symone
Best Dressed
Knock knock

I headed to the door barefoot. "Chelle, I'm coming give me 2 minutes and I'll..." I started to say as I opened the door. "Mama, hey I thought you were…"

"Ra'Chelle, I know...Hunny you look stunning."

"Thank you, but it's nothing. "

"All of my girls are gorgeous and I make sure I tell you all as much as possible," she started while I placed my diamond studs in my ears. "Besides, you never know, your Mr. Right might be here…tonight…on the other side of the door…waiting…" she kept hinting.

I swear this mother of mine could go on and on. "Mama please, not tonight ok." Buckling up my black and gold stilettos, I checked myself in the mirror and made sure my hair that was half up and half down with cascading curls was in place. I gave my body a once over before turning back to my mother. "Can we have a nice evening mama? No talks of anything that's not complimenting my home? Now, c'mon."

As we made it back downstairs, I was met with a round of applause as I descended from the staircase. "Oh, thank you. Well, I guess I should say something. Um, thank you to all of you for coming and sharing with me my new place. Thank you for your support this far. Enjoy yourself. There are drinks, food, and music. Oh, this is my baby so treat it like your own. Cause I will send you a bill!" I laughed. "Enjoy."

"Hey baby girl you look beautiful as usual," my dad said kissing me on my cheek.

"Thank you Daddy. Daddy, what are you drinking? Is that wine?"

"Don't worry about what's in my cup."

"Daddy!"

"Don't tell your mother. Hey, I'm very proud of you baby-girl," he said winking at me and scanning for my mother as he made his way to the table that held the food. Before I could make it further in my living room, Chelle pulls me towards the kitchen quickly.

"Chelle, what the hell is your problem?"

"I just wanted to give you a heads up before…"

"Before what?" I interrupted.

"Hey Symone," I heard a male voice say from behind me.

"Michael?" I squinted.

"How've you been lady? I see you've grown and seem to be doing well for yourself"

"Oh, I see you finally found each other. Symone, you remember Sis Wilson's son Mich-"

"Mama, I know who he is. How did...Did you bring

him? What did she tell you?" I started to rant.

"Symone, I know you better bring your voice down," she sternly whispered. By that time, my father had appeared.

"Daddy did you know about this?"

"Huh?" looking torn between his daughter and his wife my daddy exchanged looks with my mother and I and said, "I'm not in this," waving his hands in the air.

"Symone, don't be rude! You two talk and I'll get a drink. Ra'Chelle dear, where's my drink darling? Did you place my lime in my water?" she said walking off leaving me standing awkwardly with Michael.

"Look I'm sorry Michael, I didn't know you were coming so my apologies for being surprised at my mother's antics. If you'll excuse me, I have guests to greet and speak with but you are welcome to the food and drinks," I said before walking off and grabbing my father's arm. "Daddy, why didn't you call or text me telling me she was coming with Michael?"

"Baby-girl, your mother told me as much as she told you. I didn't know until we picked him up."

"Well why didn't you text me?"

"Now you know I have no clue how to do all that emailing, texting, whatever it is that you kids call it!"

"Daddy, I can't take her doing this today."

"Baby, look, enjoy yourself in your home. These people are here to celebrate you and this gorgeous home of yours. You know your mother won't stay long. Keep your chin up okay baby girl. Daddy's got your back ok? Now smile…C'mon…Daddy's girl…" he said pouting at me and batting his eyes like he always did to make me smile when

I got upset.

"Ok Daddy. How much did you have to drink anyway? You know what, give me this," I playfully said taking his cup.

"Take it, it's empty anyway," he smirked before placing a bacon wrapped jalapeno in his mouth.

"You know you not supposed to have that Daddy."

"Child, you are worse than your mother. Why have food I can't eat?"

"Daddy there's cheese and fruit."

"But where's the meat baby girl. The good book says that man cannot live by bread alone."

"Ok, ok, ok, Daddy I'll *turn the other cheek* so to speak, but if mama asks…"

"If your mother asks, I'll speak for myself! She don't run me!"

"Sure she doesn't Daddy," I giggled as I walked off. "Ooh, excuse me," I said bumping into a solid chest.

"Oh no excuse me," I heard the masculine voice say before I looked up to notice whom I ran into.

"Cornell?" I said.

"Symone right? Hi, sorry if I'm intruding on your party," he said with a half grin.

"No problem, I'm sure Chelle invited you."

"She did indeed. You have a very beautiful home by the way," he started to say.

"Well thank you very much. Um, if you'll excuse me, I have to make my way around…"

"Oh of course of course."

"Thank you for coming and enjoy yourself. If there's anything you need, please don't hesitate to come find me," I said before I walked off.

"I will," he nodded and smirked.

As I left, I felt Cornell's gaze on me and I felt myself blush. As I made it to the kitchen, Ra'Chelle said, "What's got you all flushed trick?" with a raised eyebrow.

■■

Cornell

Wandering Eyes

"This house is beautiful," I said while sipping my drink.

"Isn't it though! You'd think Symone had me help her with the decor, but I'll have to let her have it on this one," Ra'Chelle said before she flipped her hair.

"Hurt to say that didn't it?"

"You don't even know the half!" she said rolling her eyes. "Anyway, I see someone I know. Will you behave if I leave you alone for a while?" she asked giving me a sassy look.

"I'm the good one between us two," I laughed. "So the question is more like will YOU behave YOURSELF?"

"When do I ever?"

"Exactly".

Slapping my arm, she said, "Whatever," as she walked off.

As I marveled at the soft earth tone decor, I saw her. I knew it was her, but something about her was different. Hell, something about her had ME different. The sudden throbbing in my pants agreed. She looked stunning in stilettos, a silk blouse, fitting skirt, with flowing long jet-black hair with the light waves. "Oh that's no weave there," I murmured to myself. My eyes trickled down to her firm yet softly glossed chocolate legs. I suddenly imagined them draped over my shoulders caressing each firm calf. "Get a hold of yourself C," I snapped to myself. I headed to refresh my drink in the kitchen. Apparently, me staring at her caused me to have cottonmouth. After fixing my cocktail, I turned and bumped into the object of my attention.

"Cornell?"

"Symone, isn't it? Sorry if I intruded on your party." I had to hide the growing life that was slowly awakening in my groin region.

"Oh no problem, I'm sure Chelle invited you."

"She did. By the way you have a very beautiful home," I said trying to take my eyes off of her by surveying the little crowd she had marveling at her home, and hoping that my damn dick would go down, but even her aroma held my dick's attention!

"Well thank you. If you'll excuse me I have to make my way around and thank everyone for coming. If you need anything, please don't hesitate to find me. Enjoy yourself," she said before she walked.

I hated that she was no longer in my company, but the view I had of her walking away put a smile on my face. I couldn't help but stare and slowly get jealous of the skirt that covered her firmly round ass. It looked as if the skirt was doing its damnedest to keep everything intact. *That ass is as good as mine* I thought. I finally addressed my soldier and thought, *Down boy, in due time. In due time...*

****

Symone
Clean up

"Thank you guys for coming," I said to my last

guest as they pulled out of my driveway. Closing the door, I remove my shoes and let out a sigh of relief until I turned around to the remnants of my 4-hour house party. "Ugh, Glad tomorrow is Saturday." luckily for me Ray and Chelle stayed to help with the cleanup.

"This was actually a nice little shin-dig Symone," Ray stated while breaking down the tables in the dining area.

"Who in the hell says *shin-dig*," Chelle snapped.

"Look here you meddling, short, self-centered…"

"Hey hey," I interrupted while laughing. "Stop it now, there will not be a WWE match going on in my house."

"Whatever, I'm too cute to be fighting tinky winky over there," Chelle spewed.

"Cute? To who? Stevie Wonder?"

"Okay, now stop it seriously," I chuckled.

"That's not funny Symone"

"I'm sorry Chelle, but, yes it is! You 2 do this every time. Pull each other's hair out AFTER you help me clean my house!"

"Well that shouldn't be difficult since Ray hasn't seen hair in centuries. Hell you see the shadow from where his hair once was!"

Before Ray could hurl a quick insult, a flush came from the guest powder room. We all simultaneously looked at each other while frozen in place. "I thought everyone was gone?" I said.

"Shit me too," Chelle nervously agreed.

"Stay here," Ray instructed heading towards the powder room. As soon as the door opened, he snatched the individual by the shirt and flung him on the wall. "Can I help you?"

"Whoa! Sorry, I was just on my way out."

Running to pull Ray off of the man, Chelle ran screaming, "Get off of him!" After prying his hands away from his shirt she asked, "Cornell, are you ok?"

"I'm fine; I got lost on my way to the bathroom and didn't notice everyone had left."

"What's going on?"

"Ray was about to turn your house into the next episode of "*First 48*"."

"Always the drama queen! I was concerned about who this mutha..."

"Ray!"

"What, I'm just saying! You know, keep people OUT that shouldn't be IN. Chelle wouldn't know anything about that!"

"What the hell you mean by that?" she snapped.

"Oh let me see, revolving door, open 24-7, instant access. You know, kinda like them weeds you call legs"

"You balding muth..." Cornell instantly grabbed Chelle midair as she leapt to get at Ray.

"Ok, we're done here. Ray, I'll see you at the office on Monday," I said.

"Man if only I didn't hit women. Well, I guess this broad is an exception," he said while I was trying to push him towards my front door and away from Chelle who was still being restrained by Cornell.

"Ray, RAY, RAYMOND!" I tried to yell over his insults being hurled at Chelle. "GO HOME! My goodness GO HOME!"

Finally getting fed up, he turns and throws his hands up in surrender. "Alright alright, I'm going! Make sure you call the exterminator to have your house fumigated to rid it of fleas she brought in on that wig."

"Bye!" I said closing the door.

"UGH! I can't stand his dusty ass!" Chelle screeched as I massaged my temples while still perched on the door.

"Chelle, he's gone now. I think you need to call it a night as well."

"But what about the mess? I was gonna help you clean-up."

"Girl please, we both know cleaning isn't something you do!"

"Damn right about that! Hope the boo is up cause now I need a stress reliever," she stated while flipping her hair as she headed out.

After seeing her drive off, I closed the door and let out another sigh, but yelped when I heard, "Can I help you with this mess?"

Clasping my chest, I blurted, "Sweet Jesus, you scared me!"

"I didn't mean to frighten you," the voice carried through the foyer. "I just figured since your help couldn't, well, help I couldn't just let you tackle this mess alone," he offered.

While brushing past him I said, "Thank you for volunteering, but I think I can manage. I couldn't ask you to stay and help. It's late and I'm sure you have some place you need to be." Although the help would've been great, I didn't feel comfortable having him there alone in the first place.

"I don't mind, therefore I'm helping and I'm not taking no for an answer," he said picking up a trash bags to take them out.

"Ok Mr. Wallace, you win"

****

Cornell

Seize the Moment

As Ra'Chelle left, I couldn't help but notice the array of mess left from the gathering. *I can't let her clean this up by herself* I thought. "Can I help with anything?" I asked slightly fearing she would throw me out on my ass.

"Sweet Jesus, you scared me!" she yelped clinging to the banister.

"I didn't mean to startle you."

"Well you suck at that." She brushed past me after catching her breath. I caught a whiff of a sweet vanilla fragrance that meshed well with her body chemistry, once again it awoke my mini me. She walked with a cautious yet elegant flow as if she knew I was watching. It took everything in me not to snatch her, pin her up against the wall, and bury my face in her supple breasts that seemed like they were fighting to be set free. *Get it together C before both of us end up exposed* I finally came to and noticed that he was fully erect and making his efforts to push my pants down. . "Look Cornell, I appreciate you wanting to help and everything, but I promise you I can manage, so you can go," she said before she bent over collecting the cups and mini plates left on the coffee table.

Damn, if she stays in that position any longer she'll have a bigger mess to clean up. "Hey, I said I'll help so I'm helping," I said walking towards the kitchen trying to conceal my manhood to keep from scaring the woman.

After letting out a sigh, she stood and said, "Ok, Mr. Wallace, you win."

If only she knew the prize, I was after...

****

Symone
Worship

"Would you come to him now? While the blood is still running warm in your veins, come. The doors of the church are open as my baby, Symone Johnson sings. Would you come?" my father said after delivering a deep sermon and taking his seat behind the glass stand in the pulpit.

Apparently, since I'm the only one that sings in this family, it's become my duty to sing during the invitation every Sunday. While grabbing the microphone, I notice my mother sitting with Michael and the frustration from her ambushing me at my home with her love connection started to appear on my face.

"...Ama...zing...grace...shall always be my song of praise..." I began to sing, and left everything there. After I concluded the song, I took my seat next to the musical director before my father gave the benediction.

"Unto him that's able to keep you from falling, and present you spotless before the throne of GOD. May his peace be with you now and forever shall we all sing...Amen."

I quickly grabbed my bag and keys and tried to make a hasty exit without being stopped or delayed by my mother and her antics. "Symone?" I heard a voice call.

I turned and saw Michael's mother approaching me.

"Sister Wilson, hi"

"I know you weren't going to leave without giving me no sugar girl!" I smiled and embraced the older woman and kissed her on the cheek. "You know I love hearing that voice of yours girl, your grandmother would be very proud," she said beaming.

"Thank you. I hope so."

"So I take it you spoke with Michael?"

"As a matter of fact..."

"Sister Wilson, nice to see you," I was interrupted by my mother.

"First Lady Johnson."

"Hey Ma," Michael appeared behind my mother.

"Michael, hey baby," she said as she greeted my mother and embraced her son.

"I see you found my daughter," Mama said to Sister Wilson.

"Oh yes. You know I love hearing this child sing. Uplifts my spirits every-time I hear her. I know you and Pastor Johnson must be proud!"

"Yes we are. Um, Symone, you remember Michael don't you?"

"Hi Michael, I'm glad to see you back in church," I said with a forced smile behind the scowl embedded on my face.

"Well, how's everyone this morning?" my father asked joining us.

"Pastor Johnson that was a moving sermon! You know how to touch my spirit every time!"

"Oh thank you Sister Wilson."

"Pastor, we were just talking about how Michael

and Symone enjoyed her little soiree Friday..." my mother began to stretch the truth.

"Daddy, I'm sorry to have to go so soon, but I just can't stay," I said kissing him on his cheek before I looked at my mother.

"Well baby-girl, will we be seeing you for Sunday dinner?" He asked

"No, not today. I don't have the appetite to eat," I said grabbing my keys. "So nice to see you Sister Wilson."

"You too baby. Keep on singing!"

"Yes ma'am I will."

"Yvette..."

"Not here Symon...we'll talk in the car," my mother said to my father in a low tone as they stood at the church's entrance greeting everyone who attended Sunday service.

A Day in the Life
"I just don't know where we went wrong Dr. Johnson, I swear I don't. I do everything for this woman."

I sat analyzing a tear drenched face of a man whom I must say gave a better performance than Susan Lucci did.

"Oh get off of it Darryl! See Dr. Johnson, this is the shit I'm talking about. I need a man, not this big ass sissy!" his wife barked.

It took so much in me to keep from laughing at this woman's need to call her husband a sissy. "Ok, now, we talked about language in here. What it seems like is you require something that your husband isn't giving you," I said trying to divert from laughing at my patient questioning her husbands' manhood.

"Dr. Johnson, I am trying here but I have to just be

real and this isn't working for me. We don't work. He's too sensitive. This is a flat out pussy!" she said standing, grabbing her purse, and pointing in his direction. "I'm out," she said as she stormed down the hall and out of my building. Before I could address her husband and calm him down, he literally ran out still weeping.

"My lord, it is DEFINITELY Monday!"

Knock knock

"Ugh," I mumbled and squirmed in my chair before the door slowly crept open.

"Symone? What the hell was that?" walked in a grinning Ray.

"Oh goodness, a session that calls for a drink," I said while he took a seat on the couch

"Well I see your little pet bat has rubbed off turning you into an alcoholic"

"You know what, I'm definitely gonna need a stiff drink before I hear ANYTHING in regards to you OR Chelle!"

"You know what, speaking of *stiffs*, what happened after you kicked me out?"

Looking at Ray with my hand on my hip I said, "I did not kick you out Raymond, I...just...escorted you to the door in a hastily fashion."

Looking at me like what the fuck he said, "Woman, that's kicking me out!"

We both laughed hard as hell! Just then, my intercom buzzed. "Yes, go ahead Ashleigh."

"Your 9 o'clock is here Dr. Johnson," came through the speaker.

"Thank you Ashleigh, you can send them on back."

"Hmmmm, which one is that? The feisty couple?"

"Uh, you know that's doctor/client confidentiality young man," I stated while pushing him towards the door of my office.

"I take it; this isn't kicking me out either huh?"

"Go be productive or look like it at least!"

"Ok ok," he surrendered.

"Good morning Dr. Johnson," my client said.

"Good morning Mr. Smith. Please come in and have a seat," I said directing my client to the couch.

"Look I'm gonna get straight to it Dr. Johnson, I appreciate you for what you've done with my wife and all with these sessions but um…"

"What's bothering you Mr. Smith?" I asked noticing his hesitation to respond. "Mr. Smith, is there something you want to speak about?"

"Dr. Johnson, to be honest, I'm nervous."

"Most men aren't that intuitive about their emotions or speaking about them. They view it as a sign of sensitivity or weakness. I can assure you, everything we discuss is between you and me."

"Well there is something...." and he immediately halted.

"Mr. Smith? Hey, there's no one here to judge you. I surely won't."

"Well, first let me apologize for my outbursts during our previous session. It shouldn't have gone that far."

"These things happen when topics or issues go unaddressed."

"Well, I didn't intend on getting that angry, but I don't think my wife understands nor cares about the pressures I'm under."

"Well, Mr. Smith, you know here I encourage honesty and openness. Now, question is did you mean what you said during our last session or were trying to hurt your wife?"

Taking a deep breath, he said, "a little bit of both."

"How so?"

"Yes, I was angry and wanted to shake her up. For once I just wanted her to shut up and be attentive to me for a change."

"So, have you or are you having an affair?"

"I have had an affair."

"Her sister?"

He let out a slight chuckle and massaged his face. "No not her sister."

"Why say it?"

"Something had to shut that woman up! She thinks every woman is out to get me, but I haven't been happy with this woman in years. However, there's another woman that..."

"Wait, you've been seeing this other woman and you still agreed to doing counseling with your wife?"

"Look, I was hoping you could help me break this to her."

"Ok, Mr. Smith, this is how this works. You can't divert the issue at hand and start something new. You will indeed carry that over and this woman deserves truth, honesty, and openness. They both do."

****

Cornell

"So where did you go last night?"

"Dammit, here we go with this again," I said dropping my briefcase on the couch and adjusting my tie.

"You damn right this again."

"Look, not today okay."

"Really Cornell, Really!"

"LOOK IT'S TOO DAMN EARLY IN THE DAMN DAY FOR THIS!"

Taken aback, she said, "Baby, I'm sorry. I've just been so moody lately. I'm not really feeling good."

"Have you scheduled your doctor's appointment?" I eyed her as I sat in my lazy-boy feeling bad for yelling at my wife.

"I did. I go in next week."

Grabbing my keys, I got up and she asked, "Where are you going now?"

"I'm headed to the gym," I replied as I picked up my gym bag.

"Ok, well don't stay too long I need you to pick up the kids today."

Stopping in my tracks and slightly turning I asked, "Um, and what are you doing again?"

"Nothing, but since you're gonna be out, just swing through, and grab em."

I was starting to get hot under the collar. "You know what...whatever," I mumbled as I got into my car. Pulling out of my driveway, my phone rang. "What up J," I spoke as I hit the speaker button and put the car in gear.

"What up baby boy, where are you man?"

"Ah, just headed to the gym."

"a'ight, coo, bring yo' ass nigga."

****

Symone

"Mama, you still should have told me you were bringing him. No... Mama...I...Hi Michael," I said while rolling my eyes forcing a fake smile. My mother had yet once again placed on her cupid wings and was trying her damnedest to make a connection between Michael and me. She's lucky my last session with Mr. Smith ended an hour ago. Now, this man is rambling some mumbo jumbo about something. Honestly, I stopped listening when my mother handed him the phone.

"And I..." I heard while noticing Ray walk in my office giving me a moment of relief.

"Um, Michael, Michael, I'm sorry to have to cut you off, but I have another client that just walked in. Please let my mother know, will you. Thank you, bye," I said abruptly hanging up not giving him a chance to respond.

"Yo' lyin ass. You know damn well you don't have another client!" Ray said.

"They don't know that! I just couldn't stand to hear his voice anymore," I said rubbing my temples.

"Ok, now who is this dude anyway?" he snapped. "Is it that dude that almost got murked at your house Friday night?"

"Negro no. And who says *murked* anyway? The one you allegedly hemmed up was Cornell. That was Michael my mother brought to try and spark some love sparks."

"I see Mama Yvette getting straight to it!"

"Well she needs to chill out. It's working my last damn nerve. I ain't no damn charity case. It'll happen when and IF it happens."

"If you don't sound like your father. He would be so

proud," he mocked with clasped fingers and batting his eyes.

"Shut up fool!" I said with a chuckle.

"So then who is Cornell? Or whatever the clown's name is."

"Someone Chelle knows and works with."

"You sure it ain't someone she's layin' under?"

"Don't start that today."

"I'm just sayin. Her and rental cars have one thing in common...Unlimited mileage."

"I'm so gonna ignore that."

"Dude was bout to get it though."

"Ray…"

"What?"

"Now come on, you know you couldn't kill a handicapped fly!"

"Hell if it looked like Chelle I would in a heartbeat. I'd be doing the country a just service ridding it of major pests."

****

James

"What's good baby, hell, it took you forever," I said dapping up Cornell.

"I had to handle some business at home."

"Wifey buggin?"

"You know it."

"Well handle that ish later, what we got today?"

"30 minute cardio then back and shoulders, and finally legs. You know that part that you keep forgetting exists?"

"Ah hah, funny man huh. We'll see who'll be

laughin later nigga."

"Shut up and getcha weight up boy."

"Remember you said it."

• •

Symone

"I'm hungry, you up for lunch?" Ray asked while getting up from the couch and sluggishly walking to the door.

"Not right now. I'll take a late lunch, gotta get these files in order, and go over these notes. What's up with you, you seem so overjoyed with excitement today," I sarcastically stated.

"Don't I look it?" he said with such a straight face.

"Ugh, that bad?"

"Symone, you just don't know. These bratty spoiled ass kids and clueless parents here not sure 'what's going wrong with my little angel' and then there's that woman at home. I swear she is gonna be the death of me LITERALLY."

"C'mon, it ain't that bad."

"Why the hell it ain't! I love her, don't get me wrong, but something has GOT to change."

"Have you two talked about it?" I asked.

"It's like talking to a puppy."

"Aww, puppies are cute!"

"Focus woman. They're cute, till they shit on your carpet and act as if they didn't do a damn thang while you always have to clean up the mess."

Looking baffled at how that even made sense, I just squinted and stared as he locked his office up before heading out.

"What?"

****

Cornell

"2 more...C'mon baby you got this...1 more...push it out!" I coached my boy under the weights.

"Whew, damn I'm more outta shape than I thought."

"I've been trying to tell you man. I'm in here like clockwork," I said taking my turn under the weights. "So you shouldn't have an excuse as to why you outta shape."

"I hear you. At this point, I need to get back in here. I'll have to see what I can work around my sessions."

"Sessions?" I asked in between reps.

"Yeah, therapy sessions."

"I knew yo' ass was crazy man, but I didn't know it was THAT bad."

We both chuckled.

"Nah, marriage counseling bruh."

I stopped mid rep and sat up. "Marriage counseling? What's up?"

"I don't know man I'm just tired. Real tired," he said

"Damn bro, you know I gotcha man. Hit me up anytime"

"I hear ya C, but I guess the upside is that my therapist is fine as HELL!"

"And there it is," I said repositioning myself under the weights.

"Man, say, I thought I was gonna see some old while lady wearing coke bottled glasses smelling like moth balls and peppermints in orthopedic shoes."

"Man, aren't you supposed to be there to, what,

work out your marriage? Not trying to work the shrink?"

"I'm just doing this really for her. Hopefully she'll see that this has been over. Man I'm tellin you though, this chick is hella fine. Smooth radiant skin, Coca-Cola shape, thick thighs. Every time I walk in that office, I think about bouncin that ass. But all she wants to do is try and fix this shitball of a marriage."

"Boy I tell you, you're a piece of work!" I laughed. "Is she any good though?"

"That's what I'm trying to find out!"

"Is she a good therapist man?"

"Oh, well hell I guess. Shit, really I don't give a damn."

****

Symone

"Boy if you ever, left my side..." I sang when the intercom buzzed. "Yes Ashleigh"

"Dr. Johnson you have a call on line 1."

"Thank you...Dr. Johnson speaking."

"Ew so formal."

"Chelle, hey crazy."

"Whatcha doin' mama?"

"Oh girl, just re-analyzing and prepping to leave the office, what's up?"

"Oh just checkin on my girl."

"Is this your way of apologizing?"

"For what?"

"Really?"

"Ok fine, sorry for Friday."

Laughing I said, "That just killed you didn't it."

"You don't even know! That negro just gets on my

damn nerves!"

"Yeah, well that's fine and all but never again will it be at my house! I swear, between you and my mama, I'm gonna have more grays nesting in my hair than father time before 30!"

"Girl mama Yvette did the fool on that one Friday."

"I mean just flat out embarrassing and beyond uncomfortable."

"You don't know the half," she mumbled.

"And then she blindsided me by bringing him into my home! I haven't been in my house a good month and already it's seen unnecessary drama."

"Well, I'm sorry about my actions. I don't think mama Yvette meant anything bad about it though."

"Chelle please, she went too far."

"Ok, it was a bit much."

"And I had to clean my house because you 2 nut cases couldn't get along and I was not about to stand there and referee."

"I guess it was good that Cornell was there then."

"Whatever you say…"

"Speaking of Cornell, how long did he stay after I left?" she said as I heard the smile in her voice.

"I almost forgot he was there until I closed the door behind you. Damn near gave me a heart attack."

"What he do? Do I need to bust his head?"

"I'm good; he didn't do nothing but help me clean up since my damn cleaning crew couldn't hold it together!"

"Clean? THAT'S IT? Now I see why Mama Yvette was trying so hard."

"What's that supposed to mean?"

"Nothing. What do you think about him?"

"Who, Cornell? What is there to think about?"

"No bitch the milk man! Yes Cornell! I swear, sometimes you shoulda been born a damn boy cause you just doing that damn pussy of yours an injustice. I weep for your uterus."

"Shut it! I see, I gotta watch you."

****

Cornell

Gym

"Good set," I said to my boy as we headed towards the locker room

"So you in town this week?"

"Yeah, I am, then again you never know with this industry," I responded while unlocking my lock.

"Alright, I'll hit you later. I gotta head out."

"A'ight man, be easy." As he left, my phone began buzzing *Where are you?* But before I could respond back, it rang in my hand. "Hello?"

"Where are you?"

"I'm leaving the gym, why what's wrong?"

"Oh, nothing, I just wanted to see where you were"

"Sherrone, I told you I was going to the gym so what do you want?"

"Well, I need you to go to the store."

"For what?"

"I'll tell you when you get there. Besides, we have an engagement I have to speak at."

"When did this change?"

"I forgot to tell you about it."

"Great another last minute thing," I mumbled as I

closed the locker with my keys in hand. "Ok, I'm walking out the gym right now. I'll call you once I get to the store," I said immediately hanging up.

As I got in my truck and prepared to start up *Are you still coming over* appeared on my screen. "Dammit, I forgot. Gotta do what I gotta do," I said to myself. *Sorry baby-girl, change in plans. I can't come over today. I'll make it up to you soon though.*

My response I got was. *Alright Daddy, I'll be thinking of you tonight when I relieve myself. Until next time papi. xoxo*

****

Symone

"Ashleigh, are there any other appointments on the books for today?" I buzzed over the intercom

"No Dr. Johnson," my receptionist replied.

I made my way to the front with an empty office area. "Well, no point in sitting and waiting for nothing so you can go home. I'll finish up here."

"Are you sure? I can go through your files for tomorrow's sessions and organize them all."

"No no no, go on girl go home. I'll pay you for the full day."

Cheesing from ear to ear my receptionist got up faster than the roadrunner! "Ok if you say so. I'll see you in the morning."

Boy I tell you. When you tell a person you'll pay them to be off and watch 'em run out.

"Mr. and Mrs. Walters, we've made good progress with Aaron. Give it time, that's all he needs. Our receptionist will schedule you for our next appointment.

Sinful Secrets   M'Hogany

You all take care," I heard Ray saying coming out of his office.

"I guess that's my cue," I said. In between being lost and tickled, Ray tried to conceal his grin to see me actually at the front desk. After maneuvering my way around Ashleigh's area, I scheduled their family for their next session for the following week. "Have a great week," I said as they departed.

"So when you say you're a woman of many jobs, you really mean it huh?"

"Shut it."

"Where's Ashleigh?"

"I let her go home early. I see that was your last session on the books for today and I've been done with my clients for a while."

"Alright, so what are your plans now?"

"Well I WAS going home, but my parents want to go out for dinner since I skipped out on Sunday dinner."

"Ooooh you skipped *SUNDAY DINNER!*"

"Ooooh my ass."

"You still sour about Friday?"

"I'm not sour. But I know I'm about to put this *get Symone hitched and knocked up* movement to rest once and for all!"

"Hey now, go easy on Miss Yvette"

"There is no going easy on her. She'll think twice before putting on her cupids gear."

****

Yvette

"Michael, glad to see you made it, please come in. Pastor and I are ready to leave. Have a seat and I'll go grab him and we'll be on our way," I said welcoming him into our house and closing the door behind him.

He sits and I head into the room to ensure my husband looks presentable. I swear men would walk out looking any kind of way without a woman to make sure he's well put together. "Hunny, Michael is ready and waiting on us downstairs,"

"Yvette are you really going through with this? This is too much. Symone already made it very clear she doesn't need our *help*."

"Symon, we've been over this before. At this point, Symone doesn't know what's good for her in the relationship department. If she did, she would be married with children by now. I'm just nudging her a bit," I said adjusting his tie.

"I want you to leave well enough alone Yvette," he said as I double-check my make-up and hair.

"I will. As soon as I'm done, so let's go dear," I said as I made my way towards the bedroom door.

Symon blocks the doorway. "Yvette, we need to talk about Friday."

"Symon, not now ok?"

"No, darling, we need to talk about it. That was out of line and you know it."

"Symon, it's not out of line."

"Bringing a young man to our daughter's house unannounced pressing for a love connection and consistently trying to get her involved with this young man that she is *CLEARLY* not interested in, is INDEED OUT OF LINE!" he said and I could tell he meant business by the tone of his voice.

Stepping in closer, I placed my hands on his chest and caressed his face. "Symon, my love, I hear you and I understand your frustration. But can we talk about this another time? We have a guest downstairs waiting." I kissed him on his cheek and moved passed him. "Let's go Symon!"

"I'm coming, just grabbing my holy oil..."

****

Symone

"Ma'am your table is ready," announced the hostess.

"Thank you," I say as she shows me to the table.

"Can I start you off with something to drink?"

"Um, water is fine," I answered and then I see my parents walk in. "Oh, the rest of my party is here…" I started to say and then I saw Michael with them. "On second thought, I'll have a glass of Pinot Grigio"

"Yes ma'am."

Hurrying to greet me, my father whispers as he embraces me, "play nice baby-girl, this is all your mother's planning. Please humor her."

I had to laugh a little bit. My father knew his baby-girl all too well. He knew I would flip out, respectfully of course, if I knew my mother was bringing Michael along. "No promises Daddy, but I will try," I said gritting my teeth with a forced grin.

"Symone, hunny, how are you?"

"Hello, mother, I'm fine thank you for asking".

"You look gorgeous. Doesn't she look beautiful Symon," my mother smiled while addressing my father as he pulled her seat out for her.

"As the day she was born." And he came to pull my

seat out for me to sit.

"Michael, doesn't Symone look beautiful?"

"Yes ma'am, she does indeed. Beauty is indeed genetically strong."

"Symone, don't you have something to say?"

Inhaling and exhaling deeply "Thank you Michael." *Symone, try not to be so nasty tonight. Just make it through dinner and you'll be fine* I thought to myself.

Not even a good 5 minutes into sitting for dinner, my mother just went in for it "So Michael, please tell us about yourself."

"Well, Mrs. Johnson you've witnessed me grow up in church as you and my mother are both on the church's prayer board for the sick and shut-in. I believe there isn't much for me to tell."

"Well dear, tell us something about you as a young growing man. I've known you as a child, but I'm sure we would like to know you as the man we see before us. How about you Symone?" my mother insisted.

I swear I tried not to just spaz out, but I knew how to get her to back off. "Mother he said there's nothing else to know, so no I don't have any questions."

"Oh hunny, I'm sure you have SOMETHING in mind to ask the young man."

"Yvette," my daddy said trying to get her to lay off.

"What Symon? How else is she going to know anything about the young man or ANY man if she doesn't ask questions?"

"Yvette, stop it now," he beckoned more sternly.

"What?" she tried to innocently asked.

The waitress appeared at the table and asked, "Is

there anything I can get for you all here?"

My father placed an order for both he and my mother and Michael did the same.

"Can you please bring me the bottle of Pinot please?"

"Yes ma'am," the waitress answered.

"Symone, take it easy on the wine," my father warned.

"I will Daddy," then I turned my focus back on Michael. "Michael, my mother is correct. You won't know your company if you don't ask questions. So, please, tell me what were the grounds you were arrested on?"

Shocked at my question, my mother began to choke on her water. In between breaths, she darted her eyes at me. "Symone!"

"What, you said to ask the young man a question, so I did"

"Symone Renae Johnson! You know good and well what I meant." Trying not to take sides, my father started to rub my mother's back in hopes that she would catch her breath. "We did NOT raise you to be disrespectful!"

"I wasn't being disrespectful mother; I asked Michael here a question." I took another sip of my wine eying Michael and said, "Now leaving a lady waiting for a response is actually disrespectful."

"Actually, I would like to know the answer to that myself," my father said.

"Symon! Don't do this. This is embarrassing."

I ignored my mother's dramatic breakdown. "Michael..." I encouraged him to respond.

"Well, um, I don't think I..."

"Michael, don't you say another word. Symone, you father and I are very disappointed in you and your behavior tonight. I apologize for my daughter's rude behavior," my mother attempted to apologize.

"Mrs. Johnson, it's quite alright actually. I understand what you were trying to do and it's much appreciated, but I also understand where Symone is coming from. You and Pastor Johnson have taught your daughter very well in being cautious of whom she allows to infiltrate her inner space. I can only hope that my daughter has the same character."

I kinda felt bad for the guy now. I will admit that I've been a pure ass since I first saw him, only to get under my mother's skin, but I wasn't paying attention to him in the slightest. To hear he has a daughter just made me feel badly.

"So you have a daughter," my father interjected. I wanted to hear his response in midst of my slight guilt.

"Symon!"

"Yvette, now enough is enough. We are here having dinner, or at least trying to. You want us to get to know Michael outside of the church and we are doing that. Now I don't know what questions you expected to be asked here tonight, but Michael is a grown man and I'm sure if something bothers him he will not hesitate to speak for himself. Now sit, enjoy your meal, and let him answer the questions."

Have I mentioned how much I LOVE my daddy? The way he levels out my mother's overbearing banter while maintaining his loving and respectful tone is what I would love to have in a husband.

"To answer everyone's question, yes I have a daughter. She's almost nine now. My incarceration was due to a drug charge, however it was because of me trying to do what I felt I needed to ensure my daughter had what she needed. I got locked up when she was around two. I haven't heard too much from her mother since my incarceration and I haven't seen my daughter since then. I've made every effort possible to find them, but I've ran into wall after wall."

"I'm glad that's out and over, now we can move past it and enjoy our dinner. HOPEFULLY, there won't be any more disrespectful outbursts. So Michael, are you seeing anyone at the moment?" my mother interrogated.

Waiving the waitress back to the table I asked, "Could you bring another bottle of Pinot please?" I knew I needed to be completely wasted to make it through this dinner.

Chapter 11
Cornell

"So we have a meeting with Bangladesh and Rodney Jerkins on Tuesday in LA and we meet up with Bryan M. Cox on Thursday and artist development on Saturday," said the label CEO. "I believe that adjourns our meeting. Let's make magic people."

As the employees leave the boardroom, the CEO lingered. "Cornell, a word please."

"Yes, sir."

"Your team should stay as well."

Great, another bland speech about selling mediocre talent on payroll. These *talents* are less than that! My job is to ensure that real authentic talent gets the proper due to shine and breathe life back into a dying industry. Instead my hand is being forced to deal with these pop up, in home, one hit hot commodities. Damn, has this what my life has become? Seriously disturbing.

Buzz buzz

I need you to get off early because we have an engagement to be at.

"Cornell, can you handle that?" he spoke snapping me back to reality.

"Yes sir, I know we can."

"Alright, well thank you all for your extra hard work," he said with a smile as he exited the room.

As I made my way down the hallway towards my

office, "Cornell, are we really gonna do this?" I heard that familiar voice whisper in my ear.

"Ra'Chelle what do you mean?"

"You know exactly what I mean!"

Closing my door once I reached my office, she goes right in. "Why are we still doing this? You stand here and tell me face-to-face that this doesn't bother you?"

"Why are you so invested in the talent NOW? Your main job is merely clothes."

"You know, normally I would agree with you on that one, but this company is going down in flames quickly if no real talent doesn't come walking through these doors soon! Don't you miss real, raw, genuine music? I remember when you wouldn't put Cornell Wallace on ANYTHING unless it made sense and now look at the damn platinum plaques that mount these hallways all due to you! This basement, quick buck, excuse for music is NOT what that is and you know damn well it isn't either! If I have to deal with another Snoop Dogg wanna be with an entourage or a Beyoncé-diva-esque, auto-tuned nobody, I'm walking!"

She has a point, but I have a wife to support with pretty high standards as well as maintaining a mortgage. Neither one of us is leaving our jobs because well hell, they pay the bills. However, she raises such a good point.

"I understand what you're saying, but you have to look at it like I am. No ducks are lined in a row as far as how to approach this with the boss man. We can go to him with our concerns and walk out with pink slips."

"Well hell we gotta do something. Don't try to play me like no fool. I've learned a thing or two."

"What do you suggest then?"

"Hmmmm didn't get that far. I kinda thought you felt the same way and would take it from there. Didn't expect to snowball like that"

"Look, I hear you, trust me I do. Put something together and I'll look it over and give you my opinions on it, but you gotta have something to go on instead of just ranting and raving for change with no plan."

Knock knock

"Mr. Wallace, your wife is on line 1," my assistant said as she peered her head in the door.

"Let me get started on this proposal or whatever so you won't catch me on the 6 o'clock news for beatin the ass of one of these groupie bitches," she said before leaving back out.

"I'll hold you to it," I said following a chuckle as I picked up the line

"What's got you in such a cheerful mood?"

"Just finished a short meeting with a colleague"

"Mmmmmhhhmm, what's her name?"

"Sherrone, don't start that"

"Look I'm just on edge right now."

"And again, I told you to stop comparing our marriage to other people."

"I know I know, I just…"

"You just what?" I was starting to surpass being irritated. I love my wife, but this insecure bit is starting to wear a brutha thin.

"When are you coming home?"

"I have to travel to Kansas in 2 days then meet with the label execs in NY 2 days after that."

"Either the business is keeping you away from me,

or it's all you."

"I'm not doing this again."

Knock knock

"I'm sorry Mr. Wallace, but your 7:30 pm meeting has arrived."

"Ok, thank you," I whispered to my assistant. "Ronnie, babe, I have to go. I'll see you tonight when I get home."

"I love you."

"I love you too."

A hip-hop hopeful walks into my office, looking like the 80's threw up all over him. He looked like the love child of Flava Flav and Run DMC.

"Good evening, Cornell Wallace Senior A&R director. Glad you could make it. Let's make some music shall we?"

Restaurant

"Well, Michael, it has been an eventful dinner, but you of course were a delight hunny." my mother attempted to salvage the night.

"Mrs. Johnson I don't mind at all. I'd expect such apprehensions for a man of my past. I can only strive to be a better man and father behind it."

He's either being real sincere or he's as good of an actor as my mother is.

"Symone, hunny, we will see you later this week I hope," she directed her gaze at me

"Yes mother," I said as I picked up my glass and downed the remaining sips of my wine.

"Michael dear, are you ready?" my mother asked.

"If it's ok with you and Pastor, I'd like to stay behind and make sure your daughter makes it home safely tonight."

"Oh, no. Don't let me stop you. I'm good, so you can go ahead and leave."

That statement had my mother's eyes bright and wide like Ed McMahon was at her door with a check from the publishers clearing house! "Symone, your father and I would feel better if you didn't leave this establishment alone."

"You have consumed quite a bit of wine tonight as well," Michael added.

"I'm a big girl. Besides, I was taught by the best man I know how to protect myself. Isn't that right Daddy."

"Sorry baby-girl, Daddy's gonna have to agree with your mother on this one."

"But DADDY!"

"No buts Symone, Michael here will make sure you leave here safe and sound," he said with the death stare in Michaels' direction. "Am I clear?" he said looking at me.

"Yes sir."

While my mother stood and Michael helped her put on her shawl, my father hugged me and whispered, "You know Daddy loves you, but if this fool tries anything and I mean ANYTHING, you try your damnedest to send his ass to meet Jesus PERSONALLY!"

As my parents left out of the restaurant, I could see my mother beaming. Oh hunny she was eating this up! She just knew she made a love connection. I could see the little mouse turning in her head making wedding plans and picking out baby names!

Once my parents left I said, "I appreciate you making sure I make it out safely, but-"

"Symone as a father, I wouldn't want my little girl going home alone."

"As a father you shouldn't want your daughter out late with a stranger."

"Symone, we basically grew up with each other in the church."

"Michael, look, I'm sure you're a good guy or whatever, but we were kids then. I don't know you and you don't know me, so let's not try to act as if we do," I said grabbing my purse and leaving the table towards the exit. As I reached my car, I fumbled around for my keys. In the near distance, I heard, "I'm not letting you go home by yourself."

Spinning around I said, "first off, you're not LETTING me do a damn thing, so you can go home or wherever the hell you came from."

"I would feel better knowing you made it home safely, as I'm sure your parents would as well."

"You just don't know when or how to quit do you? Let me lay it out clearly for you ok. Make sure you stay with me on this. I DON'T HAVE ANY INTEREST IN GETTING TO KNOW YOU! Don't plan on being friends or any other thing in regards to you! Hope all goes well with you and your daughter and everything else! You may be my mother's pick, but I can select my own dates. Preferably, ones without a damn rap sheet. So for the last time, GOOD NIGHT MICHAEL!" and I turned and got in my car....

****

James
"Cornell Wallace..."
"What's good boss-man?"
"What's good J, how ya been?"
"Ah, same ole same ole. Working like crazy. How's everything on your end?"
"All good here."
"You sure?"
"Yeah man I'm sure. Question is are YOU sure?"
"Pfffttttt, man to be honest I'm tired. Maybe I can get healed by Doctor Feel Good."
"I swear you need hands laid on you."
"Hell, she can do that too. Anywhere she wants. I don't know why I'm trying to stick this out. This came to an end really 8 years ago."
"You know y'all got Sherrone buggin right?"
"Uh oh, trouble in paradise?"
"We good over here bruh."
"Yeah that's what I said. Look I gotta get back to work, but when you stop lyin to ya'self and come outta la la land, I'll give you the good ole doc's number."

He chuckled. "Like I said bruh, it's all good on this end."
"Well, it's out there."
"And again something is terribly wrong with you man," he said laughing. "A'ight I'll get up witcha later. We still down for the am session?"
"I don't know man, burning the late night oil, but I'll hit you up if I change my mind."
"A'ight big money."

Chapter 12
Symone

"Good morning Dr. Johnson. Your 9:00am has been rescheduled to noon, but Mrs. Smith came in demanding to see you. She was crying hysterically."

"Did she say anything else?" I asked my receptionist as I went through my messages and mail.

"No, she just seemed fidgety and just emotionally unstable. She was everywhere."

"Okay, hold my calls unless they are urgent or until I resolve her issues."

"Yes Dr."

Walking towards my office, I could hear objects being thrown around and broken. "What the hell," I mumbled as I neared the door.

"Symone is everything alright," Ray said confused exiting his office trying not to startle his clients.

"The hell if I know, but I'm gonna find out." I walk into an unrecognizable space that was supposed to be my office and a hysterical woman with a crystal object in hand. "MRS. SMITH!" I yelled trying to keep her from shattering the glass.

As she spun around, she spewed "BITCH!"

"Symone, I'm calling 9-1-1," Ray said.

"No, no, no. I have this under control."

"What? The hell you do! Don't try and play captain save-dat-hoe. You can't cure that kind of crazy Symone," he said tugging at my arm.

"Raymond, let me handle this. If I need help, trust me, I'll ask for it. Give me a minute."

"Symone," he urged.

"Ray...Let...Me... Handle this," I said before slowly closing my door.

"Dr. Watkins, is everything alright," I faintly heard Ashleigh ask Ray.

"I hope so Ashleigh, I hope so."

"Should I call the police," she asked.

"Let's see how she works this out, but be safe and have them on the ready. I don't touch women, but the second shit goes left...I'm layin that bitch out!"

"Mrs. Smith, I'm going to need you to put the crystal down please," I said slowly making my way towards my desk.

"Put it down? Is that what you want hoe? Why is that, so you can pick it up like my husband? Is that what I'm paying you for?" she said threw gritted teeth.

"Mrs. Smith, whatever it is we can talk about it and"

"STOP CALLING ME THAT! It's because of simple hoes like you that make real females like me act like this!"

"Okay Mrs. Smith, let's get to the bottom of this, but I need you to put the crystal down."

Dropping my expensive crystal alongside the rest of my shattered glass objects she said, "There, bitch, it's been put down."

"Mrs. Smith…"

"I swear if you call me that one more damn time,

the next thing I'll smash will be your face!"

"Ok, what do you prefer I call you?" I asked nearing the desk trying not to step on the glass that surrounded it.

"Bitch, I don't want you to call me a damn thang!"

"Okay then, you want to start by telling me what this is all about?"

"To be well educated, you sure are a dumb broad."

"Mrs... look, we can't get to the bottom of anything if you don't tell me what's bothering you or where this is coming from," I tried to reason with this woman.

"Oh bitch you already know what this is about."

"I honestly can't say I do," I said with a genuinely perplexed look.

"Funny when bitches start fuckin your husband and get caught they act all fucking stupid!"

"Excuse me?"

"Don't play coy with me tramp. I see all through your games."

"Racquel wait a second, start over here. You think I'm sleeping with James?"

"Listen bitch, I have 2 beautiful children with my husband whom I love, so back the fuck off!"

"I see we need to straighten a few things out here..."

"We don't need to straighten out a muthafucking thing! I know your weak ass tricks and I see through you! *Ok Mr. Smith, we'll start your personal sessions...blah* blah blah," she mocked. "What were you two really doing in your so called sessions?

"Now Racquel, you know I can't disclose any of that information."

"Mmmmmhhhmm doctor-patient confidentiality shit right."

"Yes that's violating doctor-patient clause."

"Oh, so the good doctor is worried about violating Doctor-patient clause? What about Marital Vows Clause huh WHAT THE FUCK ABOUT THAT?"

"Alright, I'm done trying to be nice here," I said to myself while walking around my desk coming within feet her.

"Well looky looky at the good ole doctor. You're a bold one I see," she said standing with arms folded smirking.

If I weren't in my right frame of mind, I'd slap that damn smirk right off her face. "This is what we're gonna do Mrs. Smith," I started saying trying to keep it all together and stay professional. "We can talk about whatever you want to talk about, it's your call. However we WILL respect each other. If you have any questions for me, I will indeed truthfully answer them. We will NOT raise our voices or anything towards each other. Now, if you can't abide by that, by all means you are free to go." I was done being nice, now she was gonna see hood Renae show up.

Clap clap clap "Was that your big bad girl speech Dr. Symone?" she sarcastically commented. Walking slowly towards me, I tensed up ready to scrap with this unstable lunatic. Now facing face-to-face, toe-to-toe, nose-to-nose "I know the game hunny. I've been around the block a few times so your tactics, no matter how pathetic, won't work," she said while looking me up and down "If you so much as breathe heavy in my husband's direction or I feel you are, dat ass is mine. Am I clear?" With that she smirked and gave me a once over again while heading towards my door. Snatching the door open, she turns back before walking out and said, "Have a good day Dr. Johnson."

Chapter 13
Cornell

"And this is our executive team that will be overseeing your project as well as artist development sessions. If you have any questions or feel any discomfort, don't hesitate to find me and I'll see what I can do."

"That's wassup G. If I need you I'll holla atchu," remarked the so-called-talent that was sadly signed this morning. "All dis talk is gravy, but what's up wit that advance check homie?" he quickly segwayed.

Knock knock

"Excuse me Mr. Wallace; you are needed in conference room B."

Thank GOD! I screamed in my head. "Thank you Samantha."

Turning back I said, "Sorry to have to run, but everything you need can be handled by the executive time. Welcome aboard and hope to hear great things from you," I stated as I shook the hands of what seemed like another 1-hit-wonder.

"Hey hey now, slow down there speedy."

"Ra'Chelle, I'm sorry," I said after blindly bumping into her.

"You ok?"

"I had to get outta there fast."

"Bad meeting?" she asked, as we walked down the hall.

"Not quite. This music business is just too tricky and going downhill fast. I just sat for a grueling 3 hours with the labels newest signed act who wants to rap about, and I quote, bitches dats bout dat life, hoes dat got that fire mouf piece, and getting dis paypa."

"See this is exactly what I'm talking about. We need to do something fast because this microwave music is gonna get stale."

"I couldn't agree more, however we'll have to table this conversation. I have someone waiting for me, but we'll talk later right?"

"Sure. Still working on that project," She said before click clacking down the hallway.

****

Symone

"Symone?" I heard a faint voice call out.

"Just a second," I stated trying to make my way to the door through the glass shards surrounding my desk.

Opening the door before I could reach it Ray walked in and said, "What the hell?"

"Ray, kill it okay?"

"Damn she did a number on your office!"

"Tell me about it," I said while trying to pick up the bigger broken glass chunks. "Dammit, this was my favorite glass globe from Utah!"

"So what was she ranting about that had her turning your office into hells pit?"

"Oh GOD!"

"Spill it Symone."

"Ugh, look she's having deep marital issues."

"Clearly I know that or else she wouldn't be a

client."

"She thinks I'm sleeping with her husband. It's the age old blame everyone else tactic."

"See, this is why I do family counseling."

"Don't get me wrong, I love what I do, I just get tired of these people that blame everything on the world instead of being real with themselves and face the music. Quit prolonging the inevitable."

"Now we both know that's all wishful thinking," he said while repositioning my furniture. "So does this end the sessions with the…"

"The Smiths," I finished.

"Right. The Smiths."

"Oh definitely not. We are far from being done!"

"Symone, are you out of your damn mind? This woman was a 1-bitch-demolition crew and you're still keeping them on your books? Yo' ass is crazy! Either you're charging them a shitload of money, or you got something going on." Ray stopped in his tracks. "You not messing with Mr. Smith are you?"

"First off, you should know me better than that. A man with a band is NOT attractive to me nor has it ever been in ANY WAY! Second, it doesn't matter what I'm charging them or if I'm charging them at all. It's never been about money and it never will. There are some problems within this couple and they can never move forward honestly unless they just come out with it."

"You know I agree with you on that one, so..." Ray stated as he plopped down on my couch.

"How was dinner with the folks?"

"Oh gawd!"

"Really now?"

"It wasn't that bad. Mama was just on it as usual."

"I have to give to Mama Yvette though, she does not quit!"

"She brought the man to dinner and insisted that I get to know him!" I huffed.

"Well Symone, you can be a little rude when it comes to meeting people."

"I do not! I just don't believe in wasting my time as well as theirs."

"Mmmmhhhmm, rude ass. How did Pastor Johnson take it?"

"You know Daddy. He's the neutral party until he said he had a daughter."

"Aw shit wait a minute! Did your mother know he had a kid?"

"I don't think so, hell she looked as shocked as us. Oh but when Daddy and I started asking questions, mama looked like she almost had a stroke! She wanted me to get to know him, so I was doing as she asked."

"Heffa please, even I know your *effort* had bitterness written all over it!"

Batting my eyes innocently I said, "Why Raymond, I never!"

"Oh stop it! I know you woman! I'm more so surprised that act didn't run him from the table!"

"I wish it did! Do you know he had the nerve to send my parents' home and said he would stay to make sure I made it ok, like I couldn't handle myself."

"Ooooooooooh, shame on him for being a gentleman. How rude of him. He needs to be thrown in jail.

The damn nerve of that scoundrel!"

"Don't you have a client to see right about now?" I said laughing.

"Symone, you need to just fall back sometimes and not take on so much."

"No seriously, don't you have a client?"

"Welp, that's my cue," he said getting up to leave. "Oh, uh, and Symone please refer your schizo patients to another office. You don't pay me enough to be a janitor too."

****

Cornell

"Boss-man!"

"What up Jay? I didn't know you were in town today?"

"Yeah man only for a little bit. Hectic schedule that's all."

"I hear you I hear you. You good?"

"Yeah yeah, you gotta sec?"

"Yeah, come back to my office." I could tell something wasn't straight with my boy. "Have a seat bruh. So what's going on you a'ight?" I asked while straightening my desk covered in artist's start-up packages.

"I'm in deep bro," he said wringing his hands together.

"Jay, deep how?" Now I was worried.

"Bro, deep. Like mad deep."

"J, you're not telling me anything."

"C man, she's pregnant."

"Raquel, pregnant? That's a good thing man!"

"Hell no! Raquel and I are through man! I don't know how many times I have to say it."

"Alright alright, so then who's pregnant? Apparently some chic you're seeing."

"Bro, she's been on the team for a while now."

"Ok, wait I'm confused. You buggin cause your new girl is pregnant and even though your marriage is over, like you say, you still trippin over it? Why not just tell Raquel you're with someone else and you have a baby on the way?"

"Man, Raquel is crazy!"

"And. You been knowing that!"

"Nah man, I mean like psycho cray cray. Like a screw or 3 is missing!"

"So I guess it's safe to guess that you haven't told her about shorty?"

"Hell naw!"

"Bro! You're with another woman, yet still married with no signs of moving towards a divorce? Please tell me that sounds as crazy as hell to you as it does me? And you got the nerve to be going to counseling?"

"I already told you C, this counseling thing is just for her! This marriage has been over! I want her to understand that and not hold on. I'll do for my kids, but we just ain't working together."

Ring

"Hello," he answered, "Racquel...wait...what...you WHAT?"

Click

"Damn," he yelled slamming his phone closed.

"What happened?"

"C man, I gotta cut it short," he said hastily hopping up to leave my office.

"Bro, be easy. Hit me if you need me. I mean it."

"Yeah man I'll do that. I gotta go handle some shit man. I'll see you later at the gym a'ight?"

"Yeah yeah, I'll catch you later," I said as he damn near plowed down my assistant.

****

Symone

"Dr. Johnson, may I help you?"

"Symone?"

"This is Dr. Symone Johnson, how may I help you?" I stated as I annotated my net clients file.

"So I see you made it safely," the masculine voice bellowed through the receiver.

"Excuse me? Who is this?" I asked stopping in my tracks.

"I hope all is well with you"

"Michael? How did you get my number? Wait, don't answer that. This has my mother's name written all over it," I remarked.

"Symone, don't be so hard on your mother. She didn't prompt me to call, although she gave me your number, I was just checking to make sure you were okay," Michael responded.

"Michael, I appreciate the gesture, but we both know good and well you know I made it home safely."

"I don't follow."

"So you're telling me that you weren't in the yellow cab that followed me to my street and sat at the corner of my block until my car disappeared into my garage?"

"You figured that out?"

"I told you, my daddy didn't raise no fool. That's why it took me nearly an hour to get home."

"So you had me follow you for nearly an hour with the meter running just to make me sweat?"

"I wasn't gonna let you have the satisfaction of me getting home that fast sir."

"Well, like I said, I'm glad to know you made it home safely. Even if it cost me nearly $200 dollars between following you around nearly an hour before I went home!"

"Michael, what's the real reason you called huh?"

"Straight forward I see."

"If you don't mind, I'm pretty busy."

"Well, I wanted to take you out. Just the two of us. No parents. No setups. Not a date. Just a fair opportunity to get to know each other. You can ask anything you like and you have my word that I'll give you nothing but the honest truth."

Pausing from my annotations, I leaned back in my chair in thought before responding. "Michael, what do you really want from me? You must take me for some fool! I mean what's this all about?"

"I feel like we got off to a wrong start."

"If you call being ambushed at my house and dinner as a wrong start, than ok." I was a bit rude I must admit that. I can at least give him a decent meal and opportunity to show me who he really is. "Okay Michael. I'll take the bait. When, where, and what time?"

"How's Friday?"

"Friday night is fine with me," I replied.

"Great. I'll text you the address and time later, if

that's okay with you Dr. Johnson."

"Not a problem with me," I stated.

"Dr. Johnson, there's a Mr. Smith here to see you," Ashleigh's voice rang over the intercom.

"Thank you Ashleigh, you can go ahead and send him on back."

"Well, I'll let you get back to work Dr. Johnson," he said before we departed. I sensed a smirk was on his face from the tone of his voice. "I look forward to Friday, Symone"

"Take care Michael," I said before disconnecting the call.

Mr. Smith burst into my office. "Dr. Johnson, I am so so so so so sorry. I don't know what Racquel said or did, but when she called bragging about what happened here..." and he stopped and saw the remnants of the catastrophe his wife caused to my office. "Damn, this bitch is crazier than I thought."

"Mr. Smith, Mr. Smith, calm down. Here, have a glass of water. Have a seat. Take deep breaths okay?" I tried to calm him. "Yes, your wife came and as you can see went ham! What can you say triggered this? Any ideas?" I asked.

"Dr. Johnson, I'm gonna be real frank with you. I had divorce papers delivered to Racquel today. This has been coming and she has known this for quite a while now. She's still living in that delusional world that everything between us is perfect and peachy. We're not those two little naïve teenagers trying to be grown-ups like we were nearly 15 years ago. I only agreed to sessions hoping that you would see that we definitely needed to go our separate ways. She won't listen to me, but I thought she would listen to someone with no ties to us. I was hella wrong," he recanted with a frantic demeanor while pacing in my office crunching the glass underneath his feet.

"Mr. Smith"

"Please please, James. As much as I'm paying for these damn sessions, I'd prefer you to call me James," he interrupted not stopping his stride as he continued pacing.

"Okay, James, what's really troubling you then. This can't be completely it. James, please come sit down," I motioned. As he sat down, his leg started to tremble violently. "James, what are you not saying?" I asked.

"I need her to sign off on these damn divorce papers."

I noticed that fear and rage co-mingled where hurt once dwelled in his eyes.

"Doc, look, I've been in a relationship mow for almost 2 years with a sweet woman"

"Ah, I see."

"Exactly, now I know I know, I should be involved with someone when I'm still married."

"James let me stop you right here. My position as your therapist is not to judge you, but to get to the root of the problem. So this woman, is it serious? Or would you say she was intertwined in your complex marital issues?"

"Doc, I've been with Racquel since we were teenagers. Just kids in high school. A year after we got married, she gave birth to our son James Jr. I've always been in love with Racquel. I can't pinpoint where or when it all went wrong, but when it hit, it hit like a title wave. To me this marriage was over years ago, and I started seeing this woman that made me feel alive again. It had nothing to do with Racquel, I just wasn't happy but she made me more than happy. I can admit that I'm all types of crazy over her."

"I have to say Mr. Smith; I've never seen you light up in our sessions like this. You must really really like this woman," I stated with a smile on my face.

"Correction Doc, I love her!"

"Oh well excuse me!"

"I'll always love Racquel because she's the mother of my children, but I can't force myself to be in a relationship that's not good for my children or myself."

"So, where do you go from here? Can you answer that question?"

"That's the hard part. I want to move forward with my life and give this wonderful woman the fair chance she deserves as the woman I love."

"Ok however…"

"However, Racquel doesn't make things easy doc... As you can tell," he said while looking around my office.

"I will agree with you there," I stated joining him in his scan.

"In the beginning it was mad sexy because she never made things easy. I always had to work hard to get her, which made me love and appreciate her more. But it turned from that to pure annoyance," he progressed.

"Have you talked her about it?"

"Doc, how do you tell someone like that to ease up?"

"Let me ask you this, how did she take that when you tried it?"

Dead silence

"Exactly. Now try to tell them that you are expecting another child with someone else that isn't them!"

"Wait, another child? She's expecting?"

No Symone, she's bloated. What the hell you mean is she expecting, I thought to myself. Suddenly James hung his head and slowly began to cry. Grabbing a few Kleenex from the box near the coffee table, I passed them to James. "Take your time."

"Doc I should be over the moon that the woman that effortlessly makes my world move is going to give birth to my seed, but my supposed crazy soon to be ex-wife won't free the both of us!"

"Well, James, this situation is rather unique. Does Racquel know about this other woman and her pregnancy?"

"She knows I'm not with her that's for damn sure. She knows absolutely nothing about the baby though. I don't need her stressing her out and putting both her and the baby at risk."

That says a lot I mumble to myself. "Okay, then, the living situation? How is that?"

"Well..."

****

Cornell

"Hey babe, what took you so long to answer the phone?" the female voice on the receiver stated irritated.

"I just got off with an artist's agent."

"Really, that long?" she nagged.

"Yes that long, don't start that again today."

"What time will you be home?"

"Babe, you know I can't give a definite answer to

that. I still have work I need to finish here before I'm done. You know boss man won't let me leave here without it being done," I said shuffling between documents on my desk.

"Cornell, I need you here," she wined.

"Sherrone, baby, as much as I want to be there with you I gotta work to keep things a float."

"Well, make sure you pick up groceries on your way home. Also I need you to pick up the boys and take them to get their haircuts this weekend."

"Now, wait a minute. One, I just went grocery shopping the other day."

"It's not for here it's for my..."

"Mr. Wallace you have an urgent client here to see you, and you might want to take this sit-down sir," my assistant interrupted.

"Sherrone, look, I have to take this meeting. I'll call you on my way home," I said.

"Okay, love you babe."

"Love you too, now I gotta go."

"Please send him in Samantha," I buzzed my assistant again as I scrambled to make my desk look somewhat presentable. I abruptly stood hastily and made my way around my desk to greet a music legend. "Mr. Davis, good to see you. Please come in, have a seat. Can I get you anything to drink? Water, coffee..." I asked.

"No no, I'm fine," he softly said as he took a seat.

The one and only Clive Davis, in my office. I met him last year at a showcase one of his artists performed at and once again, at least 4 months ago at one of our own showcases in New York. I can only imagine how busy this man is, so for him to seek me out was merely unexpected. As nervous as I am at his mere presence, I have to maintain my professional demeanor. "I must say Mr. Davis; it is an honor to be in the presence of such a music legend."

"Young fellas such as yourself are what make me appreciate this business. Speaking of, I told you I'd stop by sometime. There are very few businessmen in this industry that are in it for the love and craft. Most A&R or scouts are in it for that quick commission, but you, you my man, I don't get that from you. Reminds me of my younger self. The artist at your last showcase in April, oh my goodness. Her voice, her stage presence, her artistry. I only experienced that captivation and got chills from one other person. I'm not looking for the next Whitney, and frankly, there will never be another Whitney. My angel has sung her way into heaven, but for me to stop in my tracks made me more determined to figure out who was the man behind such talent." As he went on, I was taken a back at the slight mention of THEE Whitney Houston's name gave me chills. Here is the man with the best vision in the business's history. The locator, molder, and mentor of *The Voice* and he was sitting in my office giving me praise! "I'm rambling. You have that spunk that I thought died."

"Mr. Davis, all of that coming from you means more than anything. However I'm not quite sure where you're going with this."

"Here's what I'm proposing. Music isn't how it used to be and we need to get it back on track. With your youthful guidance, I need, no I WANT you to head the A&R department at Jive Records."

I swear I damn near pissed my pants. "Um, wow. I

um…I…wow," I stumbled.

"I understand the shock. I tell you what, I'll give you a month to figure it out and get back to me. How's that?" he propositioned me as he got up to leave

"Um, well…"

"Son, just shake your head yes. You can breathe later," he laughed. "I have had my eye on you son for quite a while and whatever you put your hands and name on is the truth. That's what I need. You think long and hard about my offer and whatever you demand believe I will accommodate."

"Um, thank you sir, but I …."

"Son, this decision shouldn't be made hastily. Go home. Sleep on it. Think about it. And I mean think hard. Take care son," he said as he shook my hand before leaving my office.

"Did I just get offered a job from THEE Clive Davis?" I mumbled to myself walking towards my desk.

Knock knock

"I hope you didn't forget anything," I said quickly turning around. "Mr. Davis I really am thinking about your offer but I'm gonna..."

"What offer?" Ra'Chelle said click clacking her way through my door heading towards my desk.

"Oh, it's you."

"Well, hell, nice to see you too!"

"Sorry I didn't mean it like that," I said as I took my seat behind my desk.

"Mmmmmmhhhmmm…well anyway, I came to give you my proposal. I came up with...wait...Mr. Davis...as in Clive Davis....THEE CLIVE DAVIS?!?!??!" she blurted.

"Shhhh," I motioned. I swear this woman is the loudest hood-rat here! "Yes Clive Davis," I mumbled trying to be coy about it.

"Uh, what was he doing in HERE? That man is a walking legend! Damn near everything he touches is certified success. You ain't nobody!" she went on.

"I know the man's credibility"

"Well, what's going on? You don't seem too excited that history just dropped by your office?"

"He dropped quite a load on my plate," I said removing my glasses to rub my aching eyes.

"What happened? He told you that you suck as an A&R exec?" she said with a smirk.

"Actually he said the opposite. He wants me to head the A&R department at Jive."

Suddenly Ra'Chelle bursts into laughter. "I'm sorry, I'm sorry. I just thought you were feeling yourself thinking that THEE CLIVE DAVIS came here to offer you a job."

"Actually, he did. No jokes," I said leaning back stretching in my chair.

"What the hell is wrong with you?" she blurted damn near sending me crashing to the floor.

"Well damn could you BE any louder?"

"I'm sorry it's just not everyday anyone gets a damn visit or even offer from prominent individuals! Wait a sec, what did you say?"

"Nothing."

"WHAT? You said NOTHING?" she yelled. Then she slowly approached my desk. "So let me make sure I got this correct. One of music's pioneers came into your office and offered you a position at a company that has not only seen its shares of greatness, but has birthed music royalty, and you said NOTHING? Cornell, excuse me for saying this, but, WHAT THE HELL IS YOUR PROBLEM?"

"Ra'Chelle, I understand the weight of their decision but there's a lot to take into consideration. I have a lot to take in. Why are you so aggressively concerned about the offer given to ME anyway?" When I say this woman was aggressive, I mean AGGRESSIVE.

"Cornell, I know you. We've worked together for at least 7 years now. I know your skill. You have one of the best eyes and ears for talent. This here just pays the bills. It's not what it once was and we both know damn well it won't be anytime soon!" she vented.

As much as I would hate to admit it, she has a point. "What was it you had to show me?" I asked shifting the conversation.

"Oh, right, well I brought that proposal we talked about," she stated as she pulled out a folded piece of paper from her bag. Once she returned to my desk, she rips up the paper and drops the remains on my desk.

"What the hell are you doing?" I asked baffled.

"THAT was me making things much easier for you. Here I spent time coming with an idea to revive the music scene, and here you have it dropped in your damn lap! So here is the new proposal. Pick up that phone, call Clive Davis, and say *Mr. Davis, I ACCEPT YOUR OFFER!*"

****

Symone

"Well I must say Mr. Smith; I'm very impressed at the man that came in here today. I understand these circumstances aren't ideal, but I like what I'm seeing and hearing."

"Doc, I apologize again for Racquel's behavior, but I must agree I like the man that came in as well. Is it okay if I schedule for another visit?"

"Oh most definitely, I'm here for you James as well as Racquel. Ashleigh will let you know what slots are available on your way out."

"I can't thank you again Doc," he said with a small smile as he headed out of my office and down towards my receptionist's desk.

As I sat down at my desk to update my files on James' abrupt session, my window blew in sending shards of glass flying. I covered my face with my hands trying to shield the flying glass debris.

"Symone?" Ray said rushing in from across the hall. "Are you okay?"

Before I could respond in ran Mr. Smith whom I thought was gone. "Doc is everything...Oh my goodness! Doc you okay?" he said as he rushed to my aid.

"I...I...I...I'm fine Mr. Smith."

"Oh my god," he said as he disappeared and returned with a wet handkerchief. "Here, let me see Doc," he placed the wet handkerchief on my forehead and as he pulled back to assess the damage, I notice a few amounts of blood that saturated the light towel. "You got a pretty bad nick here doc."

"Thank you Mr. Smith."

"Got dammit Symone! What the hell is going on here today...wait...Smith...Smith...Smith...Is this? Are you? Hell naw! Back the fuck away from her!"

"Raymond! Watch your mouth!"

"Symone, are you serious right now? Are you aware that your psycho bitch ass wife came in here and damn near demolished this woman's office, and you have the nerve to come here and now THIS happens! I swear on my children, if you don't leave this office before I finish my sentence, your wife will definitely become a widow, and you can believe that!"

"RAYMOND!"

"No no no Dr. Johnson, I understand his position. I should go and believe me when I say I'll get to the bottom of this. Racquel has indeed gone too far," he said and he rushed out of my office before I could get him to calm down.

"Raymond, you were out of line."

"Out of line? Look at your office! Look at your window! LOOK AT YOUR FACE! Look at..."

"What." Raymond's attention seemed to narrow in on something that lay still on the floor. He goes to inspect it and is more enraged. "Raymond, what?" He does nothing but hands me the crumpled paper that read *You fuckin with the wrong one. Next time, you might not be so lucky. Tread lightly Doc.*

"Symone, I'm going to say this once and once only TAKE THIS CRAZY BITCH OFF YOUR ROSTER!"

"Raymond, please stop using that word!"

"Look I know you take your job seriously and I applaud you for that, but this? This right here? Oh, no ma'am this is the end of the line! Now either you erase her ass off of your books, or so help me GOD I will myself! And I dare her crazy ass or her weak ass husband to say or do something about it!"

Getting up and removing the handkerchief from my head, I walk to Ray. "Look I know how you feel believe me I do, but you gotta back off and cool down right now. I'm not removing either one from my books. There is something deep down that needs to be addressed."

"Listen to you! What is it going to take for you to realize that this is bigger than you are? Is it going to take you to be tied up in an undisclosed location with half of your tongue cut out stirring in your own urine and feces for you to grasp this woman's madness?"

"Now you're going too far Ray."

"And you're not going far enough. Look, I know you want to help people. I get it. But this relentlessness you have going on with these two, you gotta give up."

"I know you don't understand it, but this will pass. I appreciate your concern; believe me I do. Now if you feel that you'll go all daddy mode on me, please leave my office now because I already have one of those."

After seconds of staring at me in sheer disappointment, Ray storms out of my office slamming the door behind him. I make my way to my desk and stare at what was once a calm and neat office. Now it just looked like an F5 tornado came in and just demolished everything in its path. *Get it together Symone; get it together!* I scroll online looking for reasonable and quick glass repair businesses and placed a call.

"Glass Doctor DFW, how may we be of service for you today?"

"Yes, this is Dr. Johnson located in University Park. I was looking for a contractor who can come and give me a quote for an office window space."

"Yes ma'am. We can locate someone out in the area to come by and assess the space within the hour. Can I have your address?"

Chapter 14
James

"Racquel! Racquel! I know you're here!" I yelled closing the door to what was once my home. When I placed my keys in my pocket and looked around to see if she was downstairs,

"Daddy Daddy!" the little voices sang from the kitchen.

"Hey Remi and JJ, where's your mother?" I asked trying to not showcase my frustration in front of my children.

"Mommy's in the kitchen on the phone you want me to go get her?"

"Nuh uh I'll go get her."

"Stop it JJ, Daddy didn't say you!" my daughter said as she took off running after her brother. I was so furious with Racquel I couldn't see straight. Although my daughter Remiah, nine, Remi for short and my son James "JJ" seven were my motivation, I was too far gone to be hurt that my own children darted off without a single hug or kiss. I walked into the kitchen to see Racquel hugging the phone to her face as usual. I can't say I don't miss those days. I was so in love with her.

"Girl I gotta go, I'ma call you later ok"

"Gossiping as usual huh," I started.

"James, what do you want? Don't you have better things to do, or other bitches should I say?"

"Racquel, don't start that today."

"Well hell James, when do you want to start it huh? You tell me! When my son sees his daddy fucking some bimbo he left his mother and sister for? You tell me when! When my daughter realizes her daddy ain't shit and feels that's the kind of man she should be with? YOU TELL ME!" she screamed. "Say something you overgrown piece of shit!"

I turned to my children that were doing their homework in the distance. "Remi, JJ, go play outside in the backyard and stay where you can be seen," I calmly said to my children although I was seething inside.

"Yes sir," they responded in unison while running through the kitchen.

Once the backdoor closed, I turned to Racquel "As long as you live don't you EVER in your life raise your voice or use that language in front of my children. I don't do it to you, and you damn sure will NOT do it to me!"

"What the fuck ever James, those are my children too! And if you love them so damn much why did you leave them?"

"Dammit I didn't leave my children, I LEFT YOU!"

"Really, you left me for who James huh?"

"I'm not doing this with you Racquel."

"Oh so you just gonna run off like a little bitch, is that it?"

"I swear you need help, prayer, something strong."

"I need help? I NEED HELP!" she paused and with a blank stare said, "It's her isn't it? I know it's her."

"Her who? Who are you talking about?"

"Where were you today?"

"What does that have to do with-"

"Did you have a session today?"

"No actually I didn't have a scheduled session, but after that stunt you pulled today it turned into one! Which takes me back to why I'm here in the first place."

"Oh so you came over her to defend your slut? Is that it? You have the nerve to come in my house and defend the woman you've been fucking around with?"

"What? I came here to see what the hell was wrong with you for trashing that woman's office! You're lucky she didn't call the cops and press charges on you!"

"Lucky? She better be lucky all I did was fuck up her office and not her damn face!"

"What is your problem?"

"You and that hoe are my problem! This is my problem," she said as she threw the divorce papers that I had sent over on the island. "Yeah, muthafucka I got em. So you're divorcing me for trifling trick after all I've done for you. I've been nothing but good to you and this is the shit you do! After all these years?"

This woman has officially lost it! "Racquel you're not making sense!"

"ARE YOU FUCKING DR. JOHNSON? Does that make sense to you?"

"What? No, I'm not doing anything with her. As a matter of fact, YOU knew her before I did! That first sit down we had with her was my first time meeting her!"

"Oh bullshit James! It's funny how not even a few sessions in we've been split into individual sessions! Then the divorce papers get delivered by a courier? I ain't no fool James. I know you're fucking the broad! I see how you look

Sinful Secrets   M'Hogany

at her!"

Well I can't deny Dr. Johnson is one fine ass doctor, but Racquel was way off at this point. "Now you tell me how the hell would I time that shit Racquel? You suggested we go to her specifically! And as far as these go, I sent them long before I even agreed to counseling."

With tears in her eyes, she slowly approached me. "I remember when you use to look at me the way I catch you looking at her. Yes I see your eyes James." as she got closer, she began to slowly disrobe. "Your eyes dance across her plump breasts," she said now standing face-to-face with her breasts exposed and pressed against my chest. "Don't you miss this James? Don't you miss the feel of my breasts against your chest?" She reaches for my hand and places it on her ass. "My soft round-brown ass."

Placing my right hand down her barely visible red thong, she leans in and whispers, "my hot juices flowing on your fingers." dipping my fingers in and out of her now oozing hot pussy juices. "Don't you miss Miss Kitty James? Don't you miss how she made you feel? How she would cum over and over on your thick dick? She's crying for you James. Make her feel good. Make us feel good."

I was torn between leaving and burying my dick deep inside her. When she licked my ear lobe, I couldn't take it anymore. "Racquel..." I managed to whisper. She looked at me with those eyes. Those eyes that I fell in love with as a teenager. Those eyes that made my knees buckle.

"Shhhh, don't talk," she said while she managed to slip her hand down my gym trunks and began to massage my dick. She didn't have much work to do because he was already standing at attention. "I know how you like it

Daddy," she moaned. "I know how wet you like it. You know how wet I can get for you. She's purring Daddy. I know you want to pet the pussy...cat."

No matter how much I wanted to rid myself of her, she had this thing about her that just pulled me in.

"Make love to me Daddy, please. Don't make me beg Daddy," she pouted.

"Racquel I can't."

Pulling my hand out from her now saturated pussy lips, she placed them in her mouth one by one. Each finger was slurped and sucked with precision. **Slurp** "Please Daddy." **slurp** "Please." **slurp** "Please." **slurp**

"Racquel I can't," I fought.

She pushed my gym shorts further down causing them to drop to my ankles and began to slowly stroke my dick going back and forth along my shaft. "Please Daddy."

"Racquel...I...can't," I panted with each stroke.

Racquel dropped to her knees and slowly took the head of my dick in her mouth and popped out the tip like it were a blow pop "Please Daddy."

"Racquel I...I...I...I..," I struggled to get out, stuttering as she places my rod back into her mouth again pushing it back further. Back and forth, she slowly sucks making it wetter than the last.

"Please Daddy," she said with the tip of my glossy head just inches from her lips.

I leaned my head back and rolled my eyes as she cupped my balls and licked up and down the shaft. She then started to hum as she placed her lips right under my sac. With each hum, I fought to keep from exploding.

"Mmmm," escaped from my lips. I know I shouldn't

be enjoying this, but SHIT! She always knew what got me going. "Damn girl," I moaned.

"You like that Daddy?"

"You know I like that shit girl." She took my now stiff rod into her hot wet mouth again and started going at it like she really wanted that nut! She sucked every ounce of pre-cum I could produce. "Shit you gonna make me cum"

"Uh uh Daddy, not before you beat this pussy."

She stood up, kissed me deeply and slowly. Is this what I have to do to get the best sex ever from my wife? File for divorce? I thought back to the first time we made love. The way she wrapped her legs around my body forcing my thrusts deeper with each stroke. The way she clawed at my back and nibbled on my earlobe. "Fuck me Daddy," she whispered as she pulled back from our intense kiss. She hopped on the island, pulled her thong to the side, spread her lips apart, and started to finger her glossy pussy for me to see. "She's ready for you Daddy. And she tastes so good," she moaned after placing her fingers in her mouth.

Before I could shove my dick into its awaiting oasis, I stepped closer and ran my fingers over her throbbing clitoris. "Mmmmm Daddy that feels good." I began to massage the vulva with my right thumb and slowly inserted my left index finger. "Oooooh yes," she groaned. Then I slowly inserted my middle finger to join its counterpart. "Shit yes!"

I simultaneously massaged her clit while my fingers danced inside her juicy sugar walls. She began to grind on my fingers wanting me to go deeper. I witnessed her head drop back in sheer enjoyment and felt her inner walls began to tighten up indicating her climax.

"Shit Daddy, I'm about to cum... yes...yes...don't stop Daddy...yes...YES...OHHHH!" right at that moment I slid my fingers out now dripping with her juices. "You know exactly how I like it Daddy," she grinned.

"Do I?"

"Oh yes you do."

I used the tip of my dick to tease her pussy lips and moisten the head. Mixing the sweet nectar releasing from her honey pot with the precum seeping from my opening. "Ah that feels good Daddy." I bent down and proceeded to lick and suck on her neck while I cupped her 38 DDD breasts. "That's it Daddy." Then I pushed through my slick threshold to glory with slow, short strokes. "That's good Daddy. That's good."

"Mmmmm," was all I could manage to get out. I have to admit, I loved Racquel's pussy. Over the years, it's formed to the perfect shape of my penis. After two kids, you'd think it would need reconstruction. Not in the least!

"Deeper Daddy," she whispered in my ear as she pulled my ass closer plunging me in deeper. "Ah ah ah! That's it! Yes Daddy YES!"

"This what you wanted? Huh? You want Daddy's dick inside you?"

"Oh yes Daddy."

I'm glad our children were outside playing because they would've gotten a full view of their parents' raw freakiness. As I thrusted deeper and harder into Racquel, she began to nibble on my ear once more. She knows that's my spot that drives me crazy! "Fuck me from behind Daddy."

Caught in the moment, I pulled out and glanced down at my heavily glazed soldier. "Turn dat ass ova," I said with a smack on her thigh. She hops down from the island slowly and turns around assuming the position. I cup her inner right thigh and lift it so that it remained propped on the island and slid into her now leaking cavity.

"Oooooh," she cooed. I started at a slow and easy pace watching as my dick disappeared and reappeared.

"Damn," I moaned. I bent over not breaking my stride and reached for her still swollen clit. I played with her clit while not interrupting my stride.

"Oh shit Daddy! Gimme that dick, gimme that dick!" she yelped. I felt her sugar walls start to enclose around my manhood signaling another orgasm. "Oh shit, I'm about to cum! Fuck me Daddy! Yesssssss!" At the sound of her pleasure, I increase my thrusts, making them not only faster but also harder and deeper. I was in short reach of my much-needed climax that I was fighting. Upon sensing my release, she abruptly pushes me away from behind her and drops to her knees proceeding to suck the orgasmic life out of my dick!

"Ahhhhhh damn!" I stuttered as I released my load in my wife's warm awaiting mouth. I was too lost in ecstasy to notice that she swallowed every drop of cum and cleaned my dick from any evidence. Slowly licking up and down my shaft and placing kisses on my sensitive mushroom tip. With each kiss, I flinched with shock waves of pleasure running up and down my spine. "Shit Racquel."

"You know I know how you like it Daddy," she said with a smile of satisfaction. She rose to her feet, kissed me gently on the lips, picked up her robe, and placed it back on. She heads towards the counter and reaches in the cabinets for the cleaning supplies carefully spraying the counter-tops and wiping them off with a few paper towels. She sprays solution on the floor and bends over to wipe it as well exposing her round brown. I swear that booty is playing peek-a-boo with me.

 Just then, I was brought back out of my moment of pleasure with the ringing of my cell. "Dammit." I pulled up my shorts, reached, and pulled out my cell to see **Bridgette** flash across the screen. I stepped out of earshot and answered my phone.

 "James where are you? You're late!"

 "Baby I'm sorry, I just got through leaving my session," I lied. "I'm on my way right now."

 "Well hurry up I don't want to do this without you," she whined.

 "I know baby, I'll be there shortly."

 "Okay, love you."

 "Love you too." **click** "Racquel, I have to go...." I said as I turned towards the kitchen.

 "Aw, you sure you can't stay a little bit longer. We can go for round 2," she said while slowly walking towards me and tracing my collar with her index finger.

 "Racquel," I stated while grabbing her left wrist. "I can't."

 "Yes you can Daddy," she said as her right hand started to make its way down my pants. I immediately grabbed her right wrist and stopped her from awaking my peacefully resting young man. I swear if she were to reach him again, he'd be ready for battle!

 "Racquel, NO! I didn't come over here for that. It

shouldn't have happened in the first place and it can't happen again! Understand?"

She instantly snatched her hands out of my grasp. "What the fuck you mean it shouldn't have happened? I shouldn't make love to my husband? What did you really come over here for then James? What just took place here?" she spat erratically.

"Racquel, calm down. I came over here to talk about your behavior earlier at Dr. Johnson's office."

With a devilish grin, she leans back on the counter with her arms folded. "So it is that bitch huh. What James, you came to fix your hoe's problem? Came to save the day? Well I guess you're just the real life Captain Save-A-Hoe then huh! She mad at her redecorated office space? I kinda like it. Made it look LIVED IN!" she said then starting to walk around the refrigerator.

"Racquel you were way out of line for destroying her office."

"She destroyed my damn marriage!"

"She didn't do a damn thing, that was all you! Our marriage ended years ago."

"No BITCH, unless I sign these weak ass papers, your ass is still MY HUSBAND!"

"What the hell happened to you?" I stated as I turned to walk out. As I neared the door, I heard Racquel follow yelling all kinds of obscenities. I just shook my head and proceeded towards my car.

"What happened to me? Nigga you weren't asking that damn question a second go when you were all up in this pussy!" she yelled in the doorway.

I placed my car in reverse and backed out of the

driveway. I connected my phone to the blue-tooth and scrolled the contacts until I saw whom I was looking for. I pressed talk waiting for an answer from the other line.

"What up Jay?"

"Aye man, you busy?" I asked while shifting gears.

"No."

"Well I'm headed back to you man."

"A'ight. You good?"

"Fuck no nigga!"

Chapter 15
Racquel

"You weren't saying that a second ago when you were all up in this pussy!" I yelled at my bitch ass husband as he sped off. I walked back into my house and slammed the door. "I bet he's headed back to tell his little bitch." I stopped and thought. *Think Racquel Think*. I grabbed my purse, retrieved my phone, and made a call.

"Hey, it's me. No it didn't work. I'm game if you are. Don't worry about the money, I gotchu. Just make sure the bitch gets the point."

"I'ma fix this shit my way," I mumbled after slamming the phone on the end table not caring if I shattered it or not.

"Mama, where's Daddy," the little voice appeared out of nowhere.

"JJ, Daddy's gone to take care of something," I said making my way towards my handsome son.

"Oh, is he coming back?"

"Soon baby soon. How about some lunch huh?"

"PB&J?" he asked wide eyed.

"PB&J it is. Last one in the kitchen is a rotten egg!" I said as he raced towards the kitchen.

Before I could catch up to him, my phone began to buzz. *In motion*. With a smirk on my face, I replied *Phase II* and returned my phone to my purse.

"Mama's a rotten egg!" the little voice giggled in

the distance.

"I'm gonna get you!" I laughed aloud as I made my way into the kitchen. *Mama's gonna get all of you…*

****

Symone
Knock knock

"Come in," I said while bent over picking up the glass shards I could gather.

"Um, yes I have a glass estimate needed for..." I heard the familiar voice say upon entry.

"No it...." I said pausing. I shot up quickly and spun around facing my door.

"Symone!"

"Michael?" I replied in shock. Okay this is getting too weird and starting to piss me off. "You know what Michael, I've had enough now! I told you before I'm not interested and I told my mother a many of times I'm not interested. What is it going to take for you two to get the picture?"

"Calm down, first your mother has nothing to do with me being here. This is my job."

"Your job?" I asked.

"Yes Symone, my job. I actually work to make a living," he said.

"Mmmmmhhhmm." I was still skeptical about him coincidentally being my contractor. "I'm having a hard time believing that Michael."

"Look Symone, you made it very clear last night that I was not the type of man you would give the time of day or even try to get to know. I got the message. I'm just here to do my job and get out of your way."

"I guess."

"I see you rubbed someone the wrong way, or you did a poor job at remodeling," he sarcastically stated.

"Just another day at the office with emotional clients."

"What? No. You're telling me someone did this intentionally? Not with your sensitive conversation and loving demeanor," he said in a dry manner as he walked towards the remaining glass window.

Something about him interested me. He didn't care that I wasn't interested. Wait, was I interested? I don't think I was. I'm not. No, I'm not interested. I convinced myself. "Well can you replace it?" I asked getting back to the reason he was there.

"I'm sure we can replace it. Let me place a call with the warehouse manager to see the process for these specific dimensions," he said taking his phone from his side holster.

"Um, ok. I'll head to the front to inform the receptionist about the work that is scheduled to take place here so we can work around it," I said as I made my way down the hallway.

As I left his presence, I wondered what were my chances of running into him AGAIN and this time it not being at the mercy or schemes of my meddling mother. I wouldn't put anything past that woman. When she is determined to get something done, she is relentless.

"Dr. Johnson. Dr. Johnson," the feminine voice bellowed bringing me back from my distracting thoughts.

"Oh, I'm sorry Ashleigh. I need you to re-direct my appointments for the next few days until I update you on the status of my office."

"Where should I direct them to?"

"My home office please."

"Wait, what?" Ray asked in a disturbed tone.

Meanwhile…

***Buzz buzz** Is everything on track?*

Everything is going as planned

Symone

"You're routing your patients to your HOUSE? Did we NOT just have this conversation Symone?"

"Raymond, keep your voice down!" I gritted through my teeth. "Ashleigh, can you make sure everything is taken care of and setup accordingly?"

"Yes ma'am, if I have any questions I'll make sure to contact you immediately."

"Thank you," I smiled before I pulled Raymond down the hall. "What in the world is your problem? I thought we talked about this already?"

"That was before I heard you were doing the stupid thing of holding sessions out of your house! You have to find somewhere else to have your sessions."

"Ray, I'm telling you for the last time, I...AM...FINE."

"I don't care if you're fine, you just had a damn deranged broad cause world war III in your office or what used to be your office, and now your window is busted! It looks like a damn war zone in there! What is really going through that pretty head of yours?"

"I see you're serious about what's going on but…"

"Apparently more than you!"

"But it's not that crucial." Before I could catch my

breath to say another word, the look that Ray gave me could have made Stevie Wonder uncomfortable.

"Not that crucial? Symone, look, I don't want you to get hurt okay? People these days are crazy and flat out don't give a rat's ass!"

"Ray, I can handle myself okay? Calm down. Besides, if I can survive having you as a friend for over 10 years, I can handle anything that comes my way."

"You laughing but I'm serious. How long are you going to have sessions out of your house?"

"Well, Michael says up to 3 or 4 days."

"3 to 4 days? Are you serious?" he yelled in a strong whisper.

"Hey, look, it was better than months!"

"Well, you have a point there. What are you going to do now since you know you can't hold sessions in your office for the rest of today?"

"While he's in here working on this disaster, I'm going to go home and get to working on the office area. Ashleigh had to reschedule all of my appointments for today to another day so…"

"So basically, you have nothing else to do for the day but just go home."

"When you put it that way…"

"Let me finish with my clients and I'll follow you home."

"No sir, you will not! You will finish what's on your books for today and I will go home alone and take care of myself thank you!"

"I'm not going to argue with you Symone."

"Nor I you! Now, go back to your office! Besides, I

need a set of eyes I trust to make sure my I'm getting my monies worth!"

Fighting the urge to go back and forth he finally said, "ok, but as SOON as I'm done here I'm heading your way. I'll call every hour ON the hour checking on you!"

"Okay okay, whatever you need to feel better. Now go!" I said as I playfully pushed him into his office.

Chapter 16
Cornell

"Mr. Wallace, you have a visitor."

"Send them in," I addressed my assistant. Just then, the door flew open.

"Aye C man," the voice frantically echoed in my office.

"J, what's going on?" I nervously asked as I dapped him up and closed my door. "You alright?"

"I need to talk to you man," he said this time pacing the floor.

"J, what's going on? Stop walking around negro you making me nervous. You need a drink? I think you need a drink," I asked headed to my mini wet bar.

Wiping his face and a shaking his leg he said, "I had sex with Racquel."

I stopped mid stride. "Oh hell yeah you need a drink," I said as I shook my head. "J what happened?" I asked as I headed started back up towards the bar.

"Man, look. I went over there to really check her bro."

"Check her?"

"She went to the Doc's office and just spazzed out. I mean damn near cleaned the place out. Shit was thrown everywhere out of place."

"Whoa, is that why you sped off in such a rush earlier?"

"Hell yeah! Luckily the doc was so understanding she didn't press charges or anything."

"She must be some kind of understanding therapist," I said handing him a drink. "So did she even say why she went ham on your shrink's office anyway?"

"Man, she thinks me and the good doc are sleeping together."

Damn near choking on my drink I said, "She what?"

"Yeah man! She thinks because the doc has us doing separate sessions we're secretly meeting to get it on."

"That's crazy. And what did you say?"

"Hell I told her ass she was crazy and it wasn't the doc!"

"That's it? You just told her it wasn't her and left?"

"What was I supposed to say?"

"How about you were in a relationship with someone else and not to mention she was pregnant! I mean, I'm no genius, but you could start there!"

"Shit the way she was going today, I couldn't get to it!"

"What do you mean you couldn't get to it? Look, I know you're mad and everything but you can't go around trashing people's office because you think I'm sleeping with her. To be honest with you, I have been with someone for quite a while now and she is expecting our first child together. How freakin' hard is that?"

"It ain't that simple C. When I walked in she threw the divorce papers down on the island! In between cussin and yellin, throwing in I moved on and had my new lady pregnant would have set things over the edge."

"Okay, so how did it go from all this turmoil, to you

two getting it in? And please no details."

He hesitated in his response, swallowed the rest of his drink, placed the empty glass on my desk, leaned back, and rubbed his chin. "After she slammed the divorce papers, she called herself trying to get a rise out of me trying to compare me to the doctor. She started reminiscing and had on this little robe."

"J, spare me."

"I told the kids to go outside and play cause she was talkin' all reckless, then as she started to come on to me, I don't know I just couldn't tell her no. I mean, I told her I can't plenty of times."

"But the little engine could," I joked.

"Man, she started rubbin on me and touching me like she use to when we were happy and started tearin off my clothes and when the robe dropped."

"Jay, whoa whoa. I get it."

"I'm just saying. I know it was hella wrong, but that woman knows exactly how to break me down," he said as he leaned forward and placed his head in his hands.

"A'ight J, look. You two have known each other since you were teenagers, hell just merely kids. You have two children, so of course she knows how to break you down. You two need to figure this out bro. Either y'all are gonna be together honestly and whole heartedly, or come to an understanding that you'll just be better off co-parenting."

"I know. You gotta point."

"Damn right I gotta point. You need to be paying me and not the damn counselor!"

"Man that ain't even the half of it."

"Whatcha mean it ain't the half of it."

"After we finished getting it in, baby girl called me while I was in the kitchen with my damn pants down."

"Aw hell naw J. I swear your damn man-card is about to be revoked."

"I got one fussin at me in one ear and now even my new lady is fussin at me."

"Now why is the new chick fussin?"

"Cause..."

Ring Ring

"Hello? Baby-girl I'm on my way. I'm sitting in traffic getting ready to exit Ross now. You know how traffic is on 75 around this time. I'll be there in 10 minutes," he lied as he rose up out of the chair he occupied. "Baby I'm coming. Calm down. I'll see you in 10 ok," he said once more before ending the call.

"J, I know you don't have that girl waiting on you."

"That's what I was trying to tell you! My intentions were to go and check Racquel and head to the doctor's office, but I got mmmmm tangled up."

"Tangled up in that ass," I mumbled. "Wait, doctor's office?"

"Today we are supposed to find out the sex of the baby."

This nigga here!

"You tellin me that after your fuck session with your estranged wife, you had the leisure to come here and chop it up with me instead of heading your bullheaded ass to the doctor's office to find out the sex of your child? If you weren't my boy, I'd kick your ass. You need to get on before lil mama get to blowin you up. Hell, she might end up kickin your ass before I do!" I said with a chuckle.

"Yeah man, gym tonight?"

"Dude we'll see. You need to handle that ish first man. Aye, stick with ya shrink and your drama man. You can't afford my damn hours and I ain't got the time to keep up with your soap opera."

I was so serious too. Hell, he's my boy, but I have my own shit to deal with.

Buzz buzz

I felt my phone instantly vibrate. *Damn, speak of the devil.* I waited until my boy left the office before I read the incoming message. *Cornell, I don't know what or who the hell you're caught up with, but you better call me ASAP.*

After reading that damn message, I rubbed my head and face in frustration mumbling, "I don't have time for this shit..."

Chapter 17
Symone

After nearly 3 hours of men in and out of my office taking measurements and cleaning up the debris, I managed to finally get all of my much-needed files and loaded them into my car. On my last trip, I stopped by Ashleigh's desk. "Ashleigh."

"Yes Dr. Johnson?"

"Can you make sure that Dr. Watkins behaves himself? See if you can keep him busy. I don't want any disruptions with the men working in my office. The sooner they can get it back into shape, the quicker they'll be out of the way! Also, if Mrs. Smith calls or comes by, call me first."

"But I thought you wanted to have your clients sent to your home office?"

"I'm gonna approach the Smith's a bit differently. Just call me if she shows up."

"Yes Dr. Johnson."

I make my way down the hall to ensure that I've gathered all that I would need to assist my clients. As I opened the door, I gasped while covering my mouth. "This looks worse than before I left!" I mumbled to myself. I stepped over bubble wrap and tape dispensers clustered on the floor in corners, as well as on tables, with tables full of glass shards. As soon as I took a step towards my desk, my heel then gets caught in the taped down plastic causing me to lose my balance and stumble. I was caught before my face and the floor became one. "Whew. Ok, Ray, sometimes you're a pain, but you came right in the nick of time," I said with a tight grip on his arm.

"Well I couldn't let you fall and face Pastor Johnson Sunday." That voice AGAIN!

"MICHAEL!" I screamed with wide eyes as I scrambled to regain my composure and bearings.

"You okay?" he asked.

"I'm, um, I'm fine."

"I was hoping to come back before you saw the debris left."

"Well, you failed."

"Don't worry princess the clean-up crew is on their way. Wouldn't want you to actually pick up something and do some work," he scowled as he walked past me.

Did this negro just call me princess? Is he implying that I'm a spoiled brat?

"Ashleigh will be able to answer any questions as well as Dr. Watkins that is across the hall," I said before I walked out and made my way home. *Smug bastard*

****

Michael

I swear that woman moves fast I thought to myself. All I saw when I turned around was the door closing. Just then, my phone rang. "Yeah...I'm on the job right now.......I can't just stop because you want me to......Listen let me get this situated first..." I struggled to get out my point across before I was disconnected.

"I gotta get this shit over and done with. This naggin and keeping tabs on a brutha is wearing thin," I stated while I placed my phone back in my back pocket. *Alright, back to work* and I proceeded to pick up the trash while waiting for the cleaning crew to come. Upon reaching the window, I noticed a folder on the floor labeled *Confidential*.

"Symone must have dropped this," I said and I instantly had a thought.

Raymond
"Hey Ashleigh, did Dr. Johnson say how long the wrecking crew would be here?"

"She mentioned that it would be a few days. Is there something I can do for you though?" she slowly batted her eyes and gave me a little smirk.

"No that was all. End of day for you?"

"Yes it is, but I have to wait until the gentlemen in Dr. Johnson's office clear out and the young man in charge brings me the key to lock up"

"Don't worry about it. You go ahead and go; I'll wait for these guys."

"You sure, I mean I can stay it's not a problem."

"Woman, if you don't get yourself up out of here!"

"Aww, my hero," she joked "Well thank you Dr. Watkins. I've logged out, my desk is locked, and I am out of here. Be nice Dr. Watkins."

"Me? I'm always a gentleman."

"No Dr. Watkins I said be nice! Dr. Johnson wanted me to make sure you're nice to these men here."

"I promise you Ashleigh, I will behave."

"Dr. Watkins," she paused with her hands perched on her hip.

"Hey, Scouts Honor!"

"Okay, but if I see you on the news, I'm gonna give you the business!"

"Take care Ashleigh," I smiled as she proceeded to get in her car and pull away. *Symone wants me to play nice, but she should know by now, I don't do nice.* I started walking down the hallway and as I neared Symone's office door, I heard a muffled voice through the door that I couldn't quite make out. That's odd because the cleaning crew hauled out the last bit of debris and glass before Ashleigh left.

I got a bit closer to hear what was being said, "No, I'm not done yet. I need more time. I'm here, but it can't be handled that quickly." I assumed it was the window repairman, since everyone else had left.

Knock Knock

I made my way inside and apparently startling the contractor that was on the phone speaking with his boss. "Oh, um, I'm actually wrapping up here. I'll let the receptionist know I'm done on my way out," he said to me.

"Oh, she's gone for the day so I'll be locking up. I'm Dr. Watkins, Dr. Johnson's colleague right across the hall," I said shaking his hand.

"Michael man, nice to meet you."

"Any idea how long you'll be repairing the space here?"

"If nothing changes, I'm looking at 3 or 4 days. I'm looking to be out of your hair no later than Saturday of next week."

"Alright, that's great to hear. I mean, can't get work done with an atomic mess in the building. No way to relax around that," I said trying to get a feel of this man. With a visit from a psycho bitch and now threats on the office, I don't trust anybody. Although he was there to work on Symone's office, I had an eerie feeling about him.

"I should be out of your hair in about 10 minutes, let me gather my things and I'll be out," he said.

"Great," I said heading out towards my office but leaving the door cracked.

****

Michael

After leaving the office, I stared at the man locking the building in my rear view mirror. *I see this won't be so easy.* I remembered the file I picked up in Symone's office and headed towards my new destination.

****

Symone

"My goodness," I stated with a strong sigh as I looked into the drab office area.

"You have your work cut out for you here Symone."

From the boxes in the corner, to the sun peering through the closed blinds, this space needed a little TLC. I had to think of something quickly before I could welcome my clients to a new space. Placing my things down on the desk that sat near the bookshelf in the north point of the room, I opened boxes and began removing my numerous plaques, awards, degrees, pictures, things that gave an office life. **Ding Dong** I heard the doorbell chime. Looking at my watch I wondered, "Who could that be? No one knows I'm at home."

Making my way to the foyer, the doorbell chimes numerous times "I'm coming I'm coming," I said while unlocking the door.

"Bout damn time!" the figure spat sashaying by me.

"Hello Ra'Chelle, please come in," I mocked to the empty space before I closed the door.

"Chile boo," she said swinging her 24-inch weave into the kitchen. "What's goin' on girl?"

"Um nothing. How did you know I was home?"

"Symone, hunny, you are very predictable. Besides, I called and went by the office and nobody was there," she said while pulling out a glass and a bottle of white wine.

"Starting kinda early aren't you?"

"It's 5 o'clock somewhere right?"

"Chelle…"

"What?"

"Spill!"

"Girl, I'm trying to keep it professional and classy at this label but they keep pairing me up with these ratchet ass, talentless, self-centered, busted, so-called rappers. And if I get another damn groupie cop an attitude with me, I'm snatchin bitches!" I couldn't help but laugh at her. "What the hell is so damn funny?" she side eyed as she pulled out the leftovers from the previous night's dinner.

"I thought you had some serious issues, yet you spazin out about some work mess."

"This shit is serious! I'm tellin you, if one more hoe reppin the boogie down Bronx or Oakland or Compton steps to me on another set with some fly shit, I'M GOING TO JAIL! Yo' ass is in DALLAS! You wanna be bad, talk that shit in west or south Dallas, or take yo' ass to Oak Cliff. See if they don't set you straight!"

"You gotta point there."

"What's going on in the office? I saw some boards up on the side of the building. You remodeling?"

"Something like that. Little repairs going on."

"Ray's face broke the mold...LITERALLY?" she said with a strong laugh to follow.

Rolling my eyes I said, "see I'm not even gonna play with you. The window is being replaced."

"That big ass window? Damn, I guess his face shatters glass too."

"Would you quit it?"

"Ok, so who did you piss off then?"

"Why do I have to be the one pissing people off?"

"Symone, that's a thick ass piece of glass. That had to be an intentional shatter."

"I don't know who could've broken it, but we found a cement block on the floor."

"Cement block? Bitch don't nobody throw no damn cement block at a window for recreation!"

Before I could say anything extra, my doorbell rings *thank GOD!* Quickly shuffling to the door, I mumbled, "great, what else can go wrong?" while swinging the door open.

"Well damn, is that how people answer doors in this area?"

"Come in."

"Look I just came over to see if you needed any help and to check on you."

"You couldn't pick up the phone and call like regular people?"

"Symone, don't try to get out this conver..." Chelle blindly spat before rounding the corner. "Shit, here this muthafucka go!"

"Symone, you didn't tell me you had Sasquatch here. Time for your monthly flea bath?"

"Ray, now you two are not gonna keep doin' this in my house!"

"I'ma need a stiff drink if this sack of shit is gonna be here," Ra'Chelle said heading back to the kitchen.

"The only piece of shit here is that excuse of a hairstyle you got goin' on on-top of your head. What is that Chubaka ass hair?" Ray shot back going toward the kitchen.

Laughing I said, "alright now, stop it!"

"Why is she here anyway?"

"Nigga don't worry about why I'm here, why the hell is your lonely ass here!"

I swear this refereeing mess is getting old and tiring.

"You know what, I came over here Symone to make sure you were okay like I said and see if you needed any help getting setup in the office. And another thing, how long are the workers supposed to be down at the office?"

"Ray I already told you. Why are you so paranoid?"

"I'm not paranoid, I'm concerned! After that crazy woman came in and tore up your office you'd think you would be a little more hesitant in leaving unknown people in your office when you're not there."

"Wait, what the hell?" Chelle interrupted.

"Oh I see you didn't let your pet Chubaka know that bit of information."

"I didn't tell her cause I knew she would blow it out of proportion."

"Can somebody tell me what the hell is going on?"

"So you mean to tell me you didn't tell cousin IT that one of your patients came in and royally fucked up your office leaving barely anything left to spare?"

"Ray!"

"Oh you did? I'm sorry. You didn't tell her about the jackass that blew out your window then?"

"Raymond!"

"Oh, you covered that too. Well, it must have been threatening letter that was left after-"

"RAYMOND WATKINS!"

"Symone? What is this negro talking about? Who is this bitch?" Chelle snapped.

Shaking my head I said, "Look it's nothing. I just had an erratic patient. It was all a misunderstanding." I shrugged it off.

"A misunderstanding? Who is this ratchet broad? Why didn't you say anything?" She yelled.

"I didn't tell you because I knew you'd act like this. Besides, I can't tell you who it is because it violates doctor-patient confidentiality."

"She violated your personal space Symone, so FUCK THE CLAUSE!"

Ding-dong

"What the hell is this, pop up on Symone day? I asked while quickly getting away from the hot seat. As I opened the door, I was slightly frozen in place.

"Symone, sorry to come over unannounced..."

"Michael...what are you doing here? How did you find out...you know what, look you have to stop following me! First, you came with my parents and that I can let that slide, then you came to dinner and we see how that turned out, then my job, now my home. I don't know how many times I have to tell you..."

"Symone, look I just brought you your file that you dropped at your office. I didn't want the crew to pick it up and go through it being that it was marked *Confidential*. I could have left it there, but I thought otherwise. I remembered where you stayed, and brought it to you since it's on my way home," he angrily spewed as he handed me the file.

"Oh, Michael I am so so sooooo sorry."

"No, don't. You said enough. Have a good one Dr. Johnson," he said as he walked off angrily.

I closed the door and headed back to Joe Frasier and Ali.

"What's eating you?" Ray asked.

"Huh, oh, nothing. You two got me being rude and stuff."

"Huh, how we got you to be rude?"

"Who was at the door? You okay?" Chelle wanted to know.

"I'm fine, I'm fine, it was Michael."

"Michael?" Chelle asked in a muffled tone. Her once warm face now resembled a deer in headlights.

"The contractor from the office? What did he want? Wait how did he know your address?" Ray asked ignoring Chelle's facial expression or lack thereof.

"He brought me some files I dropped in the office. Chelle you okay?"

"Huh? Oh yeah, I'm fine. Don't try to shift the conversation ma'am," Chelle came back.

"Symone, I don't want him coming back here. If you are gonna talk to him, it needs to be only at the office," Ray interjected.

"Ray, now you're going too far."

"Apparently not far enough. You already are running a risk of having your patients come to your house, and there's no telling how they'll act. Now you have this dude that you don't know a damn thing about popping up at your house. Something ain't right here."

"Thank you Ray, but I think I can manage."

"You can't think that everyone has good intentions and is actually a standup person."

"I know that."

"I don't think you do!" he yelled as he stormed out the front door.

"Ooooooooooh, he's mad at you!" mocked Chelle.

"You hush!"

"Don't get me mad at me. I'm just floored that you can't see how that man has the hots for you," she stated while refilling her glass.

"What do you mean?"

"You mean to tell me you can't tell that good ole Ray got the hots for you?"

"I think you're wrong about that"

"Am I? He went out of his way to come help you setup your office and check on you?"

"That's what friends do!"

"He damn near ripped that man in two, and he didn't even step a foot in the door!"

"He was concerned after earlier today."

"And you just keep making excuses for him…"

"Chelle, you know good and well I have never liked Ray or seen him in that way."

"Just because you don't like him, don't mean shit. That orangutan is crushin hard. You got monkey love girl!" she said as she shoved the last piece of chicken in her mouth.

"I done had enough drama today. I must get to my boo and relax. Besides, you ain't got shit in here to eat. TOOTLES!" She said as she picked up her purse and flung her weave out the door.

After locking the door, I head towards the couch and plop down. "Why do I have to have such overrated friends?" I yawned. I turned on the television to see a rerun of *Girlfriends*. This episode was where Joan and William finally get together.

"Aw Damn Chelle!"

Chapter 18
Michael

Status Update the text read.

Look I said I'm going to need more time, but everything is going accordingly. Let me handle this.

You must have forgot who I am and what I'm capable of it quickly responded.

I said I'll handle it and let you know when it's time.

Fuck this up and see what happens. It's either her, or you. I'll let you guess who I'm talking about. Get it done Mike and get it done fast.

That was all I could think about. My patience was wearing thin, and clearly, I'm the only one that has it.

Ring ring

The sound suddenly snapped me back to reality. Answering it, I discovered it was First Lady Johnson.

"Michael hunny, how are you?" she cheerfully responded.

"I'm doing good ma'am, and yourself?"

"Oh I'm well thank you. I wanted to apologize for my husband and daughter's rude behavior the other night at dinner."

"Oh no need to apologize. I would've reacted the same way with my daughter if I were Pastor Johnson."

"I just don't get that child of mine. We didn't raise her to be so disrespectful like that. I hope she didn't leave a bad taste in your mouth or leave a negative impression. I'm still praying for her. Hopefully my prayers for her husband will soon get answered." I could sense the smile plastered on her face.

"She was doing what I would want my daughter to. I think you and Pastor have done a great job," I reassured her, trying to end the call.

"Well, thank you darling. I wanted to contact you since you were on my mind."

"*Yvette,*" I heard the pastor call in the background.

"Michael, hunny, let me tend to this man of mine. Don't give up on that daughter of mine, because I know I surely won't!"

"Yes ma'am. You and the pastor have a good one. Don't hurt him now First Lady."

"Oh hunny, you'll learn how us Johnson women are!"

If only you knew what I had in store for your daughter!

Chapter 19
James

"What the hell took you so long to get here? Do you know how long I've been here waiting on you? What excuse it is now?"

"Baby calm down. I'm here now. Don't work yourself up and it's not good for the baby."

"The doctor will see you now," the assistant called from the door.

We walk in and I help her onto the table.

"Okay mommy, we're going to have you disrobe from the waist down and the doctor will be in shortly to begin the exam."

"Are you excited?" I asked.

"What do you think? Here I am expecting my first child and my boyfriend is somewhere doing GOD knows what instead of being here with our child and me. So excuse me if I'm not jumping for joy or bouncing off the damn walls."

I try to calm her down by rubbing her shoulders.

"Don't fucking touch me, this shit is far from over," she gritted through her teeth and before I could calm her down, the room door opened and in walked the doctor.

"Well hello hello, how are we doing today?"

"Fine," she smiled. This had to be the damn mood swings because less than 2 seconds ago this woman damn near bit my head off, and now her ass is flashing them damn fangs!

"And who do we have here with us?"

"James, James Smith"

"So Daddy I take it?"

"Yes," she dryly remarked with a quick roll of the eyes.

"Well hello James, I'm Dr. Lawson. Alright Bridgette, I'm gonna need you to scoot down and I'll do a quick pelvic exam making sure everything is ok and then we'll look at the sonogram."

I try to help her scoot down further and the second our skin makes contact; she snatches her hand away and snaps in a low tone, "I don't need your help!"

Ignoring the ever so public display of affection, Dr. Lawson strikes up a brief conversation. "So, James. Is this your first child?"

"Oh um no, Dr. Lawson. I have a daughter and a son as well."

"Oh well you should be a seasoned pro then."

"I wouldn't say that," I chuckled.

Noticing Bridgette's once more rolling eyes, she shifted the conversation once more. "Okay, so seems like everything is good. Mommy, I'm gonna need you to scoot back and we're gonna see what this little one has in store for us today." She cut the lights off and as she gets the machine in place. "So have we picked out names for our little bundle?"

"Not quite," Bridgette seemed to blow the question off.

"Are we finding out the sex today?" She said as she continued to apply the gel on her stomach and place the machine on her stomach that started to sing with a rhythmic beat.

"Oh most definitely!" Bridgette leaped at the question.

"And Dad, how about yourself?"

I was too caught up in the heartbeat of my little one to even notice that I was being questioned. I started having flashbacks to the moment I saw JJ's sonogram for the first time. My boy, my BOY! When I found out it was a boy I was running up and down the hallway of the doctor's office hugging every nurse I saw and hi-fiving every dad in the waiting room. Hell I even hi-fived the damn janitor. "

James!" Bridgette wailed.

"Huh?"

"Do you want to know the sex of the baby or not?" Bridgette angrily spat.

"Oh, of course of course," I said.

"Here are the fingers...and toes...and mouth...and nose...."

Is *this a damn nursery rhyme or what?* I thought.

"And right now she's looking at the camera waving. *Hi Mommy and Daddy.*

"Wait, did you just say *she?*"

"Congratulations. It's a girl."

Overcome with tears and emotions Bridgette said, "James! It's a girl!" She looked at me with tears in her eyes. I knew these were tears of joy.

"Ok, I'm gonna let you get cleaned up and I'll print these pictures out for you to take home. Again, congratulations to you both," she said while removing the latex gloves before leaving out of the room.

"Thank you Dr. Lawson," I beamed as she left.

"Can you believe it's a girl James? A girl! I sooooooo wanted a girl!" She blushed as she cleaned and redressed, this time letting me help her.

"I know, baby. I know."

"I wonder if she'll have my hair or your eyes. What about names? We have to fix the nursery. I have to call my mom and my sisters..." and she kept going on and on and on, and I couldn't stop laughing.

"Bridgette...slow down."

"I can't help it. I'm too excited," she proclaimed.

Then Dr. Lawson re-entered the room. "Alright I have your pictures here, but before you two go we have something else to talk about," She said as she handed Bridgette the pictures and she grinned from ear to ear goin' through the frames. Dr. Lawson pulled up a stool and began to speak even though we were caught up in our little girl's photo moments.

Once I saw Dr. Lawson pull out her laptop, I asked, "Dr. Lawson is everything ok?"

"Yes it is, but…"

"But what?" Bridgette paused yet still smiling.

"But the exam I performed before the sonogram showed that there was a drop in amniotic fluid which surrounds the baby."

"What does that mean? What are you saying? What is she saying James?"

"Bridgette, calm down," I soothed.

"Well, the amniotic fluid, in your case, is the cause of your dehydration being high."

"Okay, so she needs to stay hydrated. No problem."

"Well that and we're seeing spikes in her blood pressure. That's really not good for Mommy or baby. We can go into premature labor, and at this point, she's too soon to deliver. If she does, it'll be difficult for us to save the both of them with no harm to either's health. So what I'm heavily suggesting is to keep Mommy as calm as possible and refrain from any unnecessary stress. Other than these two things, everything should be fine. Now I'm going to be checking in on you two. Don't make me come find the two of you!" she joked. "But I'm sure you'll be fine," she smiled before leaving the room.

James can we talk please.

This is not happening to me. Not here. Not now. I thought as I deleted the incoming text.

"Who was that James?"

"Huh?"

"Who was that?"

"Oh, no one. Just work related stuff."

"James, stop with the damn lies ok. I'm tired of them and frankly, they're getting old! Now who the hell was that?"

"Bridgette I'm telling you it was work!"

Fighting my help off of the table, she was angry again. "You know what I'm sick of this shit I swear I am. Negros wanna lie to me and I'm big as a damn whale..." she started to mumble as she snatched everything from her jacket, to her purse, to her keys.

"Bridgette calm down. You heard what Dr. Lawson said about your blood pressure," I tried to calm her down.

"FUCK MY BLOOD PRESSURE!" she yelled and opened the door.

Before she could swing it completely open, I slammed it shut scaring the hell out of her. "Listen to me and listen to me good. You are carrying my daughter and I be damned if I let any hurt or harm come to her. Bridgette you WILL do as the damn doctor says and you will CALM THE FUCK DOWN!"

Trying not to cry she looks me in my face, and the lines of strain and stress began to fade. "James I am scared Okay? I'M SCARED," she whispered through tears.

"Look I know this baby. I'm scared too, but I'm here with you and we are going to see this through together okay? You are my number 1 girl! And you're carrying my other number 1 girl!"

"Well, let's get out of here because your number 1 girl is turning my damn uterus into a damn MMA octagon!"

****

Racquel

I swear on my kids, that bitch is going to pay. Bitches gon' learn not to fuck with me I thought as I went ham on my text messages while I smoked my cigarette outside the bistro. I didn't even hear Sherrone walk up until she scared the shit out of me at the table.

"Racquel...Racquel...Racquel!" She yelled damn near scaring me.

"Oh, hey girl. When you get here?"

"Girl, question is where were you? I walked up and you ain't noticed a bit of nothing!"

"Oh, chile I had a few things on my mind."

"Hell I can see that!" she chuckled as she sat down. "How's life?" She started in.

"Girl same ole same ole"

"Oh don't I know that much."

"You?" I tried to act concerned.

"Girl nothin different. Cornell working like mad crazy in and out of town. James?" she asked as she began to give the menu a once over.

"Are you ready to order ma'am?" the waiter appeared.

I'm glad his ass showed up when he did cause the mere mention of James made my pussy throb and got me hot with anger at the same damn time. "I'll just have what she's having, but with water though."

"Yes, ma'am," he said as he departed with menu in hand.

"Um miss lady?"

"What's up?" I asked eating my fruit without diverting my attention from my cell phone.

"Where have you been lately? Haven't seen much of you lately. I know James ain't got you hemmed up in the house. If he is, y'all nasty..."

If only she knew. "Whatever Ronnie," I smirked while grabbing my fourth glass of Sangria.

"How many of those have you had Racquel?"

"Huh?"

"Huh my ass, how many have you had?"

"This is just my second one," I said noticing her side eye of disbelief.

"Don't give me that damn eye."

The only thing keeping me from driving back down to that hoe of a doctor's office and fucking her up on sight is these damn Sangrias. I know that bitch is the key to James sending me those damn papers. If he thinks I'm going to just let him walk out with that bitch, they BOTH have another thing coming.

****

Symone

"I can't believe we're finally doing this. I've been trying to get you since day 1."

"Well I'm here now so prove how bad you want it," I said.

Without hesitation, he ripped my blouse sending buttons soaring across the room.

He took my right breast in his mouth and sucked on my areola then flicked his tongue over my hardened nipple. "Mmmmmmm," I moaned in ecstasy while throwing my head back enjoying the level of pleasure I was experiencing.

As he gives my right breast a tongue-lashing, his left hand slowly trickles down caressing my thighs and travels further south exploring my chocolate canvas. He proceeds to leave spine chilling kisses in a trail along my stomach and parts with my body's natural separation His wet, warm snake appears and starts making circular motions from my outer thigh slithering its way inward.

As goose bumps protrude through my now moistened skin anxiously awaiting the lashing my honey hole so direly craved, he spreads my legs apart and blows on my honey spot. I can feel my juices run immediately. He takes his forefingers and gently spreads my labia apart exposing my pink clitoris saturated with juices released from my sugar walls. I eagerly yearn for the slither of his hot tongue.

"Symone...*Symone...*"

"Yes," I moan.

"*Symone...*"

"Yes," my moans get more seductive.

"*Symone...*"

My eyes peer open. "MAMA?" I jumped damn near knocking us both off the couch.

"Baby, were you having a bad dream?" she asked.

Far from it. I thought.

"Baby you're sweating like a whore in a church house, Symon get her a glass of water," she instructed my father.

"What are you doing here?" I stated sitting up and trying to gather my bearings. As I shifted upward, I felt a sticky warmness slide in between my thighs causing my eyes to pop open like a deer in headlights.

"What's the matter baby?" she kept asking.

"Um...nothing...I think...I'm trying to remember when I fell sleep on the couch," I lied trying to ignore the gooey bubbles starting to form in between my lips.

"Me and your dad just decided to drop in on you."

"I told your mother you had to be sleep," my father interjected as he handed me the glass.

"When you didn't answer my calls I got worried and then I found you here mumbling and sweating."

I reached over, grabbed my cell phone off of the coffee table, and noticed that my mother had called me 6 times back to back. *I have got to remember to get that key back* I thought to myself. "Mama, it's 9:30. You guys live all the way on the other side of town!" *Damn did I sleep that damn long?*

"Baby-girl I told your mother we should've gone

straight home and you'd call us in the morning."

"Hush Symon. I had to see for myself that you were okay."

"Ma, I'm fine! Where are you guys coming from this late anyway?"

"Your dad and I just came from a revival."

"Well, I'm glad you two came all the way over here, but as you can see I'm well and fine. So you two need to go ahead on and go home."

"She's right Yvette, we've been here too long, and we both know you will not be driving home."

Feeling ganged up on, my mother conceded. "Ok, but I'm calling you early in the morning," she continued as Daddy helped her put on her jacket. Kissing me on my forehead she said, "Get some rest baby-girl, we'll call you when we make it home"

"Okay Daddy, love you."

"Love you too baby-girl".

Have I mentioned how much I love my daddy? After helping my parents go to their car and watch them pull off on their way home, I closed the door behind me and ensured everything was secured before I retired upstairs. As I head towards the living room to grab my phone, I notice a peach sized wet spot glisten on my couch cushion. *What the hell was I dreaming about? Better yet who?*

Chapter 20
Cornell

"1...hit...2...hit...3...hit...C'mon baby you got this baby lightweight c'mon 4...hit...5."

"Damn C! Either you tryna kill me or you on some strong shit today!"

"Man quit cryin," I joked.

"Shit nigga for you to be a small bastard, you gotta be on something!"

"You gonna cry or train, either way lift or move."

"A'ight, time out lil nigga. What the hell is your problem man? Normally I'm the one havin a damn bitch fit, but you're off your game bro," James stated while sitting on the adjacent bench.

Dropping my head in my hands I said, "Nah man, my bad. It's just been pretty rough and all. Nothing I can't handle."

"Bullshit nigga. You throwin these damn weights around like yo' ass been injectin ass shots or like yo' ass is being experimented on. You on some hulk shit nigga for real!"

Laughing I replied, "nah, I'm a'ight bro. You good to finish?"

"Nigga you gonna let a nigga LIVE? I swear between you and Racquel, I think y'all are conspiring to off a nigga. How much insurance you got out on me bro?"

****

Symone
Home Session

"Okay, I'm glad to see we're making progress Mr. and Mrs. Peoples. Continue those exercises and write everything in your journals and we'll assess and address next Tuesday we're headed in the right direction, I promise you. You two take care," I stated while closing my home office entrance.

I turn and before I could take another step, I stopped and marveled at the luxurious space decorated with leather furniture, crystals I managed to salvage, and my numerous awards. *Father I thank you for my many blessings although I am not worthy of your grace or mercy. If you don't bless me any further, or see me unfit for further blessings, you've done more than enough. Amen.*

Knock knock

"Is there a Dr. Johnson available?"

"I'm Dr. Johnson, how can I help you?"

"Please sign here ma'am. These are for you. Have a great day," and just like that, he was gone after he handed me a wrapped arrangement.

Who the hell could've sent these? As I sat the arrangement on my desk there was noise at the door again.

Knock knock

"Oh come on!" I said rushing back to the door and opening it.

"Haaaaaaaaaay boo!" Ra'Chelle smirked dancing across the doors threshold. "Well alright now Dr. Johnson. Look how you livin, or as Wendy Williams would say *How you do-eh,*" she ranted dropping her jacket on the leather ottoman. "You are indeed a mess. What are you doing here chica?" I said with a chuckle. "I can't come see my girl?" eying the arrangement on the desk "hell from the looks of it, somebody else was thinking about you too." Locking my door and making my way towards my desk to sit "I have no clue who sent these. Is there a card?"

"Nope," she mumbled taking a bite out of a chocolate covered strawberry. "Well damn, don't wait for me. Please help yourself." Plopping on the couch "so ma'am, how long you gonna be working outta this spot?"

"This week for sure. Hopefully I'll be back in my office next week. I'm not too keen on people knowing where I lay my head all in my personal space."

"I heard that. So seriously, what actually happened at the office today?" she asked while helping herself to the grapes bound together by skewers. "This patient of mine was just crazy. Came in and wrecked my office. Then after she left while I was getting my office together, or trying to, my damn window sounded like it blew up and when Ray called himself being a hero, he found a note. I don't know if it was left there or how it got there."

"Note? What did it say since you actin like it ain't shit?"

"Something along the lines of being warned and I'll get it or something..." I waved off while thumbing through some files.

"Bitch are you serious! And you ain't drag that hoe?"

"It's nothing," I shrugged not looking up from my files. "You know it was that crazy bitch E.T. was talkin' about! I don't know why you don't beat that hoe bitch ass!"

"It's not that serious"

"Why was she so damn amped in the first place Symone?"

"Girl nothing important"

"Symone, no hoe trashes an office if it's not important."

Letting out a sigh I said, "She thinks I'm sleeping with her husband."

"AWW SHIT WOMAN!" she said followed by a series of snaps! "No Chelle, it's not like that!"

"Ok ok ok, you right. But hunny you are better than I am! See, these crazy bitches swear they big billy bad ass and just as bold as shit"

"It's nothing new. These things happen when...."

"When what? ARE you sleeping with her husband? Let me find out you getting it in Symone!" she replied with a smirk "Hell no! You know me better than that! What do I get out of someone else's problem? And don't ask anything about who she was anymore or stuff like that because you know I can't disclose any information."

"Tramp I ain't asking for specific names, addresses, or the broad's DNA samples! For a woman to trash her shrink's office, the bitch is clearly not wrapped too tight and is deep in denial about her failing or failed situation. So...." she continued while crossing her arms and reclining back with a grin, "you fuckin her man or what? Is he fine and is his pussy eating game on point?" Then she sat up quickly. "Does he beat the pussy up good girl? What is he workin wit 8, 9, 10 inches?"

I mean this perverted chic was propped up on her elbows and everything. Damn near salivating at the mouth! I immediately started to scrounge through the basket that once housed the beautiful arrangement. "What are you doing?"

"I'm trying to see if this is laced with some drug. PCP, X, Weed, SOMETHING cause you are off!"

"Don't stall Symone; we're girls, so give up the juice."

Buzz buzz

Thank GOD! I mumbled while answering my phone "Hello?"

"Symone?"

"Michael?" How the hell does this man find me! "Michael, how did you get my number?"

"Well I take it you didn't get the arrangement."

I immediately focused on the basket on my desk that was being savagely devoured by my bestie. "This was from you?"

"I thought it would help..."

"Help what?"

"Did you enjoy them?"

"It was a nice gesture, but…"

"Look Symone, I know what you said. And you've said it many times. I want you to at least give me the chance to get to know me fairly. No parents. No ambush. No blindsides."

Rolling my eyes I said, "Michael, stop stop. What did you call me for...seriously?"

I just received a call from the distributor and what we thought could be done, has to be re-evaluated."

Sitting up abruptly, I asked, "what do you mean re-evaluated? How long would I possibly have to wait after this re-evaluation?"

"Possibly the initial 3 to 4 weeks."

"3 to 4 weeks? Are you kidding me?"

"I can see if we can rush the job, but that's the best I can do."

"The best you can do? I'd hate to see the damn worst. Ok ok ok, I will have to adjust this as best I can"

"Symone, I am sorry. I really am. Wait, so the dinner suggestion? You know what Michael I have to go. I need to take some time to sort some things out."

"So dinner? I swear Symone, I am completely sorry."

"Michael, please please."

"Symone, you know what I've listened and heard you rant and rave and just go on and on about me or resist me. Call it what you will. Now, I'm going to say something. We are going to dinner Friday night. I'm not asking I'm telling. There is something about you that you seem to be hiding or holding onto. You can fuss at me cuss me out, but dammit your ass will put on your best dressed, and go out. This isn't your mother's doing nor mine. Get to know me. Either way, I'm not gonna give up."

"Michael...okay. Fine. Friday...Goodbye Michael."

click I placed my cell phone face down on my desk and stayed fixated on my files for my upcoming session, while trying to avoid the piercing gaze I knew Ra'Chelle was giving. "Oh bitch don't act like I ain't here!"

"Chelle, please"

"What was that all about?"

"Girl nothing nosy"

"Bullshit Symone. Someone has you all wound up over there and the way your face looks, I don't know if you pissed or turned on. But whoever the muthafucka is got yo' ass locked down!"

"Chelle let it go!"

"You know what; you can keep your funky mystery dick"

"There's nothing to keep! And you get more dick for the both of us!"

"Mmmmmhhmmm, whatever. Well I'm about to bounce outta here and see if I can get this kitty to purr."

"Nasty ass! As a matter of fact, take this damn basket with you. Hell you don ate damn near everything in it," I stated scooting the arrangement further towards the edge of the desk. "You damn right I'ma take em. I can guarantee some of this stuff will get put to use!" she smirked and winked "Tootles," she said again flinging that damn weave AGAIN. "I swear she's gonna give herself whiplash or knock somebody down with all that swangin," I said shaking my head. *"Poor horse."*

Chapter 21
Symone

"Dr. Johnson's office, this is Ashleigh how may I direct your call...Yes ma'am she's working from a remote location while minor work is being done on the facility........I can transfer your call to her line if you would like to schedule a session? One moment please..."

"Good morning Ashleigh"

"Dr. Watkins, good morning. Just one moment *Dr. Johnson Mrs. Riley is on line 2.* I'm sorry Dr. Watkins, here are your messages," she said handing him a small stack of notes. You have one reschedule and one cancellation. Also, you have a delayed appointment today so your 7 o'clock won't be in until 9:30."

"Alright, sounds great. Has out little *house guest* made his appearance today?" I asked while signing my messages and sipping my coffee. "Not that I know of, then again he might have come through their make-shift entrance. I think I overheard him saying something was wrong or an extension on the progress of the construction."

"Oh really now, well let's hope not because we need him out of our hair and Dr. Johnson back home!"

"I agree and he can take his little dust buddies with him as well," she smirked.

"Right," I winked in return. "Well I'll be back here in my office," I said as I headed down the hallway. Once I reached my door, I stalled in front of Symone's door. I'm curious to see the what progress or lack thereof remains, so I made my way towards her door and as I reached for her handle I realized I had too much in my hands to try to sneak a peek into her office undetected. "Let me go put this mess down first." I unlocked my office and began to arrange seating and files for my first appointment. I pulled out my cell phone and texted Symone. *Hey, you busy?*

Symone: *No, just updating files and prepping for my first session. How are things at the office?*

Me: *Pretty much the same.*

Symone: *And construction?*

Me: *I think you already know.*

Symone: *Huh? You're losing me.*

Me: *Let's not play this today Symone. When did you know about a possible extension on construction?*

Symone: **sigh** *yesterday actually.*

Me: *And you didn't think to let me know?*

Symone: *Ray, it's entirely too early in the morning for this*

Me: *I'm telling you Symone, I don't trust this dude*

Symone: *Goodbye Raymond*

"I swear that woman is stubborn as hell." As I close my phone, I hear muffled voices coming from Symone's office. "I shouldn't … What the hell am I saying, YES THE HELL I SHOULD!" I step outside of my office and slowly approached her door. The voice remains muffle until I reach the door, which luckily for me was cracked. I nudge the door open a bit further not to give away my presence and notice this same nigga talkin' low. "What the hell is he whispering for when it's only him in this office?" I mumbled to myself. *Dr. Watkins, your appointment is here.*

Came blazing across the intercom in my office scaring the piss out of me. Running back to respond and cover my tracks of spying on the help, "Ok Ashleigh send them on back," I tried to respond while catching my breath.

****

Michael

"Look I understand your frustrations, but this has to be done carefully. No, it's not about the money. Wait...how much? Still I need time for this to work perfectly! You called me to do a job and I'm damn good at it, so let me do what I do and all will be right before you know it," **voices outside** I have to go. I'll keep you updated...

Chapter 22
Racquel

"You okay girlie?"

"Why wouldn't I be?"

"I don't know just had to ask. You have been on that phone for quite a while today. You have some side hustle going on?"

"Sherrone, girl you know I got a hell of a lotta side hustles!"

"So what's going on anyway?"

"You know how I do, just keeping it sexy. Had to check these little hoes out here tryin me!"

"Uh uh, bout what?"

"My man of course! These disrespectful ramps just don't know when to leave a spoken for man alone! So I have to be the enforcer!"

" I know that's right." Fanning herself "woooo, this shopping has me hot as fish grease. Let's get some ice cream..." As we made our way towards the food court, Sherrone spots what seems to be a familiar face.
"Racquel...Is that James over there?" Whipping my head around searching in the direction where she pointed. I see a tall man resembling my husband coming out of Fredericks of Hollywood. "I know damn well he isn't shopping for that hoe," I mumbled.

"What did you say?' Sherrone questioned.

"I was just saying how he must have something planned for tonight," I lied.

"Get it girl!"

"Oh I intend to," I stated as I focused on this slick ass nigga. "I'll be right back"

"No problem, I'll be here."

As I speed walked around the corner nearing the restroom, I dialed James' cell.

"What do you want Racquel?"

"Hey baby what are you doing?"

"Racquel I don't have time"

"Is that any way to talk to your wife?"

"Is there a reason you're calling me?"

"Yes, what did you buy for me then?"

"What? Are you following me?"

"Not this time my love."

"I swear you are delusional."

Just then, I noticed James coming out of Baby Depot. *I know damn well this bitch ain't pregnant!* "You better have a sister, cousin, aunt, niece, co-worker, or a damn pet that would give you any damn reason to have baby shit! Our children are well out of pampers!"

"Goodbye Racquel, I don't have time for this shit!"

click

"Muthaf...did his bitch ass just hang up on me? I gotchu and yo' bitch!" I seethed at the phone as I headed toward where Sherrone was.

"Hey girl, you alright?"

"Let's go," I dryly stated.

"What about," she started and just then, she noticed James speeding by carrying bags labeled Carter's, Osh Kosh, and Baby Depot. "Racquel, what's going on? Is there something you wanna share?" she asked smiling. "A new little special something?"

"No," I angrily stated.

"So why does James have bags from baby department stores?" Her eyes got wide like a kid in a candy store. "Are you pregnant? How far are you? Boy or girl? Why didn't you tell me? What's..."

"Sherrone STOP," I yelled damn near causing a scene in the mall.

Before she could regain her composure or bearings, I bolted to my car with her in tow yelling "Racquel...Racquel...Racquel!"

****

Cornell

"Mr. Wallace's office how may I direct your call? Oh Mr. Smith, he stepped out for lunch. I can tell him you called if you'd like...no... he should have his cell with him so you can...hello?"

****

"Pick up C Pick up Pick up Pick Up."

"J, what's going on? How'd the doctor's appointment go?"

"The appointment went well."

"So what are we having?"

"It's a girl man."

"Aww, Uncle C needs to brush off the shotgun I see."

"Hell I need that now," I mumbled "What's up with you bro, you don't sound like yourself?"

"I just ran into Racquel."

"Define *Ran Into?*"

"I was at the mall buying a few things for Bridgette and the baby when I got a call from Racquel. I didn't think much of it, until she started spazin out. The woman was stalking my ass at the damn mall C!"

"Calm down man! Look, I told you, you need to get that under control before it spirals out of it! You know her and Sherrone are damn near thick as thieves. You have to put a cap on that because I just can't take any extra drama at my house. But I'm here for you though." Is this nigga serious? Here I am damn near dodging a deranged woman, and his ass is concerned about girl talk with his wife? "I can't play these little games with her. I just want out and she's not making things easy."

"Try talking to her."

"The fuck you mean *talking to her*? This woman's mindset is equivalent to a Lynn Whitfield character."

"I told you this shit was gonna get messy if you don't handle it right away."

"Nigga, don't give me no *I Told You So*'s! Help ME! What do I do?"

"Only you can fix that J. You got yourself in that mess; you gotta find your way out of it. **Beep** "Aye let me take this call, it's wifey."

"Yeah man."

"Aye, stay up J, but you gotta get a handle on that."

"I hear you C. **click**

****

"Hello"
"Hey baby"
"Hey"
"What are you doing?"

"Oh, just finishing up with a client."

"They not working my hubby too hard are they?"

"I gotta do what I gotta do"

"Are you going to be home in time for dinner?"

"Not sure. I'll call when I'm in route. Pretty busy here as usual. They act as if they can't do anything without me."

"Before I forget, can you talk to James?"

"For what?"

"I was at the mall today with Racquel and she saw James coming out of a store"

"Baby, that's what people at malls do"

"Well not baby stores and your wife isn't pregnant"

"Really?" I asked as if I didn't know.

"Yeah. I don't know what's going on but you need to talk to James."

"Stay out of that," I proclaimed while rubbing my eyes.

"But that's just odd. Something isn't adding up here."

"Sherrone, leave it alone. Let them handle their own marriage. We are not about to let that interfere with ours."

"But they're our best friends and"

"Hey, drop it. Let them handle it."

"But..."

"Stay...Out...Of...It"

"Okay okay, I'll see you when you get home"

"Ok"

"Love you"

"Love you too." I hung up my cell phone and placed it back on the nightstand. As I look over, "hey, what's wrong with you? Why you all the way over there?"

"You expect me to be all up under you and you're talking to your wife?"

"Whoa whoa whoa," I interrupted the voluptuous 5'6" model beauty. She had waterfall curly hair that cascaded over her honey-complected face. I had to admit this Dominican-esque woman made my dick tingle by just flashing a simple smile. Video vixen for real. I met her on the video set of one of our newly signed acts while shooting a pool scene. This chic was mad fine and I just had to get it!

"Cornell!" she yelled with her thick Spanish accent.

"Oh huh?"

"Would you stop looking at my tata's and focus papicito?"

"Baby I'm sorry but you look so damn delicious!"

"No no no! You do this every time. We no talk, you just bang bang and spend dinero to keep me smilin."

Okay, so she's clearly not the brightest and her English is as solid as George W. Bush's is! "Look, c'mere," I said pulling her near me. "You know I look after you right?"

"Si"

"So let's just enjoy each other. There's nothing to talk about or pout about. We both know what this is."

"But papi, I miss you a lot. Chu can't just have me here when you want me and think I now have feelings for you." wanting to roll my damn eyes, but my dick wouldn't let me "I have feelings for you too mami."

"Really," she beamed.

"Yes, and he is feeling neglected," I stated pointing

at my little soldier. "Don't ruin the moment baby," I said pushing her hair behind her ear.

"Do I make you happy papi?"

"I don't know, do you? Show me."

With that last statement, she pulls the covers back exposing my swollen rod whose erectness is beckoning for her succulent lips. Bending down she planted, soft light kisses alongside my shaft. She extends her tongue letting warm saliva trickle down while she worked her way up, once she reaches my mushroom tip, she slightly blows cool air in his direction. The cool breeze causes me to shiver and shutter, which were recognizable by the chills. I look down and our eyes meet. She gives me that devilish grin letting me know, the best is yet to come. She licks the pre-cum oozing from my dick's peak and widely spreads her lips and lowers her mouth onto my now throbbing dick. The softness of her fluffy lips mixed with the heat and wetness of her inner jaws send me into a whirlwind. I didn't know whether to cum down her throat or snatch her off and beat that pussy into submission. "Shit," was all that seemed to be able to escape my lips. "You like papi," she asked with that wicked grin plastered on her face.

"Hell yeah," I moaned. She unwraps a condom, places it in her mouth, and returned to not only pleasure me but showcase her other talents as well. "Stop playing with him boo," I struggled to say. She climbs on top of me and in one swift move slides my swollen dick in her hot awaiting cavity. "Mmmmm," I moaned.

"Aye papi," she followed slowly riding my dick. "Fuck this pussy papi," she added bending over adding light kisses on my neck and ear. **Buzz buzz** I hear go off on the nightstand next to my ear indicating an incoming text message. I ignored it, as I'm sure it would be my boy James again. Deep in slow penetration, I cupped to go deeper. I feel her juices emerge and saturate my dick and thighs as I plunged deeper into her sweetness. **Buzz buzz** I hear again this time indicating an incoming call. Before I could reach over to answer, this woman goes in for a kiss. "No no mami, you know we don't kiss," I stopped her. Kisses are for the wifey, not the hoes you fuckin! She picks up speed and bounces that ass while clinching her pussy walls. I guess that touched a nerve sending her into overdrive. My hand was half-way to the nightstand when she dropped that ass harder and harder. "Got damn girl," I huffed. Refusing to be outdone and caused to cum before I needed to, I flipped her over face down, spread her plump honey ass cheeks, and plunged deeper inside. **Buzz buzz** "Shit," I mumbled at the frequent interruptions I was experiencing during such great nut busting sex! *Wifey* appeared on my phones call screen mid stroke. "I'll call her back," I said lost in the wetness of my lunch delight while making her cum over and over, as her screams of satisfaction rang out!

****

Symone

"Good afternoon Dr. Johnson, nice to see you in the office today," grinned Ashleigh. "Good afternoon Ashleigh, only poppin in to get some files," I returned the bright smile. "Is Dr. Watkins in yet?"

"Oh yes ma'am. He should be finishing up his clients' session right about now."

"Oh, wait I hear him coming down the hall."

"Alright mom & dad let's try and work on those

communication skills between you two and I have no doubt that our girl will come around. If anything changes, don't hesitate to call me. If need be, have her call me," he said giving his clients departing encouragement. "Bailey, I'll see you soon. Be good okay he asked the sulking pre-teen that looked somewhere around 11 to 12 years old who was playing with her DS ignoring Raymond. "Don't worry; we'll break through to her yet. You all have a good one and I'll see you next time."

"Well look at you in rare form mister. Very impressive. Encouraging with the parents and connected with the child, or good effort I guess you would say. I must admit, I'm in awe," I joked pinching his cheeks.

"I don't have time for your foolishness Dr. Johnson," he said pulling my hand away from his face.

"Ashleigh, how soon before my next client arrives?"

"Well you have one more, but that won't be until after lunch."

"Am I disturbing you Dr. Watkins or are you just ignoring me?"

"Hush woman," he said as we walked down the hall.

"Oh wait, I want to take a sneak peak at the..." I started to say looking for my keys when we reached our office doors.

"Don't go in there Symone," he startled me while grabbing my arm preventing me from moving any closer to my office door.

"Why not?"

"Cause it's not finished"

"I know that Raymond," I said with a shocked look. "Didn't you hear me say *sneak peak?*"

After he opened his office door, he placed himself in between my office door and myself. "Symone, go sit down," he said preventing me from stepping further in his newly positioned stands. "Ray I don't have time for this today."

"Well make time dammit." As he closes his office door, I plop down in his chair with my arms folded like a scolded child. "What now?" Getting straight to it, "you need a new contractor"

"Here we go again."

"Look Symone, I don't trust this nigga. I've looked around and found some other suitable contractors and...." laughing to myself "you know what, Chelle might have been on to something."

"Hey hey hey now, we don't speak of demonic spirits in my office. I don't have enough incense to burn."

"Don't start with Chelle and you burn sage to rid away spirits. But since you are so adamant, I'll bite. What, did you check his background? Google him? Do you know his blood type? DNA? Run the company's file and business inquires?" while I was joking, Ray just sat back twiddling his fingers with a straight look on his face. "YOU DIDN'T! Raymond!"

"Don't act surprised Symone. You know damn well that I was going to get to the bottom of this. Now I couldn't get past the FBI and their firewall nor get access to his medical records..." *this negro is crazy!* I thought "but I was able to Google him and his company."

"I can't sit around and entertain this," I grabbed my

belonging and stormed out of his office blindly running into a solid hard mass. "Oh I'm sor..." I started to apologize reaching for my keys and my composure still not looking up. "No I'm sorry." Snapping my head at the familiar voice. "Michael..."

"Symone...What brings you here today?" he asked still hovering in my personal space. His minty breath sent chills down my spine.

What the hell is going on with me? "Um um," I started to stutter.

"Sym-" Ray started to call after me while swinging his door open brought me back to reality.

"I just came to get some files," I said to Michael while scowling at Raymond.

Michael opens my office door, and lets me step inside before him. As he goes to close the door behind us, he looked at Ray with a sinister grin and winked.

****

James

"Jay, what up baby boy," one of my patnas greeted on his way out of the gym. "What's good Mike. You leaving?"

"Yeah man got called into work early."

"Damn man, what time you get here?"

"I was here for about an hour and a half. Me and C were doin' backs this morning."

"A'ight cool"

"Aye, I'll hit you up later."

"Yeah, let me know when you plan on comin' in bro. We need to work on them twigs you call legs..." laughing he flips me the finger. "A'ight man." As I headed towards the locker room, I heard "hurry up man that slow walk ain't considered cardio." I looked up to see Cornell on the Stairmaster. I locked my bag away, grabbed my headphones, towel, and water bottle, and met him upstairs. "You don't bro?"

"Yeah," he said hopping down dapping me up. "Let's go warm up," he said with ease. "Warm up? What the hell? How long you been here again? Yo' little ass sweatin' like 2 fat chicks in line at Rudy's!"

"I been here about an hour and a half just decided after Mike left to get my cardio out of the way. C'mon let's get to work," he said trying to catch his breath. We began to stretch out our quads and hams preparing for what would be a gruesome and intense leg workout. "So how's everything going with the baby and what's her name?"

"Bridgette"

"Right, miss Bridgette"

"Well the baby is doing well, but the doc says the fluid is low and her stress level is pretty high."

"That doesn't sound too good bro. Shouldn't it be the other way around?"

"I know. I'm trying to keep her from stressing but damn, Racquel ain't making it easy for a brutha"

"It's not all Racquel though bro. Let's keep it real here. We both know that." We moved from stretching to doing squats with the weights. "I know man, but when I go to either get the papers or get my kids I get sucked in every-time."

"Look man I know this won't be easy, but if you know you can't say no to your soon to be ex-wife and y'all can't be cordial for my god-children, then stop going to the damn house!"

"It's easier said than done C. That's where my memories of better times were made. I helped build that house."

"It's just a house J. The dream has long died. No one can steal your memories, but you gotta come to grips that the dream is over. You have to wake up."

"I just can't get past that. But you're right, besides it's just not the time to tell Racquel about Bridgette and the baby." Pausing before another set "Not the time? When do you plan on telling her? Or are you going to let the baby tell her?"

"Man, I told you how she spazed out at the damn mall when she saw me with baby shit," I said shaking my head. "What does Miss Bridgette has to say about this is what I want to know." Rubbin my head, "I haven't told her anything either."

"BRO! You are slippin' for real!"

"I know I know! I can't say anything now with her stress levels the way they are. Not to mention it could harm the baby"

"J, as my boy, I'm gonna be honest with you; you need to be worrying about them finding out by way of someone else! Believe me when I say, it's better your lady hear any damaging news from you than to hear or see it for themselves from someone else! You need to get on that like yester-year. Now, c'mon let's get off this sensitive mess and put in this work. Save all that talkin' mess for your shrink"

Chapter 23
Racquel

"Racquel"

"Hey Sherrone, what's going on?"

"Checking on you after you stormed out on me at the mall yesterday, you good?"

"Yeah girl. Sorry about that I just had an emotional moment that's all. "Hell I could tell. What's going on?"

"Chile it's too much to talk about"

"Heffa, I didn't just meet you yesterday. Talk!"

"I can't talk about it over the phone; I just need some time to myself."

"Well, okay. How is JJ doing?"

"What?"

"JJ, you know my GOD-SON, your SON!"

"He's fine as always. Why wouldn't he be?"

"Whatever you are going through must really be deep if you forgot about JJ. His breathing? Don't ring any bells?" Taken off guard by the lie I told the previous day to get my bestie off my case, I had such a dumb founded look. "We went to Walgreens to get meds for the baby?" I went in that damn store to just walk around like I was getting my sons medication. I bought cough drops, Tylenol, Benadryl, regular over the counter medication just to come out there with something. "Speaking of baby, are you or aren't you pregnant? You kept dodging my questions all day yesterday."

"Sherrone..."

"Oooooh if it's a girl we can do pink and yellows at the shower and if it's a boy we can do powder blue. I know a great place to get bedding..."

"Sherrone"

"And some cute little booties"

"SHERRONE! What the fuck is up with this 50 questions and shit? I'm fucking good over here okay, so leave me the fuck alone!"

Click

I know this heffa did NOT just curse at ma DNA hang up in my face! Grabbing my keys and purse, I darted out of the house. Rubbing my face after I slammed my house phone back down on the receiver I took in a deep breath. I know she's going to call back later, but I just needed to get her off my damn back. Then my cell phone started ringing "Hello?"

"Mrs. Smith?"

"Speaking"

"This is Rodney McDowell, PI. You contacted my assistant saying that you needed some services rendered?"

"Mr. McDowell, yes indeed. I need answers"

"Well that's what I'm here to do"

"I think my husband is cheating on me. I have the woman's license plate, home and office address as well as both landlines."

"Straight to the point I see. Seems to me that you rarely need my services. Mrs. Smith I don't usually conduct business over the phone so how about we meet say in an hour and a half?"

"I'd rather not meet in public, so could you come to

my house?"

"Much better. Could you provide me with your address?"

"Aren't you supposed to be a well-established PI?"

"Touché Mrs. Smith. I will see you soon," he said disconnecting the call.

"Now, on to the second order of business," I mumbled while hitting two and dialing.

"What the hell did I tell you earlier? I said I needed more time!" the male voice whispered. I removed the phone from my face and looked at it to ensure I was talking to whom I thought I was. "Nigga who the fuck you talkin' to?"

"Look I don't mean to be rude, but this task is not a walk in the park. You gotta give me some time on this. I can't talk right now, I'll update you later." **click** "what the fuck!" I spat noticing the abrupt disconnect. "After this is done, this muthafucka is next!"

"Mama! Mama!" I heard snapping me out of my killer daze. "Mama, we hungry," my son said entering the living room. Looking at my watch "damn," I mumbled. Okay baby, you and your sister go get cleaned up and make sure those rooms are cleaned and mama will call you when lunch is ready," I said with a smile at my baby boy. "Okay." running and yelling up the stairs "SISSY MAMA SAID GET DRESSED AND CLEAN YO' ROOM!"
Everything I'm doing is for you mama's babies. No bitch is coming between that!

Chapter 24
Michael

Click "Sorry about that. Boss-man getting estimates on another job. I um, apologize for the mess we're causing. We're doing our best to not cause more of a disaster," I stated following a nervous chuckle. "Oh, don't mention it. Be glad you don't see this place when I'm looking for lost files," she stated not looking away from the files on a shelf and stayed in that position sorting through labeled binders. She had her hair pulled up and back in a slick bun. The smell of Victoria secrets *Love Spell* invaded my nostrils as she walked past me to her desk. As she opened and closed the files on her desk, clearly in search of something, a short stack of files fell on the left side of her desk. "Shoot," she muffled.

"You need some help?" I asked.

"No no I have it, thanks." I had to find a way to keep the now rising bulge in my pants from revealing my hopeful wants and lustful thoughts. When she bent over to grab the files, the satin looking skirt that hugged her thick hips and outlined her plump backside barely moved 2 inches. Oh how I wished I was that chair or more-so that skirt. God bless that seamstress that put that fabric together to hold in such monstrosity. When she shifted further downward to collect the final files, a small pain shot through my now pulsating manhood aching to be released and relieved.

"So Michael, what are you," she started to ask. Embarrassed by my instant harden from my gawking, I immediately picked up the freshly laid plastic and began to bunch it up to hid my stiffness stumbling her mid-sentence. "You okay?" she asked.

"I'm fine," I managed to get out in a high pitch due to the pinch of a few tacks piercing through my skin still attached to the plastic. "My goodness, you need some help?" she shot putting the files down on her desk and rushing to help me. "No no no, I have it," I waved off. "Besides I don't want you to get dirty," I said heading towards the big garbage bins we had by the plastic covered window. "Whew," I mouthed. "So what do you have in mind for Friday sir since you were very convincing?" she asked while heading back to her desk. "How about I let you pick the place. I'm rather curious to see what the dear doctor likes," I stated still hiding myself behind the bin. "Well, I do have a place in mind," she stated while bending forward and scribbling something down. As she bent forward, her supple breasts seemed as if they were fighting to see who could make an appearance first. I mean those things were huge! They look like two trapped balloons filled with pudding. "Michael"

"Huh, I'm sorry what was that?" I said quickly snapping out of my daze.

"I said is 6 okay with you?"

"Oh well yeah 6 is fine"

"Ok, um, well I think I have what I need from here so I'll get out of your way. I guess I will see you later on tonight," she said as sashayed out the door. *Dammit, this is gonna be harder than I thought it would be. Get a hold of yourself Mike. Get the job done and move on.*

****

Racquel

Knock knock

"Mrs. Smith?" the 6'1" Caucasian man with receding hairline and neatly trimmed goatee stated. "Well damn," I mumbled to myself as he came inside. "Hi. I know we spoke on the phone, but Rodney McDowell," he smiled extending his hand *yes you are* I said shaking his hand. "Please come in." I think I might like this inspector gadget thing here. "Please have a seat," I said as I directed him towards the living area. "So here is what I know. My husband and I have been married for about 16 years with 2 beautiful children."

"Straight to the point I see," he said.

"My time is indeed of the essence Mr. McDowell"

"Very understandable," he nodded while pulling out a medium sized notepad. "May I?" he asked before he took notes.

"Sure go ahead"

"So your husband..."

"James."

"Your husband James lives here, no?"

"No he moved out a few months ago."

"When did you two start having issues Mrs. Smith?"

"We have a great marriage and always have so I'm not sure what the problem was. I decided we should go see a marriage counselor because James kept threatening to divorce me"

"Now wait a minute, if you two are working with a

counselor why would you want or feel that you need my services?" he asked immediately putting his pen down. "We went to see the doctor and she suggested we see her separately. I felt a bit hesitant about it, but I figured she knew what she was talking about so I disregarded it. She wanted to schedule him first and that just did something. I realized he had to be getting his dick wet with this bitch!" I didn't care that I just met this man, talkin' about this hoe mad my blood boil. "Now are you sure this woman and your husband have been having an affair?" he asked picking back up his notepad. "That's what I called you for."

"I mean, how sure are you it's her though?"

"Somebody gotta be sittin' on the nigga lap cause it sure as hell ain't my black ass!"

"Alright alright, well let's see what you have here," he said as he wrote down her license plates, car make and model, as well as my husbands. The bitches office and home location and landlines. I must say Mrs. Smith you are one well-prepared woman. I need someone like you working at my firm"

"Hey, what can I say? When I see something needs to be handled, I prepare myself for everything."

"That's what I need...at my firm that is..." he corrected turning beet red. If I didn't know better, he was flirting heavily with me.

Ding-dong

"Excuse me," I said going to my front door.

"What the hell is your problem!" the woman spat as soon as I swung the door open.

"Sherrone now is not a good time," I started to say while attempting to close the door.

"No you don't I don't give a damn what time it is, you gonna talk to me got dammit!" she pushed through. "What the hell is going on?"

"Would you lower your voice?"

"For what? What is going on?"

"Shhhhhh, dammit! I have company, I'll call you later," I said trying to escort her back out the door.

"Company? What does your company have to do with me? Unless...Have you lost your damn mind? Yo' loose ass in here with my godchildren and you got the nerve to have some random nigga up in here? Bitch did you forget yo' ass is married?" Before I could say or do anything, she stormed into my living room where Rodney was.

"Excuse me, who are you?" she rudely stated while throwing her purse, keys, cell phone, and jacket on the love seat. "My name is Rodney Mc..."

"I don't give a damn what your name is. Why are you here?" she spat with her hands on her hips.

"Mrs. Smith"

"Exactly MRS. SMITH! So that means your disrespectful ass knows that she's married. You know she has children don't you?" she viciously spat.

"Yes I do but..."

"But you are still trying to fuck up a happily married home? See it's niggas like you that need your damn balls and dicks cut off. No respect for a married union or a damn happy family. Just selfish and don't care about anyone but yourself!"

"Mama, what's going on?" my daughter came downstairs

"Go back upstairs baby."

"But I'm hungry," she pouted.

"I said take your narrow ass back upstairs. I'll call you when it's ready!" I shouted as she ran back upstairs whimpering and crying.

"Mrs. Smith, I see I need to go "

"Oh you damn right you need to leave!" Sherrone bellowed.

"Here's my card. Call me when you want to move forward and please, handle this. I don't have time for this," he stated gestured in a circular motion before letting himself out.

I turned to Sherrone. "Really?"

"What the hell you mean really? You should be thanking me!"

"THANKING you?"

"Hell yeah thanking me!"

"For what?"

"Stopping you from ruining your marriage!"

"Get that shit outta here man!"

"And with a white guy at that too Racquel!"

"You have no idea what you're talking about!"

"So you're telling me you ain't fucking this white muthafucka that just walked outta here?"

"That's exactly what I'm telling you!"

"Bull shit!"

"You know what, here," I threw the card to her and walked in the kitchen to pour a glass of wine.

"Rodney McDowell, P.I. specializing in getting you the results you need when you can't get it from the one you want," she read aloud to herself. "What the hell is this?"

she asked coming into the kitchen waving the card around.

"What does it look like?"

"Dammit Racqui."

"Sherrone tell me you're not that damn clueless."

"What are you talking about?"

I forcefully placed the wine glass down on the island, walked to the foyer, walked back to the kitchen, and slammed the manila envelope down on the island in front of where she stood and returned back to my wine.

"What is this?"

"You want to know so damn much, so there are your answers to all of your questions."

She opened the envelope, pulled out the thick document, and skimmed reading it. *James Smith vs Racquel Smith: Reasons for dissolution of marriage irreconcilable differences.* She immediately drops the document and runs to my side. "Oh Racqui hunny I'm sorry"

"Oh uh uh, don't start that shit," I swatted at her.

"When did this happen? How long have you been holding on to these papers?"

Before she finished her arsenal of questions, she saw the date on the documents. "JANUARY 2009?"

"That's just document #4, so yeah"

"The 4th one?"

"Yes the 4th one. He brought this one over himself last week but"

"But what? Wait, what happened to the first 3?"

"They made good sources of heat during the winters"

"You burned em?"

"Soon as they hit my hand," I stated while lighting

my cigarette.

"So why didn't you tell me?"

"What the hell is there to say?"

"Uh how about my husband is trying to divorce me? SOMETHING!"

"We ain't getting no damn divorce girl."

"But this is…"

"Look, he can file all damn day long but I ain't signing a got damn thing!"

"Well have you guys tried counseling?"

What the hell she say that for...

"What I say," she looked confused at my facial reaction.

"That's the fucking reason I'm in this shit right now."

"You losing me…"

"He agreed to go to counseling and I'm thinking he wants to work on our marriage…"

"So that's good."

"Until I meet the bitch that he is fucking!"

"Wait who?"

"The GOT DAMN SHRINK!"

"What the hell!"

"Ain't no way I'm gonna lose my husband to no black ass little girl playing a grown woman's' game," I stated as I pulled the ingredients out to make hamburgers for my children.

"Move away from that with that cigarette, you gonna give my god-children cancer with all this smoke."

Putting the cigarette out, I sat across the island while my bestie seasoned the meat and cut veggies.

"How sure are you that he's sleeping with this shrink?"

"Oh I know he is!"

"Have you seen the two of them together?"

"I don't have to see them together to know. Hell, I know my husband. The bitch is fly though I will say, and James does like him a fly bitch. How you think I got him?"

"Racqui, you can't assume he's sleeping with her if you aren't sure though…"

"Who the hell else could it be then? My husband ain't no hoe and I know his type. Just the mere mention of me fuckin' up her office sent him into a whirlwind," I said sipping my wine.

"Rewind, you did what?"

"Oh best believe I rearranged that bitches office," I said with a plastered grin.

"See you done lost your mind now," she said walking around the island and taking away my glass pouring it out and removing the remaining bottle from my grasp.

"What are you doing?"

"You went to this woman's office, who you think is having an affair with your husband, and destroyed it all without evidence or proof? Are you ASKING for a lawsuit?"

"Don't act like you wouldn't do the same to Cornell's ass if you thought he was cheating!"

"I don't know what I would do but I know my husband. So that ain't even a thought."

JJ then entered the kitchen. "Auntie Ronnie!"

"Hey my little Jaymers!" she beamed as she

embraced my son.

"Burgers? Mama, Auntie Ronnie making us burgers?" he asked while stealing a few pickles.

"Yes baby. Did you wash your hands?"

"Yep, just like you said. See, smell," he smirked as he shoved his wet palms in my face giving me a whiff of the Irish spring fragrance.

"JJ!"

"What? You asked Mama!"

"Did you wash the back JJ?"

"Uh."

"Boy, go wash your entire hands! FRONT AND BACK!" He ran off laughing as if it was a joke. Looking at Sherrone I asked, "How do you wash part of your hands? And tell your sister to come downstairs!" I yelled to him as he ran off. "Boys. How do you only wash part of your hands though?"

"Girl them kids are a trip. Have you talk to them about the divorce?" she asked while putting mustard on the buns like my children liked. "They don't know anything."

"Well when do you plan on telling them?"

"I don't."

"Racqui…"

"Look I already told you there will be no divorce! So drop it!"

"Mama, sissy won't come out of her room. I think she's crying," James Jr. said running back in and grabbing a paper towel to dry his hands.

"Jaymers, come eat baby. Let your mama see about your sister. Come tell Auntie Ronnie about soccer."

"But Auntie Ronnie, you don't like no soccer. You

don't even know about soccer."

"But I like my Jaymers, and you like soccer so you can teach Aunt Ronnie."

"Ok, but I don't want to lose you so ask questions and keep up," he said before he took a big bite of his burger.

I laughed to myself at the little personality of my little growing boy, before I turned to tend to my ever so emotionally conflicted growing daughter.

Chapter 25
Cornell

"Well no, that wasn't supposed to be on the docket for his session until 8 this morning. He was supposed to be with Artist Development at 9:15 and an interview with *Global Grind* at noon. Why is there a $5,000 charge for a damn chain? Is he aware where the money or this is coming from? Ok, look, handle that and I'm capping his spending! If I have to, I will attach a damn financial coach to his ass. I'm looking at the account now! Get his ass under control!" I spat with hit new clients so called team. "C, what up boss-man?"

"What up J, how's it hanging man?"

"You know low and to the left. I heard you in here ranking on somebody."

"These kids man. They gonna bleed this damn label dry."

"That's why they pay you the big bucks."

"Cornell, hey you free for...oops...sorry. I didn't know you had company," barged in Ra'Chelle. "Hey, no problem. What's on your mind?"

"I was just seeing if you were going out for lunch, since you were MIA yesterday."

"Lunch with wifey ran overboard. But I'm having lunch sent in. these damn boys and these black cards are just going swipe crazy."

"Count your blessings. I have to deal with these groupie bourgeois broads. Oh before I leave, are you free to scout tonight?"

"If it's your girl and she's gonna bless the stage, count me in! Same place?"

"Yes sir. I'll get you the green light once I put everything in place. Have a good lunch," she smiled leaving my office.

"Who was that?"

"Down boy," I joked.

"Nigga whatever. Who's the sass with no ass?"

"Ra'Chelle *Stylist Extraordinaire*," I mocked waiving my hands in the air and flinging my non-existing weave.

"What's scouting?" he asked.

"Checking out potential acts to possibly sign with the label. Kinda gives the team some fun away from work while still being on the clock."

"So wait, she's a stylist? Why is she asking about you going out to scout? How many people go out on these little scouting missions? Is she gonna dress you guys in what to wear? I'm lost here."

"Yes she's a stylist, but she's been pretty hands on with this new project."

"New project?"

Before I answered his question, I got up and went to the door. "Samantha, I'm at lunch so route all calls to my voicemail and I'll get to them later."

"Yes Sir Mr. Wallace," she replied. Closing the door, I head back to my desk. "You want Chinese man?"

"Yeah that's straight," James said looking baffled. "C, new project? What gives?"

After browsing the internet for the closest Chinese

delivery restaurant, I answered. "Okay, well, she talked me into starting my own label."

"That's what's up. It won't be easy though."

"Why?"

"Maintaining the roster as well as the projects going on here with our many artists is already hectic, but to add on the fact that I'm doing my own thing, that's a bit much. In order for this to pop off with a hitch, I'll have to keep it a wraps. Hopefully I can keep them both separate."

"So are you planning on taking or coercing already signed artists here to sign with you?"

"Man hell no! That's company and business suicide! I'm leaving them to their already certified contracts. At the rate this company is conducting business, they'll bleed them dry before they can turn over a profit."

"So who all knows about your little project?"

"Just us two, well three now including you. These old heads in here would blow a fuse and raise hell with me going my own route."

"Damn!"

"Man I'm telling you, the *talent* in this industry has gotten way out of control. People aren't putting out solid music anymore. It's either about popping Molly's…"

"Woo!" Jay yelped while dancing in his seat.

"The use of niggas or chicks wanting to copy Beyoncé…"

"Say, Jay did that though. He got a solid one with Mrs. Carter."

"Focus man. I'm looking for the Donny Hathaways, Stevie Wonders, Jodeci's, H-Town's, Usher's, Mary J Blige's, Silk, Luther Vandross...."

"Hell yeah, I feel you. Shit it's cause of them I got kids," he shook his head.

"Instead, I see these Trinidad James, Wiz Khalifa, Ray J's, Yung Bergs, Lil Zane, or these self-made local acts, expecting to hit big bucks."

Mr. Wallace your courier is here the assistant buzzed.

I get up, head to the door, and pay for my lunch. "Keep the change," I tipped the courier. I make my way back to my desk, and pass the chicken and rice with lo mein with moo shu pork to J. "chopsticks?"

"Man hell naw, you know black people don't use no damn chopsticks!" he said reaching for the forks.

"Whatever."

"So it's tonight then, the scouting thing?" he asked shoving the lo mein into his mouth. "There's a spot Ra'Chelle told me about where they do an open mic."

"That's what's up, you takin Sherrone?"

"Nah. This is work; I don't have time for her stuff."

"Oh not *Mr. I-Love-My-Wife*."

"Whatever, I do love my wife. But you know women are some fickle creatures."

"Tell me about it!"

"You know what, you should come down. Her girl sung the last time and I mean damn near tore the place down! Hopefully, she'll be on-board to do it once again."

"With shit I got going on, I need to get away. Away from Bridgette's ass. I love her to pieces though and our daughter, but them emotional roller coasters and raging hormones are KILLING ME! Then I really need to get some distance from Racquel. I just don't know who she is anymore!"

"You brought that up on yourself man," I laughed while eating my beef and broccoli. "But come on through, I'll text you the address. It's called Sankofa,"

"Sankofa...Sankofa...Sankofa..." he snapped and searched for a link to the familiar sounding name. "That place sounds familiar. Didn't it used to be on Martin Luther King?"

"Yeah, but they moved it."

"Oh word? I know the place then. They been on point. You'll definitely find mad talent in there. My ole ass might spit a few bars."

"Ole ass is right. You need to steer clear the stage and focus on that there gut sir."

"bitch everybody ain't low to the ground like yo' midget ass."

"Low? I'm 6'6"!"

"In what? Ya dreams? You and Kevin Hart could dress up like Tweedledee and Tweedledum in the hood remake of Alice in Wonderland. King Oompa Loompa."

We joked foe the next hour before I had to get back to work with these juvenile acts.

Dinner for Two and A Few

"Good evening ma'am, valet?" the attendant asked.

"Yes, please," I said while giving him my keys in exchange for my ticket.

I walked into the building in the sitting area awaiting Michael's arrival. Before o could sit down in the waiting area or go to the bar, I heard a deep voice from behind, "you look gorgeous."

I turned to see a dark 6'4" man wearing a three-piece Armani suit, staring me down with greenish blue fluttery eyes. "Thank you," I politely returned the salutation.

"Can I buy you something to drink?"

"Oh no, I'm waiting for someone, but thank you for the offer," I forcefully smiled.

"Why would any man leave a beautiful black queen waiting?" he continued.

"It's fine, maybe he's running late."

"Baby, I'd never run late if you were with me."

Okay this dude is starting to piss me off a little. What part of I'm waiting on someone don't understand.

"I'm sorry, my name is Justin, and you are?" he asked with his hand extended.

Catching a glimpse of his wedding ring, I started to scream out **NOT YOUR WIFE**. "Symone," I stated instead.

"Symone, that's lovely."

Lovely? Really? There's a million and one people named Symone. But I shook his hand anyway, even though I was rolling my eyes severely in my head.

"Lovely name for an even lovelier woman," he said and he proceeded to kiss my hand.

I took my hand and covered it with my clutch. I wanted to rip open my clutch, snatch out my travel size bottle of hand sanitizer, and drench my hands with it. Better yet, I wanted to shower in it! Thanks to my grandmother, I carried it with me everywhere!

"So Symone, what do you do?"

Where the hell is Michael!

****

"Okay look, we should be here for about an hour or 2. I'll let you know when we leave. What do you mean that's not enough time? She's not an idiot. Okay, okay. I'll come up with something!"

****

Symone

"I don't mean to be rude, but I'm just waiting for someone and I'd rather wait alone," I said with a forced smile once more.

He moved in much closer invading my personal space. "C'mon ma. We both know you ain't meeting no one here. Not dressed like that you not. Let's not front, we both grown here."

"Look I said I'm waiting on someone so please back off," I stated with a straight face. Getting even closer to the point, I could smell his over use of cool water cologne. Smelled like he swam in it and it damn near cleared up my sinuses!

"Where is he then? Or she? Hmmm? Admit it, you ain't meeting nobody here so don't play hard to get baby cause you won't win against me."

"Sorry I'm late. Had to wrap up things at the office."

"Michael," I smiled at the instant relief that I felt when I heard that voice.

"You alright?"

"I am now." I was never happier to see Michael here to save me. Hell, I would've even been okay with Ray being here!

"Say bruh, I mean excuse me, who are you?" Justin asked.

"Oh I'm sorry, Michael Sanchez," he said extending his hand. "Thank you for keeping my girlfriend company. I wouldn't want any of these thirsty bastards trying to hit on her." as he spoke, Michael wrapped his arm around my waist and pulled me in for a quick deep kiss. The brush of his fluffy lips gave birth to a tingle that seemed to bypass all of my major organs and go straight to my pussy lips. I could feel my labia quivering! "My bad, I just can't get enough of this chocolate woman here. You are again?"

"Justin, Justin Jacobs. Just making sure, she's okay. I know how these snakes are," he stated backing up with his hands in his pockets after he shook Michael's hand.

"Preciate it. It's a pretty special night tonight. You know how it is," he winked.

"Baby our table is ready," I commented with my right hand on his chest playing the role of the smitten girlfriend.

"Alright my man, preciate it again. Take care." turning back to me. "Let's go baby," he said with his hand placed on the small of my back.

As we walked towards the main room, I leaned in whispering, "thank you."

"Not a problem. I saw the distress in your face from across the room when I walked in."

We picked a little cozy table for two located in the back with a clear view of the stage. Michael pulled my chair out for me to sit down. "Thank you. I see you have some form of home training."

"Symone, really," he said with a smirk.

"Okay, okay, I'll try to be nice. I was ambushed."

"Ambushed?"

"Okay, maybe that's harsh of a word…"

"Well can I get the *unharsh* version?" he chuckled showing a pearly white smile. I had to cross my legs because of the shot of ecstasy that formed. "Well, Chelle actually brought me here to celebrate my housewarming. Just us two. Was hoping to just enjoy good food, nice music, a relaxing vibe."

"Okay so where was the ambush?"

"She brought me out on open mic night and signed me up to sing!"

"Interesting," he smiled leaning back in the chair. "So?"

"So what?"

"Did you do it?"

"I did," I confessed trying to hide my emerging smile. "But I wasn't too happy about it."

"You weren't too happy about what part? The singing or the ghost sign up?"

"Good evening, and welcome to Sankofa. Can I start you off with a drink from the bar?" the waitress safely interrupted.

Michael gestured for me to order first. "I'll have a chocolate martini please."

"Great and for you sir?"

"Crown and coke please."

"Excellent. Are you ready to order as well or do you need a few more minutes to look over the menu?"

Again, he gestured for me to answer first. "We'll need a few more minutes," I smiled.

"Sure, please take your time. I'll go place your drink orders at the bar and return shortly."

"Thank you," we said in unison.

"Chocolate Martini huh? I would've taken you for a Hypnotic on the rocks type of drinker."

"Impressive."

"But I can indeed tell you're not a big drinker."

"How so?"

"Let's see Pastors daughter…"

"Already starting off wrong there sir."

"What do you mean?"

"Pastors children are the ones you MUST be mindful of most."

"You know, you're right about that."

"Continue though I would like to hear what other thoughts you had."

"Small waist."

"Genetics."

"Smooth skin."

"Long baths."

"Nice calves."

"Stilettos."

"Over bearing parents. That all screams healthy lifestyle and occasional drinking."

"You got me on the over bearing parents portion however. I have nothing for that one. I'll say, you earned brownie points," I smiled. "Since you are somewhere in the ballpark of being humanly interesting, I'll give you a chance at seeing if you can impress me with dinner," I challenged.

"I'm up for the challenge. However on one condition."

"Condition?"

"One dance. Nothing more. Nothing less. Just one."

Giving him the side eye I said, "Try anything funny and I'm dotting your eye," I joked holding up a balled up fist.

"I won't. Promise," he said with raised hands. "Scouts honor."

"Now you know good and well you weren't a scout."

I was too...ok, I wasn't. But it was believable a little wasn't it?"

Laughing I said, "Not even close."

"Here we go. One chocolate martini for you ma'am and for the gentleman a Crown and Coke. Are we ready to order?"

I rest back in the comfortable plush seat giving Michael the *impress me* look then holding up my fist as if to say *remember what I said*. With a grin, he confidently addressed the waitress, without taking his eyes off of me. "The lady will have the grilled stuffed chicken marsala with steamed vegetables, light on the mushroom sauce annnnnnd...." leaning in on the table clasping his hands together, "mashed potatoes."

"Sure and for you sir?"

"I'll have the same," he said with his gaze still fixated firmly on me.

"Great. I'll take your menus and place these orders. It should be out shortly. You two enjoy this evening," she said smiling while taking our menus.

After she left our table, I gave a quick light round of applause. "Very impressive"

"I take it I can keep my eyes?"

"Yes you can...for now."

****

Cornell

"What's going on baby, glad you came out?" I said to James as he crossed the street. "Me too. It took me damn near 45 minutes just to convince Bridgette I was coming back and wasn't leaving for good. That's not to mention the 20 minutes trying to keep her from crying. Women!" laughing at him "c'mon man you need a drink. You self parked?"

"Hell yeah I self parked! These kids gonna milk my pockets dry! Besides everybody can't valet like you deep seams."

"Chill out," I stated following a light chuckle as I kept looking at my watch. "We waiting on somebody?"

"Yeah, Ra'Chelle. I swear women can't be on time for a single thing." As we wait outside and continue to talk, we hear a rapid amount of click clacking coming down the sidewalk. "Sorry Sorry Sorry," was all she could repeat.

"Well you clean up nicely," I said kissing her on the cheek. "Compared to what? Boo I'm ALWAYS fabulous!" I'm surprised she could breathe with the tight jeans cupping her little blemish of an ass and see through shirt showing what seemed to be a new pushup bra. "Of course you are. Ra'Chelle, I didn't introduce you to my boy James. Jay, Ms. Ra'Chelle..."

"Stylist Extraordinaire," she concluded as she took his hand. We both looked at each other and started laughing, "What I say?" she said clueless. "Oh nothing. It's almost 7."

"Oh shoot, we gotta get a table before the show

starts," she said turning around and attempting to swish her hips, more like imagination. "Is she always like that?" James leaned in and asked.

"Trust me it's not as bad as you think. You get used to it after a while, you'll be fine," I chuckled.

****

Symone

"Now that was on point," Michael stated after dinner.

"It was pretty good," I agreed.

"So I guess I get that dance huh?"

"You just might, but the jury is still out on that part."

"And when will they reach a verdict?"

"Oh you'll know..."

"Symone? That's why yo' monkey tail couldn't answer my calls cause you were out with..." and her smile instantly dropped, as she looked in Michael's direction.

"Hey, what are you doing here?" I asked.

She was briefly in a stare down and I could see her temper flare which was odd for Chelle. Something had to be bothering her, but tonight was not the night to get to the bottom of it. "Chelle," I said snapping her out of her daze.

"What?"

"Michael, I'm sorry would you excuse us?"

"Sure sure."

I pulled Chelle to the side out of earshot. "What's your problem?"

"Nothing nothing, I had a thought about something."

"You sure? Is there something about Michael?"

"No no no…"

"Ra'Chelle if there is, tell me! I don't want to be here and this negro is like crazy or a killer or something."

"Girl relax, it's nothing. I just thought he was somebody I knew for a sec. Go on get back to your little date or whatever this is you got goin' on."

"You sure?"

"Bitch yes I'm sure! Get on before he bounces out and you are the face of vintage vagina!"

"Not funny, call me later."

"Tootles!" she said waving her hands in the air. *I'll do more than call ma'am.*

I returned back to where Michael was sitting.

"Is everything ok?"

"Oh yeah, it is. Just girl stuff. Now back to getting to know you. I feel like I should apologize to you for the last time we were at dinner with my parents. I was kinda rude."

"Kinda?"

"Hey, I'm apologizing here mister!"

"Well, I accept your apology. I guess I should apologize for not refusing to come to your house with your mother as well as dinner. I don't want to be forced onto anyone. And I should have known what by your mother's insistence and your reaction," he stated.

"I guess we both are sorry for our own things then."

"So, here, now, just us, what is it that you want to know. I won't lie or run from whatever question you ask. Open target, so shoot," he confidently stated. "Hmmm let me see. When's your birthday?"

"March 23rd 1980, born at 9:30pm, 7lbs 6 oz., 20

inches long. I like long walks on the beach..."

"Really?"

"C'mon Symone. Grown up talk here. No cock-a-mami questions."

"Did you just say cock-a-mami?" I laughed with a raised eyebrow.

"Girl if you don't come on with it…"

"Seriously, what sent you to prison?" I asked.

His smile gradually faded, he sat back in his chair, took a sip of his crown n coke, clasped his hands together, and gave me an uncomfortable stare.

"Oh, sorry. I didn't mean to…I… I… I'm sorry. I was just trying...we can talk about something..." I stammered feeling like an ass *you never ask a man what he went to prison for Symone...stupid!* I lowly reprimanded myself. "No no no, it's fine. It was bound to come up right. So...I was about 18 or 19, just graduated high school doing my thing, trying to be a little hustler. And my boys and I go to a party. We meet up with some girls we were trying to impress. One chic stood out and caught my eye. I separate from the pack trying to win her over. Wining, dining, shopping."

"Oh you had your nose wide open as the old folks would say."

"Wide! I was hustlin' weed through high school and after, just to get some paper."

"Sounds typical. Not grouping you, but I know plenty of people that did the same thing."

"Well her tastes got so pricey; she was like a money leech. I had to keep her in the top brands. When the weed game wasn't bringing in what she thought she deserved, she connected me with one of her brothers who was heavy in the cocaine business. I worked my way up the ranks all to make her happy. Bought her a house, Porsche, paid trips, spa days, shopping sprees, the whole nine…"

"Well my goodness. Where were you all MY life?" I mumbled as I sipped my martini.

"Huh"""

"Oh nothing, go on…"

"Well one night we were laid up and she gets a call from her brother. She turns to me and says he needs help moving some work because his right hand man was laid out in the hospital from a botched exchange gone wrong."

"And you still went?"

"I told you she had me gaped wide open. I got dressed, kissed her goodbye, and went to make that money for my girl. Little did I know it was a setup. Armand, her brother, had been an undercover snitch for the narc team to refrain from doing heavy time in prison. About an hour into me hugging the block, I got busted mid exchange. I was charged with possession of an illegal substance with intent to sell to an officer of the law. If I agreed to plead guilty, give up my connect, and entourage, I would only get 2 to 5 years."

"So what did you do?"

"I wanted to take that deal and sing like Luther."

"So you didn't?"

"She came in to visit me and…"

"Oh God," I hung my head.

"Well she gave me some sob story about her mother being sick and Armand needing to be with them for her final days and how they wanted me to take the hit for him."

"She what? So they want a kid to do time for a grown man? I hope you did your 2 to 5 and told that broad to kick rocks!"

This was out of my character, but I couldn't stand women like that who use men for their personal gain and could care less if his life is ruined in the process.

"Well, I told you I was open wide."

"You sure are open a lot. How much more wide can you become?"

"My nose was so open I could smell the queen of England's perfume from west Dallas! Kinda like a mixture of white diamonds over musk."

"Michael," I said shockingly.

"So I took the hit."

"My lord. Well not that it can be changed, but with it being your first run in with the law did you get a reduced sentence?"

"Of course not! They pulled out the big guns. I was sentenced to 15 years."

"15 YEARS!"

"Oh yeah I would've been singing!"

As we talked, the lights began to dim. *Welcome Sankofa! How's everyone doing tonight?* A round of applause rang throughout the lounge. *Alright alright, I see some new faces and familiar ones. Again welcome to Sankofa's Open Mic Night* the host bellowed. "Oh no, I forgot it's open mic night," I mumbled to myself as I looked around to spot Chelle. *We are still awaiting the volunteers for tonight so sign-up at your free will. We will start in about 15 minutes, so grab a drink, chair, plate, and let's get to it!*

"Okay so Michael, back to you. Did you do the full 15?"

"No I only did 9."

"Well that's still a lot of time to be away."

"It is, but that's not the shocker…"

"You didn't get turned out did you?" I said giving the side eye.

"Really, you gonna hurt a brutha like that?" he said with a devilish grin.

Caught up in my own laughter. "I'm sorry; you should've seen your face."

"Ha ha but no. I should've known something wasn't right though with her. I got out finding out that I had a 9 year old daughter." Immediately silencing the laughter "What? You didn't know she was pregnant? She didn't tell you anything?" I inquired feeling like a bigger jackass for my untimely joke "she didn't say anything. After about 2 months in lock up, she stopped visiting. No letters, pictures, phone call, nothing. Just up and vanished."

"Well how did you find out you had a daughter if she didn't tell you?"

"I was on my way to see my P.O. With my boy when I saw her at a familiar corner store. We stopped for guards for my man's habit of course," he quickly passed over "Oh of course," I laughed lightly while rolling my eyes "and when he went inside, I got out stretching my legs then I ran into her. She looked like a deer in headlights. I went in on her asking what happened to her while I was doing the bid for her brother."

"What was her response?"

"She claimed she wrote me and accepted calls but I

know that was a bold faced lie. As we were going back and forth, a little girl grabbed at her asking what's going on. When I saw her, I knew she was mine. She looked like me through and through. I figured she was around eight or nine because she was so tall. I was the same height at that age. I figured that's why she stopped coming to visit me. I guess since she wasn't showing, she had to be at least a few months along. When she saw that I was staring at the little girl too long, she grabbed her hand and took off. Before I could chase after her my boy came out and talked to some sense into me that we needed to go. I couldn't risk getting violated by my P.O."

"That's crazy."

"Oh I know, that's why I'm working the way I am. My boss understood my situation and gave me a chance with the company and now I'm just working to show I can take care of my daughter."

"Take care of her?"

"I'm going for full custody." my vaginal lips began to quiver. There's nothing sexier than a man fighting for what he wants and not out of obligation.

"Really?"

"Now if she doesn't prove paternity, I'm gonna have to pull out all stops."

"She's denying she's yours?"

"Oh most definitely, but I know better. And I intend on proving it."

Alright ladies and gentlemen, our first act coming up to the stage right now to kick off our open mic is an MC from all the way..............back there the Host pointed with his corny jokes to the corner adjacent to our table. *C'mon,*

y'all show some love to Dallas's own Kada!
****

Cornell

"Miss Bridgette got you attached to that cell phone like glue I see," I teased J.

"Man she is so damn paranoid, it don't make no sense."

Before I could say anything else, Ra'Chelle came back flinging that hair "What's your deal? I asked.

"Oh nothing."

"I know that look. What's that look?" I asked.

"Oh nothing just...trust me," she winked with a smirk.

"Make sure you remember this is a work outing, not a social event."

"Calm down, I have this under control. As a matter of fact, just wait for it. You'll know it when you see it. Or better yet hear it."

"See, there's that sinister grin. You are indeed up to something."

"Do I ever let you down? Stick with me kid," she said winking and walking off. All we saw was the tail end of that hair flinging in the wind.

"Aye C, you sure you can trust that? I mean does she know what she's doing?"

Looking in the direction in which she disappeared I responded, "She better."
****

Symone

"Oh this guy is good," Michael said.

"He is isn't he?"

One more time, Kada! Show 'em some love Dallas! Next is a lady we recently heard from whom shook the house and my testicles. I mean she's just, well dammit y'all judge for yourselves. Coming to the stage, please, please, please some love to Dallas' next star...Symone!

Damn near spitting out my drink, I looked up at the host and froze.

Symone? Oh there she is. Come on y'all, show her some love

As I got up, I browsed around looking for her. This time I was really gonna kill her..........

****

Cornell

"That Kada kid was on point," James said drinking his grey goose and cranberry juice.

"Yeah he was hot"

"Alright, show time!" Ra'Chelle came back to the table grinning.

"Where have you been?" I asked.

"Damn..." J blurted out.

"Aye C man, I gotta roll out."

"You kidding me!"

"Nah man, Bridgette won't chill out. You now that new mommy syndrome," he said while dapping me up.

"Alright man. Hit me up in the morning and don't be late," I said.

"Yeah I gotcha. It was nice meeting you again Ra'Chelle."

"You too James," she said reaching to shake his hand.

"Y'all take care...*I'm on my way babe,*" *he* said into

the receiver walking out.

Next up is a future Dallas great, our own Symone..." the host bellowed.

"Wooooooooooooooo!" Ra'Chelle cheered.

Oh, this looks familiar..........

****

Symone

Approaching the stage, the host helps me and my 4 ½ inch stilettos up the stages steps. Why I chose to wear these shoes I'll never know. With each step, I'm thinking of what to sing and how I'll kill Chelle after. Grabbing the microphone, I spoke, "I was not expecting to be up here today, but my good friend ever so graciously signed me up once more."

"YOU WELCOME BOO!" she yelled from the back of the room as the crowd lightly laughed.

"I'll see you after," I smiled with gritted teeth. "Since I'm up here, can you guys bear with me tonight?"

We gotcha girl, a voice in the audience said.

I closed my eyes, said a quick prayer, turned, and looked at the head keyboardist and she gave me a gesture to go ahead.

"If I had you back in my world. I would prove that I would be a better, girl," I began to sing...

****

Cornell

"Isn't that Jazmine Sullivan's *I Need You Bad?*" I asked.

"Yes it is," Ra'Chelle snapped. "This is my Jam!" I had to have this on record. She can work a room and has much stage presence. Her style oozed sexy, but not slutty or trampy.

"Boy I need you bad as a heartbeat (bad like the food I eat)." the bands vocalists provided her background vocals "bad as the air I breathe. I need you bad I can't take this pain. Boy I'm about to go insane. I need you. I need you..." she belted. "She knows what she's doing." *When you want him so bad and you gotta get him back say ooooooooooo* "oooooooo," the crowd repeated along "She's really feeling this," I said unaware of my head nodding to the performance. "I see you boss-man!" Ra'Chelle said, snapping me back to reality. "So what do you think?" she asked as her friend finished up on stage. "We gotta get her. I can't risk her getting snatched up by anyone else! I just gotta have her."

"I bet you do," she mumbled.

"Huh?"

"I said I knew you would say that!"

"So how are we gonna go about doing this because I'm so ready to do this!"

"Slow down speedy! Let me get her on board first. You just stick to the business and I'll wrangle the talent. I'll let you know when you need to book a studio though cause I can assure you she's gonna fight me on it."

"Are you sure she'll come around?" I anxiously asked.

"Shit she better," she said before she slid out of the booth.

****

Symone

"Thank you," I said finishing up Jazmine Sullivan's hit song. *Damn! What I tell you Sankofa? C'mon, show her*

Sinful Secrets   M'Hogany

some love! She'll sang a niggas draws off! Shit you can have mine right now...oh wait...didn't wear any...well girl you can have whatever you like! The host said helping me down the stage *My My My, vocals, beauty, and booty. HALELUYAAAAH!* He said as the crowd laughed. As I made my way towards my table, I was stopped many of times with kudos and handshakes and kind words. One man actually slid me his number.

Once I made it back to my table, Michael stood and gave a light round of applause. Chelle sauntered past him towards me snapping her fingers and smiling. "Bitch don't act all shocked. I knew you would turn this piece out and you did too," she said with the biggest sinister grin.

"You're lucky we're in a public place and Michael is here," I said as she began to roll her eyes.

"Well whatever little miss snooty booty," she said with a slight tap on my ass.

"Get on girl," I said giving her a slight shove.

"Tootles," she bounced away flinging that hair to where ever she came from.

"She is indeed a character," Michael laughed as we sat down.

"Always has been."

"Now Ms. Symone that, was, amazing."

"Really," I cringed.

"I don't say what I don't mean Symone," he remarked as he drank the remnant of his drink. As we sat awkwardly and I fought to keep my cheeks from turning purple. (Y'all know dark skinned folk don't blush, we just get purple). Two more acts got up and performed. *Ok, here we'll take a little intermission so go get a drink, eat, smoke, in my case do an underwear check or buy some and we'll return with more performers. Give it to our house band Beauty and the Beats!* Then the band began to play some Al Green. Michael gets up and extends his hand towards me. "C'mon". I hesitated, but gave in. I eventually got up and followed him to the little intimate square dance floor. Before we started dancing, I look him in the face, and raise my balled up fist "watch the feet and you can keep your eyes."

Raising both hands in surrender "Fair enough," he said. He then proceeded to place his hands on the small of my back and I got chills. I moved in closer to his chest, inhaling the cruiser cologne that meshed greatly with his body chemistry. "Now it's time for you to tell me about yourself."

"What is it that you want to know?"

"I know about your family and you as the preacher's daughter, but I want to know who Symone really is." He placed my arms around his neck and placed both of his around my waist.

"Symone is a helper, lover, listener, hard worker, no BS taker."

Laughing he said, "Ok then. So where'd you get the voice from? I mean I know Sis. Johnson isn't a walking Whitney or Aretha, but let's just say, she's strong in leading congregational hymns."

Laughing I responded, "Hey, now, back up off of my mom! But anyway, I don't really know where the voice really came from. My grandmother would play gospel music in the car on the regular and have me and my sisters singing all the time. She was hard on us harmonizing and everything. It was round the clock choir rehearsals."

"Now I see. What does the pastor think about you singing non gospel music?"

"Well Daddy isn't as bad as my mom. He says to me *as long as you keep GOD in your corner, baby girl I don't care what you sing.*" I mocked my father "And what does the first lady say?" as I thought of my mom's strong disdain for secular music, my gaze became distant and I grew silent.

"Symone, hey, where'd you go?" Michael asked with a strong sense of concern.

"Oh nothing."

"You didn't answer my question."

"My mom doesn't approve of me singing anything that's not gospel," I said fighting the tears that began to well up in my eyes.

"Alright alright, we're back. If you want more of Dallas' talent to grace the stage say yeah!" the host yelled.

"Yeah!" the crowd repeated.

"Shit the Apollo ain't got nothing on us! Well other than the fact that they pay their hosts! Hell, I can't get two chicken nuggets and a side of ranch let alone a decent check! But anyway, give it up to our next act..." the host continued with his introduction.

Michael, witnessing my discomfort, walked me back to our table. "So I take it you haven't told your parents about your little vocal adventures here?"

"Of course not."

"Why not? I think they would be proud of you and the love you receive from using that gift of a voice."

"Daddy, maybe. Mama, don't hold your breath on

that one. And can you please not tell her? I know she will indeed make efforts to call you and play cupid."

"My lips are sealed."

Well if there are no more acts, this concludes our Open Mic Night Fridays here at Sankofa. See you all next week. Same time. Same place. Love, piece, and chicken grease. Goodnight!"

We headed towards the door. "Excuse me Ms. Symone?" the host came and stopped me.

"Yes?" I turned to address him.

"I don't mean to disturb you, but you have a very beautiful voice."

"Thank you," I smiled.

"I spoke with my manager and we both agreed that we would like to extend the offer for you to headline our Friday Night Open Mic. That is if you're okay with that?"

"Um, wow, um can I think about it and get back with you?"

"Think about what," Chelle mysteriously appeared.

"I was offering Ms. Symone here our feature headlining position every Friday night."

"She'll take it!" she blurted.

"Great! I'll go get the manager," and he scurried off not giving me any opportunity to retract Chelle's hasty acceptance.

"Michael would you excuse me?"

"Sure, I have to make a phone call."

I turned to Chelle when he was out of earshot. "Have you lost your damn mind?"

"Shit have you?"

"Why would you accept that?"

"Cause yo' scared ass wasn't gonna! I told you about that shy shit! You have a bad voice and badass body to boot! Here you have a major opportunity to show it off and move in your zone. So YES BITCH YOU ACCEPT!"

"Here she is our headlining songbird!"

"Ms. Symone, I'm Jack Robinson manager of Sankofa and I am pleased to have you join our family. I don't doubt you'll gain much exposure as we grow."

"Ra'Chelle Radcliffe, manager for Ms. Symone. Can you have this in writing and we will have our legal team oversee this and fax it to your office?"

"Oh yes, Ms. Radcliffe. I'll have those papers drawn up. Once you've had your team look them over you can have someone bring them back or fax them. We appreciate your time and welcome to the Sankofa family!" he said as we shook hands.

"Manager," I said through gritted teeth as we waved them off.

"Yes, you heard me correctly. Who else knows you like I do? Besides don't nobody know hot to handle you like me anyway!"

"Ra'Chelle I'm gonna go ahead and head home. I'll see you tomorrow; we have a lot to talk about."

"Symone, beautiful beautiful voice. Take care ladies."

"Was that?"

"Cornell, yes ma'am."

"What was that all about?"

"You'll see soon."

Chapter 26
Michael

"Hey, I know it's late, but we're wrapping up here and she's headed home. No, I told you to hold off until I say so. Look I gotta go, but I'll call you with more info later. Yeah I know, I gotta go."

"Michael, I'm sorry but I guess we're done here," Symone spoke with her friend in tow.

"Alright, well did you valet?"

"I did," she responded.

"Well I'll wait until they bring your car around."

As we waited, she turned to me. "I must say, you impressed me tonight. I wasn't looking forward to actually enjoying myself, but you proved me wrong," she fought to smile. They brought around a black infinity coupe. "Well this is me," she gestured.

"Nice. So being all in people's business pays off pretty well I see," I joked.

"Something like that."

As I placed her in her car I said, "I'll be right behind you."

"You don't have to I'll be fine," she protested once again.

"Haven't we been through this before?"

"Fine."

As I followed her in my Honda Accord, I got a text. *How long will you be out?*

I'm wrapping it up now, I responded.

Hurry because this pussy can't lick itself...

****

Racquel

"Is baby-girl okay?" Sherrone asked as I came into the family room.

"Yeah she's okay. I swear these kids are growing up super fast," I said plopping on the couch.

"Don't I know it? My brother's kiddos are getting so big I don't know where the time has gone."

"How is he doing anyway?"

"He's great. After his wife died, he went into a slight depression. We kept the kids for a bit until he pulled together."

"Speaking of kids, when are you and Cornell gonna make me an auntie?"

"Well we weren't gonna say anything, but we had an appointment today"

"Heffa, you shouldn't be drinking then!"

"Racqui, I'm not pregnant," she said with a look of defeat.

"Oh hunny, don't worry it'll happen. Just give it time," I said.

"Ugh, I'm so sick of hearing that. We've been married for over 10 years and nothing. Do you know how long we've tried?"

Before I could respond, my cell went off. "Hold on...hello? ...where are you? Okay... see you in 30," I said with my back slightly turned.

"I didn't know it was that late. Cornell is probably on his way home. I'll call you tomorrow," she said looking at her watch, gathering her keys and purse.

"Sure, we can go do something tomorrow," I said walking her to the door. "Sherrone, I'm sorry again about earlier," I apologized.

"Me too. I didn't mean to just go left today. I just want you to be happy," she said hugging me.

"You too hun. We both will be soon."

Closing the door I thought, *I don't know about yours, but my happy ain't too far away!*

****

Michael

Parking her car in the driveway and getting out, I parked my car curbside and followed.

"Thank you for seeing me safely home, I appreciate it. I'm sure my mom would really enjoy it more"

"Not a problem, but I'm not going to just stand here and watch until you walk in. Let's go..." I insisted ushering her to her door and inside her house. I proceed to check around the house like top flight security.

"What are you doing?" she asked.

"Checking for monsters and the boogeyman"

"And did you find any?"

"All clear," I laughed.

"Well like I said before, I thank you for tonight. You weren't too bad Michael. I even let you keep your eyes."

"Cute. Well I should be going," I stated as I proceeded to hug her good bye.

After we embraced briefly, we stood within inches of each other. "Is there anything else you need me to do or want me to check?" I noticed then she was much shorter than I thought. I noticed she took off her stilettos forcing her once 5'7" height to drop drastically to 5 feet even.

"I, um, don't think so."

Inches away from her plump breasts, pouty lips, and hazel eyes, I say once more. "You sure?"

"Yes," she whispered.

I leaned in and kissed her on her cheek and whispered in her ear, "If you say so. Sleep tight," and proceeded to let myself out. Outside I patted my pants where signs of a growing bulge were apparent. Unbuttoning the top two buttons of my shirt, I told myself, *Get it together Mike.*

****

Symone

"What are you doing?" I asked Michael as he walked around my house going from room to room.

"Checking for monsters and the boogeyman."

Cute, I thought. I took off my stilettos and put them by the front door. Being tall hurts, but I look good! Soon as I turned around, Michael was standing so close to me I could smell the spearmint from earlier that lingered on his breath. Now my 5-foot frame was standing directly in front of his 6-foot one.

"Is there anything else you need me to check?" he asked in a soft tone similar to Barry White's panty dropping bass pitch.

"I, um, I don't think so."

If he moves any closer something is gonna go down. He asked me once more, "you sure?"

"I'm sure." The warmth of his breath caused my hands to sweat, hairs on my body to stand at attention, and made my pussy quiver. "I…I…I...I...I, um, I'm sure."

Leaning over, he plants a soft slow kiss on my cheek. I inhaled his masculine musk, which intertwined with his sexy cologne. "Sleep tight Symone," he whispered before slightly brushing past me leaving me caught up in a heated and sticky trance.

Closing the door I mumbled, "Dammit." to myself. I turned off the lights and headed to my bathroom. Running hot bath water, I pour bubble bath; unzip my skirt and satin blouse, letting them fall to the floor exposing my 36D cupped breasts. As I slide off my panties, I notice the saturated stain covering my size 7 underwear as I peeled it away from my creaming opening. Gathering my clothes off of the floor, I place them into the big black hamper to be washed later with my remaining wet attire. Also removing my bra and placing it in as well. Completely nude, I walk over to my nightstand, pull out my secretly hidden drawer, and get my relaxer *Calgon*. I walk into the bathroom, pull out a drying towel, and lay it across the back tile lining the garden bathtub. Using my remote, I turn on R. Kelly's 12-Play, step inside the bathtub, lean back on the built in pillow, and reach for *Calgon*. Turning the dial to the highest speed, *Take me away* was what escaped my lips as I moaned in ecstasy coming over and over in my watery oasis...

****

Ring Ring Ring Ring Ring Ring
Jumping up out of my sleep, I realized that my house phone was viciously ringing. Using the remote, I stopped Robert over the Bose speakers and hit talk while still in the comforts of my bathtub. "Hello," I spoke aloud

while running hot water to circulate through out. "Trick! It's about damn time you answered! I been out here calling you left and right! What the hell are you doing in there? Did you get some last night? Is he still here cause I don't see no car nasty hoe"

"Chelle, shut up!"

"Well bitch you gonna leave me out here or not?" pushing another button the front door unlocked granting her access inside. "Where are you anyway? Wait let me guess...in the bathroom"

"Of course," I responded.

"Ok, I'm on my way up"

"Shut up, bye."

Shortly after hanging up, she bursts into my bathroom's double doors. "I have arrived hunny, YAAASSS!"

"Really, can you not be that extra on a Saturday?"

"Chile please ain't no turning me down ANY DAY. Question is, how long have you been in this tub ma'am," with hands on her hips. "Let me guess," looking around at the clean marble floors, the folded towel, and my wet hair cascaded on the side of the bath and *Calgon* tucked underneath. "My lord, so it was just you and Calgon last night huh?"

"Hey he took me away so I'm good"

"And you just laid up in this tub sleep"

"Um yeah"

"What the hell happened to that cup of chocolate from last night?" she spat with her arms folded. "I guess he went home"

"Clearly he didn't break you off if Mr. C had to

come out of hiding"

"Never lets me down"

"Did you even get close to cleaning the cob webs off ya pussy?"

"I don't know Michael like that Chelle. And I sure as hell am not giving him any of my cookies"

"This bitch still callin it cookies. Hell at the rate you going you won't have no damn cookies, yo' ass gonna be sittin' on a box of croutons. I'ma have to pray for you tomorrow to get laid"

"Don't play with the lord like that," I said bathing and letting the water out. I grabbed my towel and wrapped it around my wet body walking down the mini steps and stopping at the rug in front of my vanity. I grabbed my bottle of Johnson & Johnson baby lotion, but wrapped my wet hair around four times in a bun and pinned it up before I began to moisturize my body. I removed the towel and began to apply lotion over my chocolate skin, while talking to Chelle. "What's the agenda, since you're here interrupting my off day?"

"Well I brought the papers back from my lawyer from the proposal the manager of Sankofa drew up."

"Oh you were dead serious"

"And you weren't?"

"Well how does it look," I asked now applying lotion to my slightly erect nipples and breasts"

"We did some number crunching and negotiating, but we got a solid good deal"

"So what do you need form me then?" I place one leg up on the stool and began to lotion I need a few things. One, for you to sigh these papers. Two, for you to hurry up and put on some clothes. And three get ready to head out"

"First off, don't rush me, second we're seen each other naked plenty of times, and third head out where"

"Bitch see you ask too many questions," she said getting up and going behind my bathtub to the walk-in closet. I go grab a black lace panty set out of my bedroom nightstand and place *Calgon* back in his place.

****

Ra'Chelle

I know this trick heard me calling. Hell I hope she got her damn back beat in! Ain't no tellin if she got cob webs or what down there!"

"Hello?"

"Damn bitch, I hope it was good! I've been calling yo' ass all day! Is mister mister still in the house? Did he beat it up good? I don't see his car nasty hoe!" I said with a smirk "shut up," Symone responded. "Well you gonna leave bitch out here all damn day?" The lock from inside unlocked granting me access in. I walk in locking it behind me. With the phone still pressed to my ear "heffa where are you?"

"I'm upstairs in the bathroom"

"I'm on my way so tell ya boy toy to put up the sausage."

"Shut up, bye," she stated hanging up the phone. I walked upstairs into her bedroom and headed towards her double doors yanking them open "She has arrived hunny!"

"Really, do you HAVE to be so extra?" She asked still in the bathtub. "Boo ain't no taming this. The question should be did that CAT of yours get tamed?" Before I sat down across the bathroom I glanced at its neatness with spotless marble heated floors, no clothes, an empty trashcan, and I see him. "So just you and Calgon last night huh? Why the hell did you name that damn thing Calgon ANYWAY?"

"Cause he knows how to take me away," she smiled. "That's a damn shame. What happened to that tall glass of hot chocolate from last night?"

"Hell he probably went home I guess."

"See one night you gonna look for Mr. C and that damn toy gonna come up missing!"

"Don't touch my baby! He's a stress reliever!"

"If you let a nigga hit, you wouldn't NEED it to relieve no damn stress!" I spat as she got out of the bathtub. Walking towards the vanity dripping wet, she wrapped her long wavy black hair in a knot while removing the towel to dry her chocolate body causing me to bite my lip.

"So what's on the agenda that has you here on my day off?"

Relieved she said something to keep me from gawking I answered, "I have the papers from my lawyer that the manager from Sankofa had drawn up."

"Is everything ok?" now applying lotion to her dark chocolate nipples. How I wish my tongue were that lotion circling her areola "Um, we crunched some numbers and negotiated some things, but in the end it came out ok"

"Is there anything you need from me?" while placing her leg upon the stool to continue her moisturizing session traveling up her tear dropped ass and chocolate stemmed let's. She bent over to apply lotion to her ankles revealing the pinkness of her well-groomed pussy while it glistened from its own juices. Visions of me burying my tongue in and out if her wet cavity danced in my head. Her well-manicured nails playing in my curly hair while I latched on her clit until she came in my mouth. Wanting her to be my chocolate éclair in search of that creamy filling. "Chelle?" She yelped snapping me out of my daze "what do I need to do now?" 'other than melt in my mouth' I thought "oh, right, well 1) sign, 2) hurry up and put some damn clothes on so we can go", cause the longer she stays naked I won't be able to refrain from cuppin dat ass. I got up heading towards her closet to pick something out for her to wear and give myself a break. I couldn't sit there any longer with her sexy ass body exposed like that, cause the things I would do to her sound have her telling Calgon to GO AWAY! When I got up, I felt the bubbles forming in my stewed juices causing me to rush in her closet and check to ensure there were no visible wet spots. "SHIT! Now I got pussy on the brain...."

Chapter 27
Cornell

"Why is it you always wanna work on one part of yo' body dude?" I asked James.

"Nigga, I work on my bet parts!" he said while flexing in the bathroom mirrors. Taking my gym bag out of the locker getting ready to head home and shower, my phone buzzes notifying me of an incoming text message. *Can you get a studio ready for this afternoon?* Me: *I can, why, is she on board?* I texted in return. *Just book it for 6:00pm, we'll be there.* Me: *Okay, I'll send you the address* I ended. As I deleted the texts, another message comes in. *Papi, I miss you.*

Me: *What did I tell you about texting me on weekends* I responded frustrated.

I sorry papi, but I need you

"Aye yo C, you a'ight?" James interrupted as I quickly shut my phone.

"Yeah, just tryna book this studio session."

"Oh word. Went good last night huh?" Grabbing our bags and walking out the gym. "We need to see how the studio sessions goes, but hopefully it will go over smoothly. We might be able to get this label up and running sooner than expected."

"That's what's up! Keep me updated. I might be that next act you sign. And I need a fat bonus too man"

"Man please, I ain't puttin you behind no damn

mic!"

"Whatever! I'ma hit you up later"

"Alright baby boy."

As we headed out outside of the gym, **I'MA GET YOU AND YO' HOE!** was painted in red on James' car. "What the fuck!" James yells. "You GOTTA be kidding me! You gotta be FUCKING KIDDING ME!" he said while dropping his gym bag by my truck. "Damn. Storm Racquel has struck once again"

"I swear this bitch is psycho!" he yelled, "look at this shit! LOOK AT MY DAMN CAR!"

"It is bad bro." I hated to agree, but it did. His once pearly white 2011 Dodge Charger was completely defaced. Of all the years I've known Racquel, I've never seen her go to the extremes like this. "Jay, who are you calling? I cautiously asked "who the fuck you think? This woman has lost the last ounce of sense she had remaining in that damn head of hers!"

"Whoa whoa whoa," I said abruptly snatching his cell phone shutting it closed. "No no, not like this man. You need to calm down before you talk to her," I tried talking some sense into him. "Something has to happen cause this shit has to stop!"

"You know what you gotta do, but how you do it is what's gonna matter"

"C, you gotta point, but I don't know if I can keep a leveled head with her. If I saw her right now, I'd probably strangle the dog SHIT out of her"

"My point exactly! What's that shrink you were talkin' about?" I asked while snapping. "Well anyway, call her cause clearly you haven't learned a damn thing! I ain't bailin yo' ass outta jail for putting your hands on Racquel!"

"You know, lemme go cool off or something"...*look at this shit...he* mumbles while getting in his car. Picking up his phone while sitting in the car *"Dr. Johnson here,"* the female voice states. "Hi, Dr. Johnson, this is James Smith. I don't mean to bother you on a Saturday, but I really need to speak with you before I do something...oh...thank you so much. I can be at your office in 15 minutes...oh you're not at the office? You're working from home? Okay, I have a pen." He took the address down and cranked his car and headed to his new destination...

****

Symone

Hanging up my cell phone, I place it back down on the nightstand. I comb my slightly damp hair in a bun and head into my closet where Chelle was going through my wardrobe. I pulled out my grey dress pants and blazer and went to grab my black flats when I bumped smack into Chelle. "What the hell are you doing?" she asked with an arm full of outfits she put together out of my closet. "I'm getting dressed, girl move," I said trying to side step her. "The hell you are in THAT tacky shit!"

"This is NOT tacky"

"Bitch ain't no damn color or nothin in that shit!"

"Look Chelle I have things to do and a patient coming over," I said walking around her grabbing my shoes. "Client? On a Saturday? I thought you were off today?" She stood with daggering eyes. "I did too," I commented sliding my pants over my baby smooth skin and buttoned with ease. As I put on my blouse I just got a call that sounded like an emergency, so I can't just dismiss it because it's supposed to be my off day."

"This is why I don't have your job," she responded while quickly putting the clothes back. "Don't put those shoes on since you're so hell bent on taking clients," she said grabbing my black 5-inch wedges. Looking at her phone, "I gotta go, since you throwing monkey wrenches in my plans. But make sure you wrap that shit up by 4 because you need to be ready by then and don't ask no damn questions just be ready."

"Yes ma'am," I mocked.

"Tootles tramp!" she said clacking out down the stairs.

After I heard the door close and the bass from her car dissipate down the street, I comfortably placed the wedges back in my closet and placed back on my flats. "Professional and comfortably cute," I stated. I made my way downstairs towards my office doors in time to hear the buzzer go off. Quickly running to the door, I open it and before I could get out "Mr. Smith"

"Doc I swear I'm gonna wring that bitches neck!" he spat rushing past me.

"Hey hey hey, now wait a minute. Slow down. What?"

"I came out of the gym with my boy and the **BITCH** spray painted my GOT DAMN CAR!"

"Wait, who?"

"Catchup with me doc! Racquel!"

"Okay okay, calm down," I tried.

"No Doc, come see this shit!" he said opening my office door and grabbing me by the arm damn near dragging me out with him. "See, do you see this? DO YOU

FUCKIN SEE THIS?" I've seen a lot in my years of being a counselor, but this is a first! I mean she definitely is a different type of woman. "Okay, Mr. Smith let's go inside," I tried to calm him down a bit more turning and redirecting him towards the office entrance of my house.

Click click click click click

"Have a seat Mr. Smith," I encouraged "Where do you think this is stemming from with your wife"

"Wife? EX-WIFE! And Doc I really like you, I mean I really do. But, you gotta come with something else cause I ain't in the mood for that intelligent dumb ass question. It's past time for you to be straightforward. Last I checked, you were one of us," he said pointing to the back of his hand.

"Okay, Mr. Smith."

"James."

"Okay, James. Off the record, I'm gonna give you what you want. What brought this on?"

"Doc look, all niceness out of the window. This bitch is crazy. First, she fucked up your office. Then your damn window got busted. She accuses you and me of messing around. And you got the damn nerve to ask my black ass what caused this?"

"Okay James, enough is enough. Your wife destroyed my office. I'm not sure if she is the cause of my damn window being fucked up, yes I said it, but I feel like you're leaving some things out."

"Look, I'm sorry. I honestly don't know where Racquel's mind is anymore or when it got there," he panted with his hands clasped and his leg shaking violently. Yes, a man's body language says a lot even in times like these. "The only way we can move forward and fix this is to address it!"

"This? There's no fixing THIS!" he yelled back in his irate rage.

I poured a glass of water and placed it on the table in front of him. "James, I will NOT have you yelling at me in my home or anywhere for that matter."

"I'm sorry, I shouldn't be taking this out on you Dr. Johnson," he tried to calm himself down.

"Now getting back at it, did you two talk about your first outburst?"

I tried, but she automatically assumed that since I wasn't sleeping with her sister...that..."

"That what?"

Hanging his head further into his hands

"What is it James? I asked heavily concerned.

"That I'm in a relationship with you and have been…"

"Oh, oh no!" I slowly responded as it registered late. "Isn't she aware that she sought out me and my services?"

"I mentioned that to her numerous times! I just agreed to go to the sessions so she could get off my back and get a way out!"

"Now, have you informed her about the real new lady in your life?" I asked

"Bridgette? Of course not? I'm not stupid! That's suicide!"

"James, you do see a problem there right? What's

wrong about her assuming that you and I are an item but right about you not telling her that you've indeed moved on?"

"Doc, look, I know Racquel okay. It's either her way or no way alright. I can't risk my relationship with Bridgette and our daughter because Racquel is just hurt because we didn't work out. I mean, I'm hurting as well because I didn't expect to fall out of love with the other of my children and first love. That's life."

"I understand and I commend you on being such a stand-up guy," I pushed myself to say. "And recognizing that staying would bring the two of you down, but in order to move forward you have to be completely honest and open. The last thing you want is for what is basically happening now."

"You don't know Racquel like I do though."

"James, it doesn't matter how well I know her. Truthfully, this woman you speak of is a woman that you truly don't know either! Only you can rectify this and set it right. Does she know that Bridgette and you are expecting?"

"Hell no!" he said with a bigger attitude.

"So when were you going to say something about that to her?"

"Doc, I don't know okay!"

"Are you still in the home with Racquel and the children?"

"I haven't lived in the house in years."

"How does Bridgette feel about that?"

"Well she's okay with that, since we live together."

"So how long have you and Bridgette lived

together?"

"About 2 years now."

"Wow, 2 years. That's quite a lengthy amount of time James. And you still haven't gotten around to telling your ex-wife? Do you see the unbalance in that?"

"Doc, I've sent her divorce papers year after year but she either rips them up, burns them, or just won't sign them. Now with our daughter on the way and Bridgette's health being a major concern, I can't take the added stress."

"Her health?" I asked.

"Her doctor says that her stress level is high and could harm our daughter so she needs to remain as stress free as possible."

"Oh my I see. This is quite a challenge…"

"Exactly!"

"However, James, tell me this. What will you do or have you thought about if Racquel finds out on her own?"

"How do you honestly expect me to keep others from being hurt Doc? I can't be everywhere."

"Let's just start with you and Bridgette. I know your concern is her and your daughter. You don't want to go into a new situation carrying the woes of an old one. Would Bridgette be ok with a session with you and her on Monday?"

At this time, James was fighting the tears that began to well in his ducts. "I don't know how this mess got so out of control," he grumbled.

"We can sort this out and get everyone on the same page or at least near it."

"Doc, you think so?"

"I'm determined to see everyone through this."

"Let me talk to Bridgette and see what we can come up with. But I have to get this cleaned off of my car before it causes a more permanent stain."

"Take care of yourself James. My phone line is always available," I reassured him as I escorted him to the door.

Before I could lock it, my cell began to ring. I noticed a car parked three houses down. I peered down the street and it seemed as if there was slight movement in the vacant vehicle as if I was being watched. Then again, you're liable to see anything adjusting your eyes from dimly lit to bright sunshine. Not giving too much thought to it, I closed the door and headed back to my desk. Again, my cell rang. "Hello?"

"Well damn, took you forever!"

"What Chelle, I was with a client."

"For damn near 4 hours? If this mofo has to sit on YO' couch for that damn long, his ass just needs to be on some damn drugs! Hell he making ME feel depressed and shit!"

"What do you want girl?" I asked while annotating James, I mean Mr. Smith's file and sending Ashleigh a follow-up email to look out for his call.

"I told you earlier to be ready when I called"

"What time is it?"

"Heffa it's nearly 5:30! Bring yo' ass on! I sent the address...and put those wedges back on! I know you took 'em off!"

"Alright, let me lock up and I'll meet you there."

"Tootles"!

"Bye."

I shut down my computer, lock my office doors, head back upstairs, and grab the wedges from in front of my bed and head back downstairs. I head towards the garage and set the alarm before getting into my car. I take the address Chelle texted me and plugged it into my cars navigational system embedded on the dashboard and see that it is 20 minutes away from my house. As I place my car in reverse, I let the garage door down and get a notification that the house was secure. In route, I head towards my calculated destination and I pass the car I noticed earlier. It looked as if no one was in it, so I just assumed it was someone's who resided at the house or visitor and went about my way.

Ring ring

What is this bug Symone day? I thought to myself while answering the blue-tooth on the dashboard. "Hey Mama."

"Hey hunny, what are you doing?"

"Driving."

"Where are you headed?"

"Meeting up with Chelle."

"What's that girl got up her sleeve now?"

"Mama, you know I don't know."

"That chile needs some serious prayer. Anyway, so have you spoken to Michael since that disrespectful dinner?"

"Ma, really, now isn't the time to talk about that."

"Make time Symone. I was really disappointed with your behavior."

"MA! Not to day okay, I've talked to Michael and it's okay."

"Well why didn't you say anything. What did he say? Have you two setup for a date?"

"Mother...I gotta go; I made it to my destination." I was not going to continue with cupid here but I was seriously at my destination.

"Alright baby, well don't be out too late cause you need to be at church early in the morning."

"Yes ma'am," I said rolling my eyes.

Chapter 28
Cornell

"Didn't you say your girl was on her way?" I asked.

"Hold on, she's downstairs. Let me go get her," Ra'Chelle said leaving the studio.

When can I see you is what the text read. This woman is really working my last nerve. *Papi I need to see you and feel you*

Me: *look this isn't working out for me anymore. You do understand I have a wife* I texted back.

But papi, I thought you loved me.

I hated that I lied to her, but that ass was worth every one. However, now she's becoming way too clingy for me. Hell I also found out she was letting other niggas hit too! *Papi you said we would make a baby.* "Aw Hell Naw!" I blurted out loud. Luckily, no one was there to hear it. What the hell I look like having a baby with this jump-off. What the hell will my wife say? This trick is crazy and Cornell don't do crazy. Yeah I definitely gotta cut this chick loose.

"Cornell," I heard snapping me out of my internal rant. I look up to see Ra'Chelle walk in with a huge smile plastered on her face with Symone in toe. "Hey ladies. Symone, welcome to the hit factory." The look Symone had on her face said this was a surprise to her. "I take it you didn't know you were headed to a session," I asked peering at Ra'Chelle.

"No I didn't. All I was told was to meet Chelle at this address and she brought me up here," she responded with arms folded shooting daggers towards Ra'Chelle.

"Hey now, you're both here, so let's not worry about HOW you got here. It's time to put this voice on wax."

"I'm sorry Symone, if you want to call it quits, we can. I don't want you to be here if you're uncomfortable. There's no pressure to start anything if you don't want too," I apologized.

"The hell she will! She's here, so there's no need for her to leave. Can we move this along," Ra'Chelle blurted.

"Excuse me Symone, Ra'Chelle can I talk to you for a minute?" I insisted pulling her to the side not giving her an opportunity to contest. "What the hell is your issue," I harshly whispered out of Symone's earshot. "Are you trying to RUN her off?"

"She's not going anywhere trust me, you have to push Symone, or she'll procrastinate and just sit on it!"

"You can't push like that Ra'Chelle! We can't afford to have her feel forced. She can totally back out and mainly I'll be assed out a hell of a lot of money," I barked.

"Look you worry about the talent. And as far as Symone goes, you let me deal with her how I know. Trust, she won't be going anywhere. I can guarantee that."

"You'd better hope so!"

"Look, she's here isn't she?" she spat flinging her horses mane. I had to admit it, she had a point.

"Do something with that hair. You gonna have people coughing up fur balls," I swatted as the strands slapped me in the face.

"Whatever!"

I could see Symone slightly grin as she sat in my engineer's chair. I almost got choked up by the slight smile causing my pants to agree.

****

Symone

I can't believe this tramp set me up once again I mumbled to myself. Not only did she set me up twice at Sankofa, but now she got me here in this studio. I noticed Cornell pulling her away to address her. I hope he gives her ass the scolding of a damn lifetime! As I went through my schedule plans, Chelle and Cornell seemed to diffuse their intense conversation where Chelle flung that damn hair again. This time, Cornell caught the tail end of the weave toss. "And do something with that hair. Hell, you gonna have people coughing up fur balls," he spat while he swatted the strands from his face. Smiling to myself. I told her about that damn hair

"So, you ready chick?" she asked me.

"Ready? For what?" I snapped from my planner looking up at her. I could see Cornell shaking his head in embarrassment behind her. I guess she was going against his better judgment, in pure Chelle fashion.

"Bitch what you think? We ain't here to knit or hold hands!" she sarcastically stated. "Just go and put something down so you'll know where your comfort level is and Cornell can give us some input on where to go from there."

Thinking heavily I asked, "Well, what would I sing? I didn't have anything prepared."

Snapping she replied, "how about that gospel song. You know, the one Kelly Price did that you sing"

"See, you most definitely need to be in somebody's

Sinful Secrets   M'Hogany

church tomorrow," I joked placing my things in the seat I was sitting in. "So, Cornell, is it alright?" I asked.

"Oh, please! I'd love to hear what you have," he gestures towards the booth. I step inside, place the headphones on my head, give the mic a quick test "one...2...check...1...2", then get the thumbs up from Cornell at the board, while Chelle grinned like the Cheshire cat. I say a quick prayer and channel what my granny taught and started singing. "I don't know...about tomorrow...I just live, from day to day..."

****

Cornell

Hoping she would finally come on board, Symone took off her jacket to her suit and placed it in the chair with her other belongings. "Cornell is it alright?" she asked.

"Please please go ahead. I would love to hear what you have," I said.

She turned to step into the booth as I got a glance of her body and I must say it was well put together even in office wear. The smoothness of her ass outlined in her pants woke up the sleeping beast within. *I would love to work that out!* I thought as she stepped in the booth. "1...2...check...1...2," she said testing the microphone. I instantly became jealous of the microphone being allowed to be that close to her glossy lips. I give her the thumbs up, and she opens her mouth releasing heavens best kept secret. I felt chills engulf my back, arms, groin, and legs. I even felt the oozing of precum seep from my stiffening rod. Now, I felt ashamed and bad. I was not only getting aroused by this woman, but while she was singing a GOSPEL song at that! Shaking my head *there's a special place in hell just for me.* Gawking at Symone, I nearly forgot Ra'Chelle was in the room until she startled me. **Clap** "what the...." I said coming back to reality, "You were over here mumbling something," she said with hands on her hips. "I was saying are you sure she's NEVER been in a studio before?" I played off. "I told you," she smiled. *Many things about tomorrow. I don't seem to under...understand...* Symone continued to belt from the booth. "Damn," slipped from my lips. Ra'Chelle backhands my arm. "What the hell was that for?"

"Stop cursing on a gospel song!"

"If you don't stop hitting me...." I laughed *For he knows what lies...ahead....* Symone wrapped up. She looks up with those hazel eyes. Between her and Ra'Chelle, there wasn't a single dry eye. I wave for her to come on out. "How was that?" she asked picking up her belongings and sitting back down like she didn't melt the damn studio with her blazing vocals. "You're kidding right?" I asked her with raised eyebrows. "She's kidding right," I voiced as I turned towards Ra'Chelle. "With that voice, you shouldn't even have to ask. I haven't met a person yet who can sing like that. I can only imagine what you can do with a non-gospel song."

"You two talk amongst yourselves, I gotta take this call," Ra'Chelle stated while stepping out the studio. "So tell me honestly. Is this your FIRST time in the studio?" I asked her while making a copy of her singing for her to take home. "I've been TO studios before, but not behind the mic for myself."

"I just don't understand why a woman with such a gift as yourself just doesn't want to use it"

"It' not that I don't want to use it I'm just cautious about singing. My family is very critical"

"I remember you briefly speaking about that. You still have my card?" I asked I do"

"Please please use it. I want to help get you out of that comfort zone and embrace that gift. If you don't want to sing gospel per say, that's fine. We'll work on something you can shine at "where would I start?"

"Who are some artists that you enjoy and their songs?" as she was deep in thought I tell you what, next weekend come back here and we'll put something down and go from there. Your choice," I said staring at her chocolate face. "Okay, I can do that. What time next weekend?" she asked. "Call or text me what time is okay for you."

"Alright, I'll let you know when my schedule is open," she said with phone in hand. "I'll leave you to your time. Early morning for me tomorrow. Thanks again for your availability," she stated as she put her jacket on and came to shake my hand.

When our hands touched, I couldn't deny the surge I felt from our skin connecting. "Take care, and I look forward to hearing from you soon."

****

Ra'Chelle

"Hey. Yeah I'm at the studio now...yeah she made it. Hopefully it'll work out like I want it to. Don't worry, I know her very well. If I have to drag her ass down, I'll do what I have to just to get it going the way I want. The way WE want," I said on the phone. "No, no, not now. I'll let you know when the time is. You gotta let it build." I looked in the tinted window and saw Symone and Cornell shaking hands. "And from the looks of it, it's building pretty quickly," I smiled turning away from the door.

As I continued my conversation, the studio door swung open and out popped Symone. "Hold on," I whispered in the receiver.

"Hey you leaving?" I asked.

"Um yes ma'am. I have an early morning tomorrow. You'd better be there yourself missy."

"Have you eaten yet?"

"No, I was gonna just grab something on the way home"

"Oh no ma'am. We have to celebrate. Let me grab my things and wrap up here and I'll come pick you up from your house since you're closer than mine," I said.

"Okay, I guess I can do that. Call me when you're on your way," she said stepping into the elevator.

"Hey, I'm back," I said after the doors closed. "Babe don't worry, I have it under control. I'll text you later. Get some rest cause when I see you, you'll wish you had! Love you," I said before ending the convo.

"So boss-man, how'd it go?" I said with a smile on my face walking back into the studio.

"You know how it went! That' girls voice is golden! Ra'Chelle whatever she does musically, I WANT IN!" Cornell stated with a serious look. "Really," I stated while placing my hands on my hip "I'm serious Ra'Chelle. I don't know how long you've been sitting on her voice, but I'm dead serious. If she excels musically, I want to be a part of the team. Not for money or notoriety, but because I believe in her talent. Even if she doesn't work with me in the future"

"Well ok Mr. Wallace! You really believe in her that nus?"

"Ra'Chelle, I've been doing this for quite a while and trust me when I say I have never heard someone sing with such passion and conviction like her. Half of the artists that come on with the label make me just want to throw up my hands and give up. But Symone? That's a breath of fresh air right there!" he boasted. He seemed to light up when he talked about Symone. Seems like this was going to be easier than I thought it would be. "I'm glad to see you back to that guy that was so passionate about music. I missed him," I said with a pouty face. "So what did you two talk about while I was out anyway?" I asked "just dropped some ideas for her to think of some artists she likes to sing to and their songs and we can try them out," he said wrapping up and shutting down the system. "So she needs what, instrumentals then?" I asked grabbing my purse and workbook heading towards the elevator. "Right. Nothing major just a few to start with and we can go from there. We can pick whichever one she's more comfortable with, lay it and just loosen her up behind the mic," he said as we exited the building and got into our cars "I'm headed to pick her up from her house and go out to dinner, so we'll brainstorm while we dine," I said before putting my car in gear. "Keep me updated," he said.

"Will do. TOOTLES!" I waved as I burned off towards Symone's' home"

****

Symone

Driving home, I couldn't help but slightly blush at

my moment at the studio. Once I arrived home, I went upstairs and looked myself over in the mirror "It's just dinner with Chelle, but I'm feeling pretty good," I said looking in the mirror. Feeling pretty comfortable, I removed the band that held my hair in place and unraveled it from its tight bun. I ran my fingers through it as I waved up and fell past my shoulders coming to my waist. I looked at my watch "she should be here," I stated as I walked downstairs with hair flowing in the wind. I head to the kitchen, pour a small glass of Moscato, and turn on the television. Before I could get too comfortable, my house phone rings "hey, you ready?" Chelle yells over Tank serenading to *Sex Love & Pain* in the background. "What? Turn down the radio!" I yelled while rinsing out my glass and placing it into the sink. "I said are you ready?" she repeated. "I'm coming down the street now."

"Okay, let me lock up and I'll be out," I said before disconnecting. I grabbed my purse and cell and walked outside to see Chelle's 2012 candy apple red Audi circling up into my driveway. "Oh, somebody's feeling herself tonight I see," she said fluffing my hair.

"Whatever," I laughed. She pulled off and headed down the street. "Sooooo…"

"Soooo what?" I asked. "how did you feel about the session?" asking before Tank re-committed to moistening women's panties all up and down my street. "Surprisingly, I do. You know what, thank you for that"

"WHAT?"

"You know what. If you didn't push me like you do, I would've never even touched a mic."

"You know, I remember Mama Johnson and her

voice. You sound too much like her to not do anything with it. You know she would have a fit!"

"Yeah, I know. I miss her so much though. I know she's only been gone for a year, but that woman meant so much to me"

"Yeah, me too. I loved her like a second mother. Enough of the mushy shit! You not finna have me crying again!" she said while we pulled up to the Olive Garden. As the waitress showed us to our seats, we ordered the house wine and placed our orders. As we wait for our orders, I talked with Cornell after you left"

"Okay, and..."

"And he said to me *If she does anything musically, I want in on it!*"

"What does he mean by that?"

"He wants to ride with you trick! I mean he's willing and wanting to work with you even if you don't stay with him."

Almost choking on my wine I asked, "he what? So let me get this straight, he wants to work with me on projects even if I work with someone else. Like if I'm *DISCOVERED?*" while using air quotations.

"I told you a long time ago heffa your voice is golden and Cornell knows his stuff. So if anyone is to take you to the top, he's the man." she smiled while our dinner arrived. I was really excited and shocked. I'd have to really think about it and make my decision from there.

"Now that THAT'S taken care of, what time am I picking you up for church in the morning?"

Chelle's eyes got wide while she was shoving a fork of Alfredo pasta in her mouth. "What?"

"Don't talk with your mouth full and don't give me that look. You got over on me twice, well shoot, three times so yeah you are GOING TO CHURCH TRICK!"

"You know what, fair enough. But the minute your mama starts in on me, I'm out! I don't care if I have to WALK HOME!"

"Girl whatever, just be ready when I get there and you better not act like you aren't at home either!"

"Who me? Never!" I gave her a side eyed stare. I knew her all too well. After dinner, laughs, and drinks we departed from the restaurant. As we neared my house, I saw the same weird car parked on the curb "Hey, what's going on with you? You got quiet all of a sudden. What's eating you woman?" Something about that car just had me weirded out. "Huh…"

"What's wrong? You went from being all talkative to straight silence."

"Nothing, something just caught my eye." I diverted as I took a glance in the side mirror at the sitting car. We pulled up in my circular driveway "so 7 am, be ready"

"7 am, what the hell? Bitch I'm barely rolling over at 7!"

"Well you better roll into some church clothes!" I said before I closed the door. I waved Chelle off after opening my door. As she drove off, I caught view of the car once more before she passed. I got a weird and eerie feeling in the pit of my stomach immediately. "No more wine for a while," I mumbled grasping my mid-section while locking the door. I went and poured a cup of water and headed upstairs. I pulled out my clothes to wear for church the next morning when my phone rings "Hello?"

"Hey baby."

Rolling my eyes I said, "Hello mother."

"I was calling to see if you made it home in time and were in bed. You know your father and I look forward to seeing you in the morning." taking a deep breath and sighing "yes mama. I know and I'm fine. I'm safe. Going to bed," I retorted with all short answers.

"Did you set your alarm? You know how you sleep."

"Yes mother"

"You pull out your church clothes?"

Okay now she was getting on my nerves. "Good night mother."

"Okay okay, I'll see you in the morning. Love you," she tried to pull back.

"Love you too," I said before hanging up.

As I stood in the center of my walk in closet, I assessed the purple blouse and knee length skirt. "This would go good with my purple black and silver wedges," I thought aloud. Satisfied with my wardrobe selection, I placed the water on the center console, removed my clothes, and placed them in the baskets to be washed. After placing my shoes in their color-coordinated spaces, I grabbed my water and headed towards the bathroom. Now feeling lightheaded, I stand before my vanity in a light daze. "How many drinks did I have?" I stood there in my brown matching lace panty and bra set, and I start to finger comb my wavy hair. After taking down the band, I let the other half fall and began to play around with it to see what style I wanted for church the next morning. "I think you look gorgeous with your hair up," a voice barreled from my doorway scaring the piss out of me. Scared shitless, I spun around to see Michael standing posted in my bathroom walkway. *How did he get in my house? How long has he been standing there?* Ran through my head. Instinctively, I grabbed my robe from the stool and quickly wrapped it around my now shaking body. "Michael, what are you doing here?"

"You know what, when you wear your hair down it brings out your eyes," he stated uncrossing his arms and slowly walking towards me

"Michael, what are you doing here," I asked again.

"The waves of your long black hair cascading down your chocolate skin with those little sultry hazel eyes," he continued as he inched closer and closer

"Michael, what are you doing here," I persisted with a trembling tone.

Once he reached me, I felt backed into a corner and had no idea what was going to happen. Fighting tears, "Michael..."

"Shhhhhhhh," he stopped me. "You're shaking. Do I scare you Symone?" he asked and the closer he got to me I could see the lust in his eyes.

"MMMMMMichael, what...are...you...doing...." before I could finish, I ran to the sinks vanity and vomited all of tonight's contents. I felt a set of masculine hands pulling my hair away from my face while sweat formed beads while I felt like the hurling would never end. After what seemed like forever, I felt myself fall limp and became one with the coolness of my marble floor. I began coming in and out of consciousness "Symone." Michael said laying opposite of my staring gaze looking into my

Sinful Secrets   M'Hogany

glossed over eyes. "Michael." my eyes whispered with paralyzed lips. Michael was then gone and I couldn't move. **Blink** The room was dim as I came to realize I was fading in and out. **Blink Blink** suddenly Michael appeared once a gain and I felt myself being rolled onto my stomach still lying on the cool floor now slightly heated from my pressed body. Michael positions himself to where he's now facing me. He smiles and strokes my hair moving it away from my face and moves in to kiss me on my cheek. I wanted to snatch away from his touch, but I was immovable. All I could do was blink, and THAT was even becoming difficult. **Blink Blink** looking and fading in and out Michael laid looking in my eyes. Suddenly he broke his gaze of lust from my gaze of fear, looked up, nodded, and returned to my eyes. My legs then parted, the towel got pushed up, and my once favorite lace panty and bra set were moved to the side and there was now something being inserted. *Is this really happening to me? Am I really here? This must be a dream that's no longer worth dreaming! Wake up Symone! Please wake up!* I thought to myself. *Please PLEASE wake-up!* Still gazing at me and stroking my hair, Michael stared and didn't say nor do a damn thing. I couldn't move, couldn't even create a frown. While this stranger invaded my most sacred lady parts with his nearly there invisible excuse of a penis. A tear fell from my eye and crossed my face. Michael reached over and wiped it away. "Is he serious?" I thought. So much was going through my mind. This just couldn't be happening, not to me! It seemed that as soon as the mystery man started, he suddenly stopped. **Blink Blink** And I faded in out. What seemed like forever to blink, my eyes straightened to open.

Michael then was suddenly gone. I still didn't move. My legs were still spread apart, but there was something latched onto me. Without warning, the penetration started, but this time the strokes were slower, deeper, and the thickness of whoever's penis and presence was felt and apparent. Still paralyzed, whatever was latched on to me appeared "JUSTIN." my eyes screamed. What the hell! Did he just...Was this...I WAS SETUP! That HAD to be the explanation of how this man was in here sucking on my tits and raping me. RAPE. OMG. This can't be happening. Another tear fell and then another and they just kept coming. "Aye man, why this bitch crying." was the last thing I remembered hearing before everything faded to black.

Chapter 29
Cornell
Lasting Impression

"Babe...Baby...CORNELL!" Sherrone yelped snapping me out of my daze. "Yes baby"

"Did you hear what I said?" she asked.

"No mama, I'm sorry. What did you say again?" I honestly asked getting undressed. "I stopped by Racquel's place and I swore she was having an affair with this guy"

"Sherrone! Didn't I tell you to stay out of it? Damn! We don't need this extra." I said placing my shoes on the shelves. "I'm not gonna leave my girl out like that and you know it," she snapped while pinning up her hair before placing the scarf around her head. Shaking my head as I placed my shirt in the hamper and approached the bed to remove what seemed like a million pillows from it. "Anyway, I was so sure she was having an affair when I walked in and see some white guy sitting on her couch. I lost it. She had this man in the house with the children not too far away," my wife continued. "Sherrone, I told you to not get involved. We have our own house to tend to. Besides Racquel is a grown woman who can have whomever she chooses over at their house." I said still removing the pillows off of the bed. "How many of these things are even on here? I just want to go to bed!" Finally, I got all 60 million pillows off and proceeded to climb in our bed. "Cornell!"

"What?"

"I know you are not getting in this bed ignoring the well-being of those children!" I rolled over to the awaiting face of light evil that started to warm my wife's face. "Baby, look, I'm tired and that's between Racquel and James. Not us"

"Speaking of James, do you know he filed for divorce?"

"Sherrone!"

"For real, you need to talk to him. He's about to leave his devoted wife and two children for some broad in a skirt"

"So you've really gonna talk about this"

"You damn right I am, better yet we ARE!"

"WE aren't gonna do a damn thing but let ME get some sleep! I have a long day ahead of me and I need a good mind to do it. So goodnight!" And I rolled over. I should've known that was going to ignite an argument I had no energy for. "Cornell Damon Wallace!" Dammit not the middle name. "Sherrone look." I tried to roll and say "No! Here our friends are going through hell and high water and you're not in the least bit concerned. Hell for them or the children. OUR GOD-CHILDREN!" *I just want to sleep GOD!* I screamed in my head. ." I am not saying I don't care about them but that's their business. Yes, those are our Godchildren, but those are THEIR children. They aren't dead! Leave it alone and go to sleep!" I rolled back over and tried to ignore the continuous banter until I passed out. When I wake up the next day, Sherrone was still sleep. *Meet me at the gym in 20 minutes* I texted. "Where are you going?" the sleepy whisper called from the bed as I placed on my shoes. "I'm going to the gym, go back to sleep." I said walking around the bed. "How long will you be out?" she continued with closed eyes. "I'll call when I leave, not sure how long I'll be, but get some sleep." I said kissing her forehead before I headed out of the bedroom. Once I reached the front door, with gym bag on, when my buzzes, *On My Way.* I hop in my car headed towards my destination.

****

Symone

Coming to, I find myself in my bed with my pajama pants on with matching wife beater. I reached upward to grab my head due to the blinding light from the sun creating a light headache. "That couldn't have happened. I just know that couldn't have happened." I mumbled repetitively. Bits of flashes ran across my mind. Images of Justin vaguely appeared. Then Michael. Then Justin. Michael. Justin. Michael...just the thought of this dream made me feel dirty. I couldn't rush to the shower fast enough. While in the shower, flashes of that brief nightmare still lingered around. "That felt too real." I mumbled before I was startled with the **Ring Ring** from the house phone system startling me out of my thoughts. Stepping out of the shower, I use my remote to answer the phone connected to the sound system. "Hello?"

"Girl, you okay?"

"Ra'Chelle?"

"Bit...I mean who else would it be? You didn't notice me calling you? How much did you drink last night?"

"What are you talking about? Wait, what time is it?"

I asked as I scrambled to get to a clock. 9:45. "9:45!" I yelled. I rushed to get dressed. Thank GOD, I pulled out my clothes the previous night. I was worried because you were supposed to pick me up at seven. You're never late and not to mention your mom has been blowing up my phone! You know good and da... you know good and well I don't do early morning wake-ups! She lucky it's Sunday cause I was finna cuss yo' mama out royally!"

"Oh no. okay let me get dressed and I'll come get you." I stated nearly out of breath from rushing to be at church before 11:00. "I'm already downstairs outside. I been here since 7:30! You lucky I didn't call the cops or beat this damn door down!"

"Okay let me catch my breath then."

"You gonna unlock the damn door?" I hung up after remotely unlocking the door. After placing my remote back down on the nightstand, I plopped down on my queen constellation bed and rubbed my face to collect my thoughts. "What happened to me." bursting into the doors "what's going on heffa?" looking at the distressed look I tried to conceal, Chelle quickly sat beside me "what's wrong? What happened? You okay?" she asked.

"Yeah, yeah, I'm fine. Just tired I guess. Stress of the job. Let's go before my mother calls either you or me!"

"No ma'am. We are going to make sure you're okay." getting up, putting my hair up in a wavy ponytail with strands left out, and lip-gloss, I grabbed my glasses, clutch and keys "I'm fine, let's go." I said following a convincing yawn. I walked past Chelle as I yawned because this girl could tell more than anyone could when I was lying.

****

Cornell

"Aye C, what's up?"

"Look bro, I know you got a lot on your plate, and I really really feel you, but you gotta get shit under control"

"C, whoa, what are you talkin' about? What's going on?" We stood outside of the gym for the next 10 to 15 minutes or so talking about the conversation our spouses had. "This has gotta get resolved man." I said "wait it was who in my house?"

"Look we both have things on our plate already. You my boy and all, so I'm gonna keep it straight with you. Handle up on that!"

"C, I understand man. See I didn't know all of that though. Trust I'll get that taken care of"

"Alright man, cool. Now let's get this workout on. NO mercy!

****

Symone

"May the lord watch between me and thee. While we're absent. One from another. Shake someone's hand and tell 'em I love you." as the church dismissed and mingled with each other, my mother approaches me. "Symone, are you okay?"

"Yes mama I'm fine. Why wouldn't I be?"

"Something doesn't feel right."

"Are you okay?"

"It's not me that feels odd, it's something about you. I just feel it in my spirit." She couldn't have been talking about my dream. "I'm fine mama as you can see"

"Symone, beautiful voice sweetie. Just beautiful."

one of the members said hugging me interrupting my conversation. "First lady you and pastor must be so proud of her."

"Yes we are." my mother smiled. I see Michael over the congregation with his mother. My heart dropped into the pit of my stomach. "Michael darling, how are you?" my mother almost plowed down the church member just to get to him. I swear you'd think she knew how he laid the pipe. "Ugh." I shrugged at the thought of my mother getting it in. "Let me find out my mama a freak." I mumbled to myself. "Hello first lady. How are you?" he smiled and hugged my mother "oh I'm so much better now that I see that face of yours." she beamed as she grabs his face like he were an infant. "Symone, look it's Michael." she smiled so hard MY damn face hurt. "I can see mother. Very well." I sarcastically stated. "Hi Symone. How are you today?" as soon as he spoke to me, that eerie feeling returned. This time I became nauseous. "Can you all excuse me please?" I stated briskly making my way down the aisle heading towards the nearest exit. As I walked, I tried to contain myself and quickly get out of the admiring accolades and repetitive *God Bless You's* being passed out from numerous members amongst the congregation. Once I made it outside, I went to the nearby shade tree to block the sun that beamed down on my chocolate skin. "Get it together Symone. You're okay. Just a bad dream that's all. Just relax!" I kept telling myself. "Symone, are you okay?" I was startled by the male voice that crept behind me. Wiping my face from the tears that secretly escaped my lightly puffy eyes, I feared my father followed me outside inquiring what happened to his baby-girl.

"Michael?" I surprisingly yelled.

"Are you okay?" he asked.

"What are you doing out here?" I asked trying to regain my composure.

"I noticed that you looked bothered and unwell. I insisted on making sure you were okay to keep your parents from worrying. Your father took more convincing than your mother who pretty much pushed me to come out here."

Chuckling I said, "I wouldn't put it past her. Well thank you Michael for your concern. I just had a bad night I'm sure and my sleep probably has just been off. I'm sure it's nothing. Again, I thank you." I said touching him on his arm and side stepping him. I still couldn't shake this nauseating feeling, but either the fresh air or Michael's concern helped it start to subside. As I started to walk back towards the church "Symone, actually, can I talk to you for a moment?"

"Um, sure Michael." I said turning around mid-step. "What's going on?" he looked uncomfortable wringing his hands together and rubbing his freshly cut hair as I waited to hear what he had to say, I took in how well he cleaned up. Nice gray 2-piece suit with matching tie and Stacy Adams shoes. I couldn't quite hear what he was saying due to him either mumbling, rambling, or the wind whipping through, so I stepped closer. As the wind was making his cologne molest my nostrils, I felt the opening of my lady cavity trickle in excitement. Until I realized what he said "I'm sorry Michael...what did you say?"

"Symone I said I want to apologize for yesterday." slightly confused "yesterday?" what could he mean by yesterday? Being late? The kiss? Invading my personal space with his tongue? Honestly, there wasn't anything to apologize for. In my opinion, I should be the one apologizing to him for being blatantly rude and not giving him a chance. Hell aside from Calgon, that's the most excitement I've received in GOD knows how long! "Last night." he stated again with shifty eyes while placing his hands in his pockets. "Oh no, the kiss Michael? Don't worry about it. Desperate times called for desperate measures"

"Not that Symone"

"Um, you being late? Don't sweat that. I understand your position and working late is called for at times. Believe me I know I mean I sometimes forget to call Chelle..." I started to ramble.

"No! Later! The...you know..."

"The what Michael?"

"Look Symone, I know it was wrong and honestly I don't know why I went along with it. The look on your face just broke me as a man. And that will forever be on my conscience." he started again... truthfully; I was still lost as to what he was talking about. Was he really feeling bad about making me wait or was it the kiss? Those were the only things that happened that night. "Michael, I told you it's okay. To be honest, I rather enjoyed it. I haven't been out in a while and surprisingly I actually enjoyed your company." I smiled. With a perplexed look on his face, "Symone, I don't think we're talking about the same thing." he took his hands out of his pockets. Placed my hands in his and moved in closer. "Symone I am apologizing for last night. For, Justin. For startling you in your home. For my..." **SLAP** I tried my DAMNDEST to knock this niggas teeth down his throat so he could bit his own ass! With tears in my eyes that confusingly held frustration and the highest level of pistivity, I realized that what was haunting me as a bad dream was indeed my horrid reality. "Symone, I deserve that but let me..."

"Let you what? What are you goin' to say Michael? Huh? I'm sorry for setting you up? I'm sorry for breaking into your house? I'm sorry for invading your privacy? Or how about my favorite one I'm sorry Symone for raping you? Is that what you're sorry about? Huh? Is it?" I fumed through gritted teeth. By this time, members were still filing outside of the church. "Symone I'm sorry I really am "do you really go round doing this to women?"

"No...well...no...I felt bad when I saw your eyes. I never expected..." **SLAP** Once more, I gave him the hardest slap I could conjure up. "You don't get to feel ANYTHING!" I tried so hard this time to slap his ass unconscious. Once I turned to walk away from him, I noticed I had an audience of holy rollers nosily staring in their best dressed. As I made my way back to the church to gather my belongings and leave, I ran into my father. "Symone, baby-girl, what's wrong? Are you alright?" he said with a concerned look. "I'm fine Daddy. I just need to go"

"Hey hey, what's wrong with Daddy's girl? Clearly you're upset." he insisted wiping the tear remnants from my eyes. "Daddy, I'm fine." and before I could continue convincing my dad that I was good Michael appeared..." Pastor my apologies if I upset ...." The look my father gave him then had me worried. I was worried for my father, his congregation, my mother, my family, and somewhere so far down the line, worried for Michael. "Young man, what did I tell you before? Did I not tell you that if you so much hurt my daughter in any way possible..."

"Symon." my mother softly spoke as not to alarm the congregation that was still dispersing. "Symon, not here. This is not you. Let it go." my mother gives me the eye of disapproval and continues "whatever the issue is , not here," she continued while placing her hand on my father's chest. "Come on, we've gotta get you out of this wet robe and into some dry clothes. You know you shouldn't be out here in this air after preaching..." she lightly scolded as he turned and walked with her towards his study, but not before giving Michael the staring eye of death. "Symone"

"Michael." I said turning so no one could hear my statement "if you value life in any way, I'd heavily suggest you put distance between you and I." I said before quickly walking back to retrieve my things. "Hey chic!" Chelle intercepted. "Oh, hey. Let me get my purse and keys and we can go."

"What's wrong?" she asked stopping me like damn near everyone else, "nothing, I'll be back"

"Symone, what the ……" Ra'Chelle isn't a holy visitor therefore, I knew that in seconds, she would let that lethal tongue of hers flow with not so sacred words and she wouldn't care. She'd dare one of the members to correct her too! Keeping her from possibly starting another ruckus, I pulled her to the side "You better come wit it too cause you know I would turn this place out!" she spat with hands on her hip. I didn't know how to it. I just couldn't form the words. I didn't want to be a victim. I wasn't a victim. But

for some reason, the words just wouldn't form. How was I going to say this to my best friend? "Symone?"
"Huh?"
"Heffa you better start talkin'. What is going on?"
"Michael..."
With raised eyebrows she asked, "Michael what?"
"We went out and had a good time and talked..."
"Symone, skip the middle man. Condensed version boo," she said snapping.
I blanked out.
Snapping again "SYMONE!"
"Let's go. I can't talk about it here"
"Well here I got your purse and things so." Chelle handed me my things and we turned in the direction of where I parked my car. Next thing I knew, Chelle was no longer walking with me. When I looked around to see where she was, she was heading in Michael's direction. "Hey!" she yelled across the parking lot. "Oh no!" I mumbled aloud. I reached my car in time and ran in my four inch wedges across the parking lot to grab her and trying not to fall at the same time. Before I could reach her, **SLAP** she struck him just as hard as I did. "No no no no no Chelle no no no no!" I said grabbing her hand before she readjusted the other side of his face. "Now we can go!" she said as she turned around and flipped her hair slowly strutting back towards my car. "And if you want it again, feel free to come see me!" she boasted without interrupting her stride. I didn't feel bad for him at that time. Hell at any time. He deserved all the slaps possible. No it wouldn't change anything, but he deserved them. "What was that all about? What did he say? What did you say?" I asked as I

pulled off out of the church's lot. "I didn't know what he said or if he said anything. I just know that if he did something to you it was gonna be hell to pay and I made sure he was well aware of that. He sounded like his ass was whining which is probably why I slapped his ass. Hell I don't know"

"So you just slapped the man?" Don't get me wrong, I'm glad she did. But I know his face has to be humming. "Don't nobody wanna hear no grown ass man whining and shit!" I shook my head as we exited Skillman and turned into Michelle's for some southern cooking. "Not going to Mama Yvette's again huh?" Chelle stated closing my door and walking in "after what just happened, oh no ma'am. My mama is team Michael all day and wouldn't believe he actually did what he did." I blindly spat. I completely forgot about what had happened and almost blurted out to Chelle and the people in front and back of us. "What did he do again?" *May I help you?* "Yes, Salisbury steak, mashed potatoes, green beans..." *Cornbread or roll ma'am?* "Roll please." *And drink?* "Water and a bowl of lemons please." I eagerly leapt at the chance to dodge answering Chelle's question. The waiter took her order and we found a corner seat for two by the window. "So"

"So what?" I said knowing good and well she meant. "What did Michael do? Heffa don't make me ask you no mo." I held up one finger pausing her mid question, bowed my head, and said grace. She was ok with that because she knew I was going to bless my food and if she in the least bit interrupted, would be some problems. "Amen"

"Damn girl, did you and Jesus catch up over lost

time or something?" ignoring her I quickly cut a piece of my tender Salisbury steak and scooped up a spoonful of my mashed potatoes. "Omg, this is so good." I mumbled diverting the inevitable conversation. "Symone"

"Hmmmm." I mumbled trying not to talk with food in my mouth. "What, you not hungry? Now THAT will be the day! You know you can't rid yourself of NOBODY'S food." I joked trying to get her mind off of the subject. If anything could, I know it would be food. And the way Michelle's cooked; I brought her to the perfect place. They had that *shut up and savor the flavor* type of cooking. She picked up her fork, took a scoop of her candied yams, placed it in her mouth, put her fork back down, crossed her arms, and stares me down. "What? You don't like it? Is it nasty? Is there a hair in it? Bug? What?" I said taking another bite of my steak. "Don't sit over there and act brand new with me Symone. Start talking. What did Michael do and you better start before I turn this mutha out!"

"Alright, alright. Calm down." I said nervously putting my fork down and taking a sip of water. "The other night, Michael and I went out to get to know each other fairly."

"Fairly?" she asked.

"You know his mom and mine are like bosom buddies and are determined to make a love connection. On two too many occasions my mother has snuck Michael and I together. I was rude I must admit and honestly wasn't giving him a chance. I was surprised when I needed a contractor for my office and he came."

"He's your contractor too? Damn, Mama Yvette is serious about this thing ain't she?"

I didn't plan for that to happen and I thought that too about my mother, but yes. Anyway, he sent the fruit arrangement to my home office."

"Oh THAT one?"

"Yeah, the one you scarfed down? Yes"

"Oh uh uh hunny, he knows your location way too much for me boo"

I decided to go to dinner with him to at least give him a fair chance."

"Was that when y'all were at Sankofa? See you too nice boo"

"Yes it was the same day you set me up AGAIN!"

"Girl boo, anyway"

"Don't forget you got a beat down coming for that too"

"Chile please, next! I'm still trying to figure out what he did wrong?"

"Well while I was waiting on him to get there that night, there was this guy who started talking to me."

"I swear Symone; you are such a damn prude!"

"How am I a prude?"

"A man talking to you shows interest trick."

"Not when his ass is married! You need to be interested in your wife!"

"Last I checked, there's nothing wrong with talking to a woman or anyone that's not your spouse"

"Well, I do when you're hitting on me. Anyway, I kept telling him that I was waiting on someone and he got all in my space saying *You and I both know you're not waiting on anyone* like he was gonna get something and I should just give in and go with it."

"Oh uh uh, he bold."

"Apparently the look of distress was clearly visible on my face because Michael came in and acted like an apologetic boyfriend. He also insinuated that we were celebrating something special. The guy..." snapping my fingers to trigger his name. "oh Justin, backed off."

"Ok I'm still lost. Were you mad cause he was acting like yo' boo?"

"No. well, you remember when we went to the olive garden?"

"Yeah why?"

"Well, I was feeling odd on the way back home. Just eerie"

"Is that why you shut down on me?"

"When I got in the house I started feeling weird. I thought it was the wine so I turned in. like clockwork, mama called making sure I didn't forget about church in the morning."

"girl yo' mama don't play about that church thing chile," she said while eating her smothered pork chops I pulled out my clothes for church, but started feeling dizzy and lightheaded. I didn't know what it was, so I just took it as it being a long day. I got ready for a bath and while I was in my underwear waiting for the tub to fill, I was playing in my hair for potential hairstyles."

"I swear Symone you should write a damn book!"

"Why you say that?"

"Cause you're the most damn detailed person I have ever met! You make a bitch wait for the ending! Even though I'm tired of reading, I wanna see what happens!"

"Shut it! Anyway! While I was doing my hair, I

heard *You look beautiful with your hair pulled up.*"

"You hearing voices now? I told you at some point listening to all these people's issues is gonna make you go crazy"

"I turned around and there was Michael standing in my doorway"

"In your house?"

"Yes!"

"Did you call him after I left? I know that monkey was in need, but damn. Calgon runnin' low on battery life huh? Oooooow! Get it!"

"No ma'am. I didn't even talk to Michael that day, I don't think"

"So wait, how'd he get in your house?"

I don't know! I freaked out as he started walking closer to me. I quickly remembered I was barely wearing anything and started reaching for my towel."

"What did he do after that?"

"He walked towards me and I was nervous as all get out"

I would imagine"

." he looked kinda out of it with somewhat bloodshot eyes like he'd been either crying or drinking"

"Chile that negro ain't been no damn crying"

"Well there you have it I guess"

"Go on"

"It kinda gets fuzzy there"

"Fuzzy? What the hell you mean by *fuzzy*?"

"Fuzzy! Like unclear!"

"Trick I know WHAT it means, I'm just saying"

I started feeling more dizzy and light headed and

before I knew it, I blacked out." upon hearing me say I blacked out, Ra'Chelle sat up abruptly in her seat "BLACKED OUT?" she yelled.

"Shhhh, lower your voice girl!"

"You better start talkin' then. You know I don't play that shit!"

"When I came to, I was on the floor"

"The floor, what the fffff...Okay backup. What? Where was Michael?"

My mouth got dry and I took a sip of my water.

"Symone, where was Michael?"

I took a deep breath before I spoke. "I vaguely remember…"

"What DO you remember?"

I remember feeling the coolness of my bathroom tiles on my chest and face. I remember seeing Michael's face appear out of nowhere."

"While you were on the floor?"

"Yes"

"He didn't help you up off of the floor or at least try?"

"No. actually he laid there with me and started rubbing my hair"

"You layin on the bathroom floor and he layin there playin in your hair?"

"Exactly."

"What the hell is in this nigga's head? And you just laid there!"

I couldn't move"

"What the hell you mean you couldn't move?"

I was numb from the neck down and couldn't move.

I could still feel, but just couldn't move. All while he was rubbing my hair and staring me in the face I couldn't move. Then my...my...."

"Your what?"

"My legs got spread apart and something or someone replaced themselves where my underwear was. With wide eyes full of tears, Michael still didn't move. He just laid there staring. Just laid there. Then no sooner did it start, it was over. Well, I thought it was before Michael disappeared." I spoke lowly while looking out of the window trying to figure out what has come of my life up to this moment. Shaking her head "disappeared"

I thought he felt bad cause while he saw my tears he wiped them from my face until he got up and then someone else took his place."

"What? Place? Who? Did you see his face? Do you know him? Was it a him?"

"Ra'Chelle…"

"Seriously, did you though?" As she awaited my answer, my demeanor shifted and I grew silent and directed my focus back out the window. "Symone," she said with a concerned whisper "What happened."

Letting out a deep sigh, I continued. "My legs did a repeat. Spread once more and I was still unable to move. I felt the feeling of a presence different from the last. This time, I could actually FEEL it. Then I zoned in on the fact that I was being nibbled on. I knew damn well I didn't have no ants or bugs cause I kept a clean house"

"Don't I know."

"when my eyes traveled down to what was gnawing at me, I couldn't believe my eyes, but the same guy that was trying to spit game at Sankofa was latched on to me like a nursing infant"

"What the FUCK!"

"Ra'Chelle!" I reprimanded. We were still in the restaurant but I knew the continuation of this conversation wasn't gonna be able to be had in this establishment. "You know what, we're done. C'mon let's go cause I see my outbursts are about to get further out of control..." she said while grabbing her purse.

****

Cornell

"Cornell?

"Yeah baby"

"What are you doing?"

"I'm in the studio"

"Can you come up here please?"

"Alright I'm on my way." I headed upstairs. She caught me in mid production of a few demos to show Symone. As I headed upstairs, I walked in to see James sitting on the couch. "What's good Jay baby. I didn't know you were comin' over"

"Neither did I, but I got a call saying you needed me to come by." Immediately I stared at Sherrone in the kitchen saying "did I now and did I say what reason I needed for you to come by?"

"Just that we needed to talk"

"Really." I said with my eyes fixated on Sherrone. Before I could continue, the doorbell rang. "I'll get it. You boys excuse me," she said quickly exiting the kitchen to the door. I walked over to James "C, what's up?"

"Look man, I told you Sherrone and Raquel are

very close and you gotta nip that shit in the butt. Sherrone knows about you filing for divorce and is determined to work shit out between you two." I tried to quietly reason before Sherrone returned. "C, you know it's not that simple"

"I know it, but Sherrone don't know that I know." as we talked lowly "alright fellas we ready to get started?" we look up and instantly Jay jumps up "What the fuck is going on?"

I know you didn't call me over for this bullshit C!"

"James wait." my wife tried to say. I just shook my head and tried to calm my boy down. "Jay, chill man. Hear what she has to say"

"If her ass ain't apologizing for damaging my shit, my ears ain't receiving a got damn thing her mouth is serving!" he said, "I ain't apologizing for a muthafuckin thing! Tell yo' BITCH to apologize for ruining my family!" Racquel spat back. I don't know what Sherrone was trying to get accomplished but this is the shit I was afraid of. "C, look man...." he said while pulling me aside "look, I know Sherrone and you mean well, but this shit is so far left..."

"Jay, I'ma stop you right there. I didn't have anything to do with this. This is what I was talking about though. Nip this shit man here and now before it gets worst. This right here, I'll deal with her once you guys are gone"

****

"What the fuck does he have to talk about? Why the hell I gotta apologize? It's his hoe that's breaking up this happy marriage." Racquel spat. "Racqui, calm down. First off, what did you do where he feels like you owe him an apology?"

"I didn't do nothing his bitch ass didn't deserve."
She yelled "Racqui, what...did...you...do?"
"She tagged the fuck outta my damn pearly white car! IN RED PAINT! That's what the crazy bitch did!"
"C'mon Jay, that's the mother of your children." I said "Next I'ma yo' hoe and you can bet that!"
"Whoa, you sprayed his car? What has gotten into you?" my wife tried to intervene. I told you Sherrone I am NOT down with no bitch stealing my husband!"
"Nobody stole me! I FUCKIN LEFT." he yelled. I just about had it with all of this childishness in my house. My wife and I already have a serious conversation to have, but this right here has got to come to an end. "Okay, everybody calm down." I said. "All of this yelling and cursing isn't getting us anywhere?"
"Cornell is right. I ain't apologizing for anything cause I did what any loyal and faithful wife would do!"
"C man, I gotta get outta here cause I'm seconds from shakin the shit outta her and hoping for the worst!"
"Jay, don't be like that." I tried to say as he headed towards the door. "Don't stop him Cornell. Let him run like a little bitch. He's probably gonna run to his little slut. They can be bitches together for all I care. They gonna end up missing bitches fuckin with me." with that remark James, who was at the door at this time, frowned, turned and said "what did you just say? You threatening me?"
"Jay you know what, you're upset. Let's just go outside and cool off. Don't do anything you'll regret!"
"Nah C." he said swatting my hand away "nah you wanted me to talk, so that's what's gonna happen." redirecting his attention towards Racquel "look, I've been

trying to be civil with you for a while. I moved out and come to see our children regularly until we worked out something. But your unruly ass seem to be so stuck on you, nothing seems to get through. So let me put it to you like this. WE'RE DONE! We BEEN DONE! I've moved on and I'm very very VERY happy! As far as your little threats...." Jay steps closer to Racquel but I stood in between him and he speaks over my shoulder "Fuck with me if you want too." and he walked out of my house.

"I told you to stay out of this Sherrone." I leaned and whispered to my wife as I walked towards the door as Jay slammed it rubbing my head.

"Did you hear this negro! We are STILL married and he just admitted he's with someone else! Why is it he didn't just say it was that bitch? You know what, you sho right..." she said clapping with every syllable.

Why do black women do that anyway? She grabbed her purse and got ready to bolt.

"Where are you going? What are you about to do?" Sherrone started to ask.

"Hunny I'm going home to my children. Don't worry about Racqui though, I never lose." she said with a wink before she left as well. **Sigh** "Well THAT went well." my wife said plopping down on the couch. "Oh no you don't. I stressed to you NOT to get involved, but you did. I told you NOT to do anything, but you did!" I started "what do you expect us to do? Let them just self-destruct?"

"It's their marriage! If it falters, that's for them to figure out! We didn't marry them. No matter the relationship, we have to support our friends. But not in our home!"

"I can't believe you would stand here and be okay with this!" she yelled. "Look, I hate it for my boy, but hey it's his decision to make. I can't change that man's mind"

"Are you serious?"

"I'm going back downstairs to the studio. I don't have time for this...." as I headed towards the studio my phone began to buzz. *Studio...Tomorrow...7.* I knew it was from Ra'Chelle but my smile was more so from the anticipation to hear Symone's voice once more. I sat at my board and ended up daydreaming of her voice bouncing off of the speakers. I could hear her voice so clear the hair on my arms stood up at attention. I got chills. I remembered that I'd recorded her voice in the studio as a rough draft and had it on my flash-drive. I uploaded it and had it on repeat. Soon as her voice began, so did the leakage in my pants. "Any woman whose voice can bring a man to cum HAS to be on my team!" But with this feeling I was feeling, she had to be my special project. I wasn't going to take NO for an answer either...

****

Symone

Ra'Chelle and I headed out of Michelle's, drove to Oak Cliff, and strolled around Glendale Park. "Um ma'am, why are we here? You know I don't do no walkin? And I ain't walkin in these Giuseppe's!" she complained.

"See this is why I always keep a spare pair of tennis in the car and flip flops."

"You know I wouldn't be caught dead in a pair of tennis!"

"Girl get over it and get out! After all we ate; we need to walk some of this off."

We started our round and continued our conversation.

"So back to you boo and this toddler on your tit…"

"Justin."

"Right Justin. Damn name sounds perverted. Now while he was latched on, Michael was dicking you down." I stopped talking and shook my head "I swear you have such a way with words Chelle"

"You do know what that's call Symone though right"

"Chelle, don't." I said as she caught up. "No, you know what it is! That's Rape Symone!" When she said it, I went numb. I knew what it was, but I didn't feel like a victim. When people speak of rape, they victimize the word and the person attached to it. I was nobody's victim. It shouldn't have happened, but there's nothing I can really do about it. "Have you gone to the police about it?"

"No no no." I quickly responded.

"And why not? Symone something needs to be done!"

"I know, I know."

"So what are you going to do?"

"Nothing"

"Nothing? NOTHING? Did we not just agree that something needs to be done?"

"Look we can't change what's happened, but GOD will have the final say"

"Here you go with this shit!"

"Watch it Chelle"

"Okay, I know you want to leave it up to the big man upstairs, but these muthafuckas gotta know it's wrong and pay. But if you don't wanna do anything about it, we won't."

"Thank you. And can you please please PLEASE not say anything to my parents? I can't afford to bail everybody out of jail"

Chapter 30
Symone

"Dr. Johnson's office, how may I direct your call." I heard Ashleigh say as I collected my messages and flashed a smile before heading to my office. Once I reached my door with latte in hand, I glanced at Symone's door. I know it's bee, what, a few weeks already, but this is just ridiculous. Unable to shake the feeling that something was just not right, I went into my office and placed my things down. As my computer loaded, I wanted to know why it was so damn quiet in Symone's office. I mean I'm glad the noise is gone, but she's not back, so there needed to be something going on in her absence. She may be a big girl, but I don't like this activity. "No, no, no. Leave it alone ray. Leave it alone." I coached myself. I pulled my files up and arranged my office for my upcoming sessions. After a whopping 10 minutes, I couldn't take it anymore. "To hell with this. Symone will just have to be pissed at me later." I go across the hall and burst into Symone's office hoping to catch someone in the middle of doing something foul. I wasn't sure how to feel walking into a clean and empty office with no trace of prior damage. "What the hell." I mumbled. The plastic that use to line the carpet was gone along with the tape that lined the carpets. The tarp that draped alongside the window was absent from the pane which was now replaced with a large thick Corsica window. I didn't know if I should be upset or relieved. I went over to her desk and looked around for anything misplaced. As I stood there baffled, I heard voices in the hall. Well, one voice really. Feeling trapped, I quickly slid under her desk. "Got dammit." I groaned at my aching knees, but kept my pain under wraps to no reveal my presence. "Yeah I'm' here. No no, it's all clean and finished. I will definitely let her know she can come back to her office." the voice I heard was familiar. It had to be that joke she hired as her contractor. "I told you if you gave me more time I would deliver didn't I..." More time? He must be talking to his boss about the work he'd done in Symone's office I had to admit that she was kinda right. He did a great job on her office, but I wasn't gonna tell her that shit though. I'm big enough to eat crow however. "Huh? Oh yeah. Most definitely. I can't say we'll do it again, but it was indeed a tight fit. I know you don't want to hear about it, but we have to be on the same page if this is going to work well. Her mother is a very determined lady I must say though. If the saying is true, then the pastor needs to keep tight tabs on his beloved wife. You know the juvenile song *She Get It From Her Mama*. Of course I did, you know I had to get me a piece of it too!"

"*Piece?* What the hell does he mean by *Piece?*" I whispered to myself. "No, I wasn't alone. My boy Justin helped me out. You know he got his in too. But that nigga dick so little she didn't notice he was there. No, she didn't say no or stop, but it kinda doesn't matter now does it?"

Is this nigga talking about smashing Symone?

"It worked well. She couldn't do anything. I thought that's what you wanted? Wait, why you getting mad though? I mean she saw my face so I couldn't just leave her on the floor! Yes, I put her in the bed but I don't think she remembers anything. Calm down. We can move on to phase II now," he said with a fading voice indicating him leaving the office and for his sake, he'd better be leaving the fucking area!

"Ain't this a BITCH!" I said punching under the table unaware that I punched a hole in it. *Dr. Watkins your first appointment is here to see you.* "I swear Ashleigh tends to have the best timing when a brotha's on a mission." I said shaking my head as I left Symone's office. Now I have to put on a great face and demeanor to keep from canceling all appointments for today, finding this nigga and his bitch Justin whatever, and winding up on channels 4, 5, 8, and 11 in Lou Sterrett for murder. I know one thing, as soon as I see either one of them bitches; I'm fuckin 'em up ON SITE!"

Yes Ashleigh, you can send them in..."
***

Knock Knock

"Who is it?" I asked as I got up from my desk heading towards my office door. Today wasn't really the day I needed to have pop ups. "If this is Michael I swear got GOD..."

"Dr. Johnson, I need some help..."

"Well, come on in James. What's going on? Sit sit..." I said surprised to see Mr. Smith here in my office.

"Doc, um are you busy?"

"Don't worry about my schedule. Sit. What's going on?" I asked.

"Well, I was at my boy's house yesterday and his wife had the most brilliant idea to get us together to 'hash out' this thing that me and Racquel are going through."

"Ok go ahead"

"Long story short, I told her to apologize for my car's damage and she justified herself, or tried to at least, by saying how she was going to do something to me and my woman."

"Now by woman does she mean Bridgette? Or is she still?"

"She still is convinced that you and I are an item."

"Have you had a talk with her?"

"Oh I did last night!" *Something tells me I'm scared to ask what was said.* "I know that look Doc."

"What look is that James?"

"You want to know what I said don't you?"

Damn was I that transparent? "Now James, you know I don't pry. If you feel like sharing that's your position to do so." I lied. I wanted to know what he said like the next person.

"Well, once she started threatening me, I didn't care what I really said to her to be honest. I just remembered telling her that if she was bold not to fuck with me," he said.

"Oh my goodness. I don't know what to say."

"Well I do. I want to say thank you."

"For what?" I asked shockingly.

"Well because you have done something that no one has been able to do in years. Before coming to your office, I didn't say much of anything. If it wasn't for Racquel suggesting we visit your office, I wouldn't feel this good about life. I'm happy with the woman I love, my children are all doing great, and I'm just in a happy place. I haven't been here in a long time."

"Well, I would say you're welcome, but there's still something that needs to be done"

"Doc you keep pushing for me to just be honest with both of them, but I don't see why I should"

"Let me break this thing down for you, on your terms, James. Do you love Bridgette?"

"Yes I do"

"Do you love her enough to marry her?"

"God knows I want to"

"Do you love your children?"

"More than I can breathe"

"And you want them to have the best life they can"

"As free as possible"

"Then you have to lead by example. Don't lead either woman along any further and you can't bring secrets into your new relationship. That's a recipe for disaster."

"Doc, I know what you're saying is true and right, but I'm scared of what Racquel would do and I fear Bridgette would leave me and I'll never see my daughter."

"Fear is only what you allow it to be."

We sat and talked further for another 3 hours and as much as I hate to see a marriage crumble, this union should've been over years ago. "Doc you indeed have opened my eyes to a lot of things possible and got me thinking. Can you do me a favor?"

"Um I don't normally do favors, but I'll hear you out. I might know someone that could help you better than myself"

"Would you be our marriage counselor, if she accepts my proposal of course?"

"My my Mr. Smith. As much as I would love to say yes, let's just wait and see what is laid on the table before we get to talking about future plans."

"I can agree to that." Looking at his watch "oh damn! I didn't know it was that late! Bridgette is going to damn near KILL ME! Doc I'll definitely be in touch," he said walking to the door. "And Symone, please look out for yourself. I loved Racquel once, but I never put anything past her. Take care"

"I appreciate that Mr. Smith...James. Take care yourself." I said in the doorway as he got into his car and started down the street.

Ring Ring

"What now?" I said before I picked up my cell phone. "Hello?"

"Hey hot mama."

"Hey Chelle, what's up?"

"Gotta call from Cornell and he wants you to come by the studio tonight around 7."

"7? That's in 45 minutes?"

"Well I guess you better get to moving then huh!"

"Ugh, let me at least change"

"No ma'am! You can't keep him waiting! This is how these execs process. Whatever you do, DO NOT KEEP HIM WAITING!"

"Ok ok, I'm locking up now and headed to the studio."

"Great, call me when you leave! Tootles!" **click** *I mean this woman is something else* I stated as I locked up my office. I then got into my car and headed towards the studio. As I headed down the street, the car was no longer sitting in front of my neighbor's house. For some that wouldn't be alarming, but to me something just didn't add up. Later. I'll deal with that later...

****

    I get out of my car at the studio building and head inside. As I approached the floor, which housed the studio, I ran into Cornell at the same time. "Symone."

"Cornell hey how are you"

"Can't complain and yourself?"

"Good good. I must say I was pretty surprised yet excited when I heard that you requested me to come to the studio." I said as he began to unlock the studio doors.

"Me? I received a text message telling me to be here at seven. I assumed you were ready to work on some music. At least that's what I got." he said.

    We entered into the studio, both of us stopped in mid stride, and I had to admit, tears began to fill my eyes. On every table, there was a medium size bouquet of white short stemmed roses and lit vanilla fragranced candles were the only light source. Standing in amazed awe, we both whispered "Ra'Chelle." I mean there were candles in every space you could think of. Even inside the booth on short tables. I hope you all have great insurance." I said trying to get my composure back to where I wanted it to be. Shaking his head and going to put his belongings down and bring up the system, Cornell checked to ensure that everything is actually safe but goes into the booth and blows out nearly half of the candles lit. "It's nice, but there's too much expensive equipment in there to keep those lit. I mean, did you want them still lit? I didn't even think to ask," he said stopping before he got completely out of the booths door.

"No no no, I'm actually in agreement with you on that one. I'm surprised that the sprinklers haven't gone off with these in here." I said before I sat down. "Well from the looks of it, they must have just been lit."

"How can you tell?"

"The wax hasn't liquefied enough to signal a timely burn." Interesting. "So." he said as the board and system was logging on "Did you and Ra'Chelle come up with some songs to cover?"

"We brainstormed over a few and I picked some that I liked"

"Okay great, what did you have in mind?" Pulling out my blackberry 8830i, I scrolled to the notes section and pulled up my saved annotations "*Almost Doesn't Count* by Brandy, *Officially Missing You* by Tamia, *I Need You Bad* by Jazmine Sullivan, *Hero* by Mariah Carey, *Never Let You Go* by Faith Evans..."

"Well I see you come well prepared Ms. Symone.," he said with a smile. "Let's stop with at Faith Evans because I have a feeling there is indeed more. Out of the ones you just mentioned, sort them from most likeable to least likeable and we'll record in that order. Do you have any of the instrumentals?"

"No, is that a problem? Ra'Chelle didn't mention that I needed any."

"Not a problem at all. I can pull them up easily." as I sat and sorted the songs from these female greats, both of our phones seemed to buzz in unison. We both stopped what we were doing and checked our messages. *Glad that you two made it together. Hope you like my ambiance and decorum. I'm sure as of right now half if not all of the*

Sinful Secrets   M'Hogany

candles in the booth are blown out, Cornell, and you two are brainstorming on which one of Symone's many songs are going to be sung. "How does she know all of this?" I thought. *Symone, stop worrying and just let go. Before I'm done, there's another song that I thought of but I know Symone didn't 'Spend My Life With You' By Erica Benet and Tamia. I'm sending you the track now Cornell. Oh, don't think I haven't heard you in your office boss-man This is a duet with your name all on it. Let's make music people! Tootles xx.* I couldn't help but just laugh at this heffa, hell we both did. "Well I guess we know what song is up first." he joked. Before he could search for the instrumental, his inbox buzzed with an incoming message. "My goodness that girl works fast." Ra'Chelle had already sent the instrumental to his inbox and along with it had the male lyrics attached. "This girl has thought of just about everything," he said as he extracted the track. "So what we'll do is listen to the track first and get a vibe of it then we'll lay it down. How does that sound?"

"Sounds great to me." We sat there for nearly 20 minutes listening to the track and forming our own versions to the song without changing the originals. I never heard Cornell sing before, then again, I haven't spent time with him so I'm' just hoping he doesn't sound like trash. If he did, I already had a few male vocalists in my head to replace his with. "Well Mr. Cornell, I do believe that the first verse is yours." I said. "That's right it is isn't it. Well Ms. Symone, would you mind managing the boards until I came out?"

"Um sure"

"Don't worry I'll show you quickly what to do. It's

very simple actually. Come sit." he waved over. I sat in his seat and he stood directly behind me. Why did he have to stand directly behind me lord. The cologne invaded my nostrils and once more, my pussy lips began to tremble. I don't know what it is with men's cologne and me. "Okay so this button here starts the tracks over from the beginning. I've already set the equalizer so there shouldn't be any major adjustments that you need to worry about. And this button here will start the track and record at the same time. You ok so far?"

"I think I have it down."

"Ok, now don't make any funny faces if I sound bad okay. I haven't sung since I was in high school so be nice"

"Stalling are we?" laughing "ok ok, I'm going." As he walked into the booth and placed the headphones on, he signaled to me that he was ready. I pressed the button he showed me would play the track and record at the same time. The song played and he began to sing, "I never knew such a day could come, and I never knew such a love could be inside of one...." I was indeed amazed at his vocal abilities. I sat back in the chair and listened to him lay Eric Benet's vocals. He had a smooth tone about him that wasn't too high or too deep but in that realm that would definitely cause you to have moist panties. Once he hit that first high falsetto, my heart dropped and bypassed my stomach and went straight to my already awakened vagina. *Now this is what I'm talking about!* I said in my mind as I grooved in the studio and zoned out. Once he finished his verse, he placed the headphones on the stand and came out of the booth. "Not bad Mr. Cornell, not bad at all. Didn't know you had that in you sir"

"I don't make it a habit to let people know about my **clears throat** skills per say"

"Well, you have a very nice voice." I complimented. "Well thank you Ms. Symone. Now I do believe it's your turn at bat."

." Oh well, ok." I got up and stepped inside the booth. The lingering smell of his cologne was all up in through this booth. *Concentrate Symone Concentrate.* I told myself. "Let me know when you're ready." he said on the intercom. I said a little prayer, took a deep breath, shook my arms (as if that would connect to my nerves), and gave him a thumbs up. He played back the track with his vocals. I had to zone out and not get caught up in his voice and miss my cue I bobbed my head and prepared for my part "........I never knew till looked in your eyes.....I wasn't complete till the day you walked into my life......."

****

Cornell

"...and baby I'll never find any words that could explain. Just how much my heart, my life, my soul you've changed..." Symone belted in the booth. Damn, she had vocals for days. Every time she hit that high pitch note, my dick throbbed. It was something different about her that I just couldn't put my finger on. Either way, I wanted her. I had to have her. I needed her. "...can I just see you every morning when I open my eyes..." *Yes, you can* I thought aloud. Luckily, no one else was there to question my rebuttal. She finished up the song and I waved her to come on out. "So how was that?" she asked.

"Beautiful as always. Just beautiful"

"Did you want me to mix it tonight?"

"If you can that would be great! It'll give me something to listen to and critique on my way home."

"Critique? What is there to critique?"

"I feel like I was flat in some areas and could've given stronger vocals. I sounded a bit winded as well."

I spun around in my chair and stared her gorgeous chocolate face down.

"What?" she asked.

"Are you serious? Were you just in there with yourself?"

"Of course I was in there with myself"

"You couldn't have been. I didn't hear anything pitchy or winded. If I didn't know any better, I would've thought Tamia was in there herself singing!"

I appreciate that, but I still could've done better"

"You are one tough artist I see." I spun back to the board and began to merge vocals play around with them on the board. "Symone, do you mind me calling you Symone?"

"Sure that's fine."

"This is going to be a while; would you like to order something to eat?" I asked.

"Sure, whatever you prefer I'm ok with."

Before I could get up to make a phone call, there was a knock on the studio's door. Looking at my watch with a baffled expression, I go to the door and open it to see no one standing there. Before I stepped out to get a better glance, "Cornell wait!" Symone yelled stopping me in my tracks.

"What's wrong?"

"You were about to step on that bag on the floor."

she said grabbing me my waist slowly pulling me back. The touch of her hands caused chills on my arms instantly. I turned facing her thick frame and found myself staring in those hazel eyes. "Cornell," she said quietly.

"Yes"

"Are you going to pick up the bag or leave it there?"

"Oh right." I said leaning over picking up the bag. As I bent over to pick up the bag, I noticed her well-manicured toes in her wedged heels. *Keeps her nails and feet done I see. Nice.* "You say something?" she asked. I just noticed that this was a to go bag from chipotle."

"This has Ra'Chelle written all over it if you ask me," she said with a light shake of the head.

"Well let's see how well she knows the both of us then." I said putting the bag on the table and taking out its contents. There were two salads one with brown rice and one without. One with black beans and one with pinto and they both had chicken as the meat. One with very little Pico de Gallo and sour cream. And the other with corn, mild sauce, lettuce and cheese. "Well I must say I am very impressed at Ms. Ra'Chelle." looking at the bowls "yes she knows me very well"

"And apparently she does me." I said. Symone sat at the table where the leather couch was and began to slowly eat her food. Even the way she eats made my dick swell. Her lips. Her tongue. My dick was doing flips! I was aching to feel her tongue intertwined with mine. "Something wrong?" she asked snapping me out of my trans. "hmmm, no no not at all. Just wondered if you needed any napkins." I covered up "yes please, and thank you." as I turned and went back to the board I patted my pants *down boy you gonna get us in trouble*. As I began to sync the vocals together and take out the dead air we started up a conversation "so Symone, tell me what's the significance of these song suggestions."

"What do you mean significance?"

"These aren't just random songs pulled off of the radio. You strike me as a lyrical vocalist. You become one with the words of the songs which better helps your performance."

"Well look at you sir. It might sound corny, but I view myself as a hopeless romantic."

"There's nothing corny about that"

"I love ballads and I know that I can transfer my feelings into one and connect with the audience."

"Nice. But that wasn't the answer I was looking for"

"Really, then maybe you should restate the question," she fired back *Sassy too, I like that.* "*Almost doesn't count, Officially Missing you, I need You Bad, Never Let You Go*, these titles give a brief summary of what you might have gone through. These aren't just *I like these songs* choices. I don't mean to pry, but I feel like we've known each other for quite a while. So I feel comfortable asking, what has happened?"

"What has happened? What do you mean?" she said "See that, there. The deflection. When I get personal or too close, you shift. You get antsy. You seem uncomfortable. The first few times we met, you weren't this way. What's going on?" I asked. Oh yes, I was a very attentive man. She sighed and put her half-eaten salad in the bag. She took a napkin, wiped her mouth, and took a drink of water that was on the counter. "Well, a few days ago something happened that I'm not sure actually happened but apparently it did"

I want to say ok, but I'm not sure I understand." I said. "Well last time Chelle and I left here, we went out to eat dinner. I am very cautious of my alcohol intake even if I'm not driving. We left the Olive Garden and headed to my house. I had been feeling sick since I left the restaurant, but shook it off as excitement mixed with nerves from actually being in the studio."

"Could it also have been something you ate?"

I thought that as well. I got home and prepared to go to bed." *Damn. I wish I would've been a fly on THAT wall* "mmmhmmm." I said now much more interested in the story. "I started feeling more and dizzier."

"Has that happened to you before?"

"Never. I'm a very cautious drinker and only had 2 small glasses of wine at the restaurant."

"That sounds odd, but please continue."

"I thought it was due to maybe the amount of clothing I had on, so I undressed to my underwear to at least get ready for a bath." *Shit if she continues with her description of getting undressed I'm gonna have a slow shower of my own in my pants.* "I became hotter even just in my underwear." *And the leak has begun* "then I hear a voice that tells me how beautiful I would look with my hair"

"A voice? Male or female? Was it Ra'Chelle? Your dad? Brother?" I asked now a little concerned "Well, if it were my brother I would be ok, but I have no brothers so that scratches that out. Chelle was long gone and my dad is an early bird so he's in the bed before 10 o'clock. But yes it was indeed a male's voice." just then a frown started to creep on my face "so what happened?"

"Well there's a guy that my mother is trying to basically marry me off to. Well long story short, it was him. Now mind you I didn't invite him to come over"

"So he just appeared in your house out of nowhere?"

"Apparently so. Well as startled and scared as I was I became very unstable I guess you could call it."

"Unstable? Now you have me worried."

"After that feeling it got very fuzzy. I came in and out just non coherent."

I don't think I'm liking where this story is going. No, I KNOW I don't like where this story is going. "Well what do you remember aside from this man being in your house?"

"I remember finding myself on the floor unable to move."

"Symone...are you...don't..." and without word, I threw the closed bottle of water against the wall. I didn't know what came over me, but I was completely enraged. "So you mean to tell me that this guy raped you?"

"Well, he and another."

My eyes got wide. "It was 2 of them? Do you know the other guy? Dammit!"

"I'm sorry if I upset you," she retracted

"No no, I'm sorry. It's not you. I just hate to see men, well males, take advantage of a woman. A GOOD woman at that. What can I do?"

"Nothing. I don't want anyone to do anything." I

never met a woman that thought the way she does. "I don't want the hassle of filing reports and doing tests to prove my allegations, then there's my family that I don't want to even begin to deal with," she continued.

"Symone, I am so so so sorry that you had to experience that. No person should ever have to experience that."

"Thank you, but there's nothing you have to apologize for."

"I feel I do"

"Well, again, thank you."

"So what does that have to do with your song selections?"

"Well, I actually started to feel this guy and give him the benefit of the doubt before all of that went down. So"

"Aaahhhh makes sense now." I said. Just then, the system had completed the mix and mastering of the song we recorded. "Well, if it's okay with you, I would love to see you again this week say Wednesday to put at least 2 or 3 of these songs down."

"Actually that would be great."

"Perfect. Well here's your copy and I think we can call this a night. Again Symone it was more than my pleasure." I said shaking her hand. "Here, I'll walk you out." I suggested.

****

Symone

I don't know what came over me to just open up to him like I did, but there was some form of comfort that he had over me. Or maybe it was just me needing to get it off my chest. Either way, if we were going to be working together, he had to know certain things about me. Cornell volunteered to walk me to my car like a gentleman. After he threw that bottle, I didn't know if he was capable of being such of one. I was kinda taken aback as to how emotional he got from me telling him what happened to me. As I grabbed my bowl and its remaining contents with my purse and headed outside to my car I felt somewhat secure and safe. "Thank you again for seeing me outside Cornell. You are indeed a gentleman. So Wednesday same time?" I asked.

"Yes ma'am. You come and bring that voice and I ensure you we'll have a hit on our hands in no time." he said with a smile.

As I placed my things in the car, he reached over and gave me a hug. Okay, nothing wrong with a hug. As we pulled back from our embrace, he locked eyes with me and slowly leaned in and gave me the most passionate kiss I'd ever had. My heart fluttered. My stomach tied in knots. My legs became weak. My mind was yelling STOP but my heart was telling me to proceed. Instinctively, my arms wrapped around his neck and he pulled me in closer as if we were determined to mesh as one. For a minute, I forgot where I was and lost myself in that moment. Once we parted lips, we both exhaled deeply. He kissed me on the forehead and made sure I got in my car safely. Before closing my door, he leaned in once more, grabbed my chin, tilted it upward, and placed a series of kisses on my lips before saying, "have a nice night Symone. Drive safely and I'll see you later"

"Okay." I said in a tone I've never heard before. As

I pulled off headed home, I was completely overwhelmed. I couldn't stop smiling actually. I arrived home a few minutes later and once I walked in and secured my house I ran a nice bath and turned the Bose system on to my assorted mixed slow jams. Just then, Omarion's "O." came on. I had *Calgon* nearby and before I could turn HIM on, an incoming call came on. "Hello?"

"Just checking to make sure you made it home safely"

"Cornell?"

"Yes Symone. I don't want to keep you any longer so get some rest," he said.

"Thank you, be careful going home yourself." I said. "Goodnight," he said "Goodnight." I returned. As the called ended, I reflected on what was just said "be careful going home." *Home* I thought. His wife. Dammit! I forgot about him being married. Now my stomach was doing those tricks once again. "What were you thinking Symone? You should've slapped the dog shit out of that man! How does something so wrong feel so right? Oh lord I'm going to hell!"

Chapter 31
Ray

"Good morning Mr. Watkins." the receptionist said. "Good morning Ashleigh. You're in such a great mood I see." I take it you haven't heard. Our little house guest won't be returning back! It's a great day all around!" she beamed. "That is a great thing indeed! So any word on when Dr. Johnson will be returning?" I asked as I took my messages. "She should be in her office as we speak. She beat ME here this morning." she looked surprised. "Oh really now, well thank you Ashleigh. See you later." I said as I headed down the hall. I noticed Symone's office door was closed so I went into my office quietly and placed my things down and prepared my office for my first session. After I took my jacket off, I went across the hall to give little Miss Symone Renae a piece of my mind! "Ray, hey. Long time no see," she said in such a perky voice. "Don't Ray me." I spat "what the hell happened"

"Ray what are you talking about and why are you so hostile?"

"Symone save it for somebody else. What the hell happened?" I demanded. "Honestly I don't know what you're talking about so either you explain what has you all hyped up or I suggest you go get prepared for your sessions for the day." she diverted. "So you want to play innocent I see. Okay let me see if this rings a bell. Michael."

"We went over this already Ray. Michael was my

contractor and if you haven't looked around, he did a marvelous job. So back off of it already." she said going through files on her desk"

"I figured you would say something like that. Look, I was all about eating crow and telling you how you were correct about Michael and his work ethics. He did indeed do a marvelous job on your office; I'm not ashamed to admit that."

"Thank you, now can we just drop the Michael topic, please. We both have a busy list of clients today and we need to be in the best mind frame possible," she said.

"Okay Symone, I'll give you that and I'll get off of the subject of Michael." I said with my hands in my pockets.

"Thank you..." she started.

"Now, Justin on the other hand..." and as soon as I mentioned his name she stopped in her tracks and looked away like a dear in headlights.

"Oh, did I strike something? Name sound familiar?" I said with a frown. Just then, she gets up and quickly walks to her door and shuts it.

"What do you know about Justin?" she said with a frown.

"The question isn't what do I know about him it's what DON'T I know and how I didn't get it from you?"

"What are you talking about?"

"Symone, why didn't you tell me you got it in with this negro? And to add insult to injury, you added another nigga?"

"What the hell are you indeed talking about? Have you lost your mind?" she damn near yelled.

"If you must know I overheard that nigga Michael bragging to someone about him getting a *piece*. And he added in a Justin too. So my question still stands, you had sex with not one but TWO niggas? What has come over you?" I was indeed upset but didn't seem to recognize the tears in her face. Before I could say anything else, Symone hauled off and slapped me damn near blind!

"What was that for?"

"Because after nearly 15 years of friendship you would even think that I would freely let 2 men run a train on me! Because that's EXACTLY what you are suggesting. If you must know." she started to speak through her teeth, "my sexual encounter with both of those 2 was not consensual!"

Feeling like an ass, I slowly wiped my face and went to her side to apologize. And as I approached her, she swatted and pointed with tears beginning to weld up in her eyes. I hated to be the cause of her hazel eyes drowning in heavy flows of water.

"No! NO! You don't get to apologize and make things right. NO! You don't get to console me! No! You don't get to do anything but leave. As my friend, you should KNOW what I don't do and don't allow! Here I am going through and you automatically assume..." and she frustratingly walked to her desk and just ignored my existence.

I went to her side "Symone, look. I'm sorry all I heard was that ass Michael talking to someone on the phone about how they did something to you and I just went in from there. I hadn't heard anything from you and this joke of a guy was still here. In my defense, I've been telling you to get this guy checked out thoroughly. He's making it seem as if he's accomplished a big task or as if he's conquered a big obstacle." looking up at me after fanning her eyes and making sure she was straight. "Is that your defense? You *told* me to have him investigated. Ray, if this is your *Good Friend* act I'm gonna need you to work a little bit harder on that," she scolded.

"Okay, I give you that. I'm new to this okay. Hell I know we both are." I sat on the edge of her desk. "Symone, we go back as far as being teenagers. I love you like the little brother I never had." I joked.

"And I you like the big sis I never wanted but got stuck with," she rebutted.

"So to see someone hurt you or do something harmful to you that you don't deserve is utterly disturbing to me. I'm sorry I reacted in a way that wasn't rather conducive to how I should have. From the depths of my heart, I truly apologize. If you need anything, you know where and how to reach me." I said really apologetic.

"Well I do need one thing," she said pulling her folder out of the draw opposite of where I sat.

"What's that?"

"I want you to clean off that ass print you're leaving on my desk."

"Oh shut up!"

"I'm just saying I don't want to be sitting with my clients and fighting paying attention to their issues and smelling ass to the point I can't function!"

"You know what, that's my cue to leave I see." I said chuckling as I headed towards my office with Symone in toe. As we reached her door "Hey, thanks for your concern. I appreciate your friendship I really do," she said with a sincere face. "You my girl, you know I'll always have your best interest at heart."

I know. Catch up with you later," she said before closing her door.

As I made it back to my office Ashleigh buzzed me. "Yes ma'am Ashleigh."

You have a Bailey Branson to see you for a session

"Thank you I'll come get her in just a moment." I concluded.

This was a first for me with Bailey, but hopefully we'll make good strides. "Bailey, nice to see you. No mom and dad?"

"No sir, um, Dr. Watkins can I talk to you. It's rather personal really and I don't know how to tell my parents," she confided in me.

"Sure sure, come on back." As I sat down in the office with Bailey I could see the fear in her posture. "Bailey, what's going on? Is school okay? Relationship with mom and dad ok?"

"Well everything is fine at school and Mommy, Daddy, and I are getting there. But something happened and I don't know how to talk to them about it."

"Well, whatever you wanted to talk about we'll work through.

****

Symone

After walking back to my desk after that little emotional tiff with Ray, I appreciated our friendship a little bit more. I never had anyone more upset than me about MY own well-being. As I sat at my desk preparing to go over my client's charts and progress, I heard my cell ringing. "Hello?"

"Hello Beautiful"

"Cornell." I said with a grin "How are you?"

"I'm a lot better now that I hear the voice of an angel." I'm not sure if I was blushing or not but I know I was smiling. "Um, thank you I think." I said. "I was headed to get breakfast on my way to work and you crossed my mind and I just had to hear your voice," he said. "Well, that's nice to hear. But I'm sure your wife feels the same way every morning as well"

"But I'm talking about you Symone"

"And I am flattered."

"I just want to get to know you a little better. Especially if we are going to be working closely"

"I understand. Cornell, if you don't mind, I have clients coming in so can we continue this conversation another time?"

"Sure we can. Have a good day Ms. Symone"

"You too Cornell." I said before disconnecting the call. *Dr. Johnson your 10 o'clock has arrived* my intercom buzzed. "Thank you Ashleigh, please send her on back." I replied before I got up to head to my door and greet my client...

Chapter 32
Cornell

"Well looks like someone has a great smile on his face!"

"You know what, today is a good day! And you my friend are a very cleaver person!"

"Why me? Oh and you're just figuring that out?"

"I don't even want to know how you got her to come to the studio, but I will say that it was magnificent! Her voice is like nothing I've ever heard! It makes you melt just listening to her sing. Now I'm gonna overlook the candles and roses, but you sealed it with the Chipotle salad bowls." I grinned.

"I don't know why y'all always second guessing me and my skills! I know you Boss-man and I know Symone like the back of my hand!" Ra'Chelle said flipping her hair.

"Ok, so since you know us so well, let me in on the gist of the candles."

"Well I know you work better in a relaxed environment and since when do candles not relax a person. Hell they have lit candles in massage parlors," she said applying her lip-gloss.

"Okay I can give you that"

"So how did it go?" she asked.

"A big part of me says to refrain from answering that because you already know how it went."

"And how would I know that sir?"

"The same way you would know when to have the food dropped off. It was still warm and sure as hell wasn't sitting there when we got to the studio."

"Well ok, maybe I'm psychic a little bit."

"Psychic my ass." I joked.

"Well Boss-man I have artists and their entourages to style so keep me updated. If there's anything I need to do, you know where to find me! Tootles!" she said with her signature hair toss.

As she left my office, I couldn't help but think about Symone. "Beauty, talent, and humility. Very hard to come by now days." I said as my desk phone began to ring. "Cornell Wallace, A&R Exec how may I help you? Oh yes, please, put him through. Mr. Davis, sir, yes I've given much thought to what you've offered. After much thought I've decided to accept your offer, however after I finish my tenure here. Yes sir, I understand and...well...I understand...well I'm sorry but these are my terms sir. No disrespect, but I can't back down from that request. If your office can't accommodate my request then I guess that's my denial to the offer.

****

"So you see Dr. Johnson, I'm the other way around. He the one who's more tired and I want it all the time," my client spoke.

"Well, how often do you climax when you two have intercourse?" I asked while taking notes.

"You know what; I don't think I really do to think about it." She said perplexed.

"So have you spoken with him about it?" I asked.

"Um no, not really."

"So how do you plan on fixing this?" I asked.

"Well that's the problem; I don't think I really want to fix it."

"Please explain."

"Dr. Johnson, I'm tired of being the man in this marriage. Our sex life is relatively boring. Same thing all the time. I have tried creams, oils, chains, whips, videos, outfits, role-playing, and our last go around I suggested another party."

Uh oh, never a good idea I thought to myself. "And how did that work out for you two?"

"You know what; it worked out greatly for me!"

"Okay, then what's the problem?"

"Basically, I don't want to be married to my husband anymore. The other party was more interesting than he was. So I just wanted to see if it was something that I needed help with, but I see what I need to do is rid myself of him in this marriage so that the both of us can truly be happy with someone deserving."

Finally a couple or someone in a relationship that has seen some sort of light. Granted it, it wasn't much time put in, but if they feel this is what is best for their relationship then so be it.

"Okay, well if you've come to the terms of that on your own, why me? Why come here?"

"Well, I just don't want to up and leave and not say anything. I think he deserves to know everything. I have to at least give him that. Also, I wanted to know if you would do the couples counseling for me and my new love."

"Wow, well um sure. As far as your husband, I think you're on the right track with him. Question is are you prepared for his reaction to what you have to say to him?" I asked her.

"I think I am. I've taken everything you've said in our sessions and I've applied them and I've realized that I have been the selfish one in this marriage and I've been holding him back from being utterly happy. I don't want to do that with my new relationship. I want to have a clean slate. I want happiness all around. But is it possible to tell him here? I mean can we have our last session here and we all come clean?"

Don't do it Symone! Don't Do IT! The little voice in my head screamed. "Sure, whatever you two want to do." I said *Stupid just stupid* the voice responded. "Once you head out, let Ashleigh know about your last session and she'll schedule you."

"Thank you Dr. Johnson for everything."

"Oh don't thank me just yet." I laughed. "We'll see you next time." I said as she left my office.

I walked back to my desk and heard my cell going off once more. I took it out of my purse and saw yet another text message from Cornell. This has to be the 12th message he's sent me *Just checking in on you and hope you have a great day*

How much hope does this man have? Just about every text is like that. Right then another text came in from guess who?

Cornell: Can you meet me at the studio after work? If I say no, he'll probably keep asking so let me just go and maybe we can get some other songs on wax.

Sure, I'll head that way once I leave here I responded.

Three more hours with another bickering couple that doesn't listen to each other at all but wants to point the finger at each other later, I was completed and drained for the day.

"How was your first day back Dr. Johnson?"

"Oh Ashleigh it felt like I never left. I guess it's better they come here than at my house then huh." I joked.

"Oh yes ma'am. Tomorrow you have just as hectic a schedule as today. I'll forward the charts over to your email so you can prepare for them tomorrow. Also I have your confirmation from the relationship convention in ATL for next Monday I'll also forward you that itinerary."

"Oh goodness, I forgot about that!"

"I figured you did but I went ahead and sent out an update to all of your clients that you'll be gone on a 3 month tour and have updated them on your trusted referral therapists. I also sent them updates that you will still have access to their files and how they can reach you if it's a dire need."

"Ashleigh you are indeed a gem. I wish you could go on the road with me." I said pouting

"Oh no ma'am. I've seen the crazies you encounter daily and I must say I will indeed pass on that. But have fun though!" she smiled and waved as I left the office.

I got in my car and started to drive off. As I hit the first light, my phone rang. On the wireless blue-tooth, I noticed the number was Cornell's.

"Hello?"

"There's that voice."

"Hello Cornell."

"I can't wait to see you today Symone."

Just from that statement alone, I got knots in my stomach. Good and bad. "Is there something I'm missing?" I asked.

"You'll see when you get here," he said with what sounded like a smile.

"Um, ok I guess."

"Believe me you'll love it, I'm sure of it." he said.

"Pretty confident I see."

"Always," he responded.

"Well, I just turned down the street of the studio so I guess I will see you momentarily." I said.

"Okay," he said and we disconnected.

I got out of my car and headed up to the studio. The building seemed to be empty today, which was rather odd. "Cornell, hi. Um I have a question."

"Sure what is it?"

"Is it always empty on a daily?"

"Yes and no. Most of our artists here mainly come on the weekends and during late hours."

"Oh ok. Well what was so important that you had to see me today?" I asked.

"Well I would like to see you every day, but I'm sure we'll get there."

"Confident I see."

"I wanted you to hear this track and get your opinion. Please have a seat. Get comfortable," he said as I went to sit on the plush leather couch. He went and grabbed the remote control for the system and came and took a seat next to me on the couch. "The sound is much better from this side," he said and pressed play.

As the track played, he bobbed his head to the

instrumental and as soon as I heard the 808 bass race through my chest, I closed my eyes and began to feel the beat travel through my body. As I became one with the instrumental I failed to recognize that, I'd gotten very comfortable on the couch with my head on the pillow and feet in the cushions with my 5-inch heels on the floor in front of the couch. Once the bridge hit, I started humming unconsciously.

After the song wrapped up, I noticed Cornell smiling catty corner my position. "What?"

"I take it you enjoyed that."

"How could you tell?" I asked.

"Well for one, you were humming after the second chorus space. And two, you got super comfortable."

"Oh I'm sorry. But I really like this instrumental."

"Well, I'm glad you enjoyed it because it's actually a song I've been working on for you."

"Are you serious? Cornell please don't play with my emotions right now. I've had a long day of work and I don't have the mental strength to be disappointed."

"I'm very serious when it comes to music. I told Ra'Chelle that I would support you and your voice no matter what and I mean that." Sitting closer to me, he began to play in my hair as he spoke. "I've never and I mean never heard anyone with such as voice like yours, and most of the ones that are as talented as you are the most arrogant. You are different. You rarely use the gift you've been blessed with, and sometimes down talk your talents. You are so hard on yourself. I wanted to do something for you and I know and believe you will kill this song."

"Well I thank you completely." I said slowly

moving his hand from my hair. "It's getting late and I have to get home. I have files I have to prepare and chart for tomorrow and I have other files I have to prep before I leave for my convention." I said as I put my shoes back on.

"Convention?" he asked as he helped me put my shoes on. Well he actually wasn't putting my shoes on. Once I said my convention, he took my feet and began to massage them. I'm ticklish on my feet and it took everything in me not to gut check him or laugh extremely hard. "What's with the convention?" he asked.

"well as a counselor I am a part of this panel of relationship therapists that hold a convention in Atlanta every year."

"And what is topic or main message?"

"what we do is give a listening ear to couples that relatively couldn't afford to sit in a therapists office as well as give them various opinions on how to deal with their spouses per say. My take on everything is deal with self first before you can deal with a counterpart." I said trying to ignore the foot-massage that was getting a little too good for me to take.

"Well, I guess I should invest in that session huh."

Then I remembered the band he wore and the woman he must go home to and felt just as bad once more. I removed my feet from his lap and heavenly hands and once more attempted to place them in my shoes. Succeeding to do so, I grabbed my belongings again and stood up.

"I really do have to be going, and I'm sure the lady of your house is wondering where you are as well. I appreciate the thought of me for the track and it is indeed beautiful." I said as I made my way towards the studios doors.

"As I said Symone, it's yours," he said before I turned around to say thank you again.

As I placed my hand on the door to open it, his hand covered mine and that shock of electricity ran from my head to my stomach. I looked back at him innocently and the next thing I knew my back was pressed up against the studios wall.

"Symone, I've never met anyone that does to me what you do," he said inches away from my lips. "I've wanted to kiss you from day one," he continued.

"You already did remember," I said in a daze.

I didn't recognize that I'd dropped my purse. Hell I don't remember where it was to begin with. Standing there, inches apart from each other's lips, we stood marveling in the chemistry that was overbearing.

"I can't Cornell." I tried to fight.

"You can't what?" he said not backing away intensifying the chemistry.

"This is wrong. You're married. I just can't." I again tried to fight.

"Can you really fight chemistry?" he asked as he whispered in my neck.

"I...I...I...I...I just can't." I kept trying to fight.

"You sure?" he asked before he placed light kisses on my neck. I fearfully felt my knees begin to buckle under me, but I dared to give in.

"Cornell...I..." and before I could finish resisting his charm, his lips were wrapped around mine. I felt every fluid in me rush south and begin to saturate my already none existing lace underwear.

As if instinctively, my hands traced his biceps and noticed the tone that accompanied the muscularly chiseled chest. He knew just the right amount of pressure to apply and the more I tried to resist, the more he inched against my frame. As I tasted his succulent cloud nine lips, I heard a multitude of things. I heard music playing and seemed as if I felt fireworks going off. I would've thought I was going crazy, but I couldn't think of anything at that moment but his lips and mine.

He then lifted me up from my post on the wall and carried me to the couch where we were once placed in deep conversation and laid me down not once breaking from kissing. He ran his fingers through my hair and kissed every inch of my chest and neck before he returned to my lips. He savored my lips as if they were his life support system. He cupped my right breast with his left hand and began kissing on my spot once more. I felt the juices from my candy slowly seep out. Thank goodness, I was wearing a dark skirt. He spread my legs apart and laid himself atop of me again managing his weight not to crush my frame. He returned to my lips and began devouring them.

He paused and asked me, "Can I?" and I shook my head no. As if I hadn't turned him down, he goes back to devouring my lips. He sits up, looks at me for a moment, and then goes back to placing kisses on my neck. As he is caressing me and I must say it feels great, I get a glimpse of his band. A sudden shot of hellish guilt shot over me and I instantly push up from him.

"What's the matter? Are you okay?" he asked.

"Um, not really. I have to go." I said trying to put

Sinful Secrets   M'Hogany

my shoes back on once more. I have got to invest in simpler shoe attire. I scanned around looking for my purse and saw it on the floor by the door. I stood up and briskly walked to go retrieve it, unaware that Cornell was right on my heels. As I bent over to pick up my purse and came back, I was staring smack dab at Cornell and his dreamy bedroom eyes.

    "Are you okay?" he asked once more.

    "I'm fine. I just have to go." was all I could say.

    "I understand," he said as he finger combed my hair back.

    As I was looking for my keys, he leans back in and kisses me once more. Damn his lips are lethal and addictive.

    This time as if not to waste any more time he placed my purse on the table and locked the door in one smooth motion. He picked me up once more and carried me over to the couch again without breaking that kiss. He pushed my skirt up with his legs and found my soaked spot. "Someone's wet," he said as he placed his finger in between both of our wet lips. He removes his finger, continues massaging his tongue with mine, and uses that dampened finger to massage my already swollen clit. I gasp and his kisses become more intense.

    He slid my lace underwear to the side as he massaged my clit in a circular motion. Feeling the hot substance seep out of my opening, he inserted his finger and I shuddered in delight. My head leans back in pleasure as he attacks my spot. He then whispers with his finger still inserted and his eyes locked on mine.

    "Can I trust you?" he asked.

And without second thought, I responded, "yes."

He goes back to devouring my mouth once more that I feared I would need CPR after this! Somehow, along the way my jacket was removed as well as his shirt exposing his muscles and various tattoos.

With his dry hand, he smoothly popped my buttons on my blouse exposing my 36 DD's. As if instinctively, he began to lick my breasts while they were still held hostage in their supported confinement. He slowly pulled them out one by one and gave each one its fair share of tongue-lashing.

In between each breast, he made his way back up to kiss me deeply and passionately. After the second kiss, he winks at me and dives down between my legs. Oh my goodness I knew that tongue was good but my lord he was GIFTED! He slowly made little circles around my clit. Then he played with it to see me squirm. He flicked his tongue back and forth rapidly. Then he ran his tongue from the top of my clit to the opening of my honey hole. Then he inserted his tongue in an in and out motion. Now I've seen this before in porno's a just thought those women were acting, but there was no acting going on here! The more he inserted his tongue the more turned on I got and wet I became.

He slowly went back up to my clit and latched on like a baby to a bottle until I came. Mid orgasm, he inserted that finger once more and just went for the gusto. Unaware of what was to come, I felt myself get wet and hot a lot more.

"That's right baby, squirt for me." I heard him say while fingering me.

Squirt? I'm a squirter? What is this man doing to me? ran through my head, but not for long because another wave came over my body and I felt the need to push again.

"That's a good girl. Let it go," he said removing his finger.

He reappeared and started kissing me once more. Now I wouldn't normally kiss a guy after he's devoured my lady parts, but something was different about him. I rubbed and caressed his face clueless to what was coming next. He brought his finger in between us again and this time we kissed and licked around my juices that saturated his finger. As this was happening, he slowly inserted his dick into my hot cavity. We both shuddered in pleasure.

"Damn you feel so good baby," he said in my ear.

He slowly began to stroke my pussy as our kisses became more passionate and full of life. He then buried his face into my neck and wrapped my legs around his back. His strides began to pick up rhythmic speed. He returned to kissing me and I kissed him as deep as I could. Then he sat up while in mid stroke to admire my body and caress my breasts. When he did, he noticed me grab the side of my face. With a smirk, he noticed that holding my face was a sign that I was indeed coming. He looked down to see that with every pump followed a spray of clear hot liquid.

"Don't stop wetting me up now baby. Give it all to me," he said digging deeper.

In fear of losing his load quickly, he turned me over and I instinctively assumed the position. Y'all know it, face down ass up...

"Ahhhhhhh," he moaned when he re-inserted himself.

He tried to slow stroke as much as possible without either one of us losing it. With every slow stroke, a small squirt followed. So his strokes picked up and as they picked up so did the water works.

"That's it," he said enjoying the view.

After what seemed like forever he flipped me back over and pressed his body on mine and kissed me softly and passionately all while inserting himself once more. He picked up speed slowly and deeply. "Cum for me baby. Give me that one. I want that one right there. That's it. That's it. Good girl," he said in my neck.

I tried my best not to claw his back up as he made me cum over and over and over. He sat up then and didn't stop his strokes. I want you to watch me," he said as he started going deeper and deeper I felt myself cum again but this time it was much bigger. I felt him swell more than he already had.

"Look at me, look at me," he demanded before his eyes rolled back in his head as we both came together hard............

3 Months Later

"Dr. Johnson, so great to have you back. How was the convention?" Ashleigh asked as I picked up my notes from the front desk.

"It was interesting." was all I could say.

"Interesting?" she asked.

"Ashleigh, trust me when I say, interesting. Be glad you live in Dallas." I said smiling as I headed to my office laughing. "See you later."

"Alright," she said.

Once I got back to my office and opened the door, I

saw a bouquet of white roses on my desk. I put my briefcase and purse down and looked for the card while I smelled the fragrance of the arrangements.

"Hmmm, no card." I said.

"Well look who's returned and seems like you have an admirer as well. Hope you didn't go to ATL and meet nobody." Chelle said coming in looking at the arrangements on the table. "Oh hunny these are gorgeous. You holding out on me?" she asked with a side grin.

"No ma'am you know these are my favorite flowers. Besides, you know I buy myself roses all the time. I don't need a man to do that for me when I can do that for myself."

"Yes we know this Symone. I see R2D2 isn't at work today. Did he go ahead and croak?" she asked.

"If you must know, Ray was summoned to be in court today."

"Damn, well he's still breathing so I'll have to go with plan B. They putting him in jail for his face? I told him to look like that is against the law."

"No funny girl actually he's a witness to one of his clients. His child client came to him a few months ago and told him she didn't know how to tell her parents she was being raped."

"What? That's sick!"

"Yeah, bad thing is she didn't know how to tell her parents because she was being raped by her uncle."

"Oh see that's sick as hell. How did they find out? He said something?"

"Well yes and no. He didn't say anything until she told him she didn't know why she missed her period. She thought it was because GOD was punishing her for something she did." I said.

"That poor little girl. Well hunny I came to gather the details on the ATL. What were the men like? Clothes...Wait, scratch that. I've seen how you dress. Never-mind," she said leaning smelling my roses.

"You know what; just cause I don't dress with my ass out doesn't mean I don't know how." I defended with my hands on my hip.

"Oh please Symone; you are queen of pants suits. You don't mix much of color with a damn thing," she said.

"Hey, I have to have things that compliment this chocolate skin. I can't wear every color. You remember that time I work canary yellow in high school. I thought I was cute!" I said.

"And looked like a damn bumble bee." she laughed.

"Exactly! Not happening anymore! But the fashion scene there is questionable. But other than that, chile they are more of a mess than we are here."

"Shut up!"

"Girl yes. At the conference, this gay couple of guys got into an argument over who called the other fat and when someone else was siding with one of the men they both ganged up on the guy. I mean it was just crazy. Then there were more people there that just wanted to complain and get an attitude with you when you don't agree with them. I'm like boo boo you came to me and YOU'RE the one that needs the help not me." I said.

"Uh oh look at you. Gone for 3 months and coming back speaking street lingo and bourgeois talk. Aw her-ca-leez her-ca-leez," she said mocking the Nutty Professor and clapping.

"You know what, shut it." I said.

"Well dahlin I just wanted to stop over and check on you before I drop by the boo's place."

"And when am I gonna meet this *BOO* that you keep so hidden?"

"The same time you introduce me to the mystery man who dropped these roses in your lap," she snapped before pulling out her shades.

"I told you I bought these for myself ma'am. You saw there wasn't a card." I defended.

"Hunny please, save that for Spock across the hall, I know better! Tootles!" she said flipping her hair and strutting out.

I can't say where these came from. Hell I'm still a bit floored where they came from myself. But I had an idea. Just then, my phone buzzed. "Hello?"

"Good morning beautiful how are you?"

"I'm fine." I said with a smile as I sat down in my chair.

"Did you make it in safely?" the voice asked.

"Yes I did." I said.

"Did you see your gift?" the voice asked again.

"Yes I did. They're beautiful." I said as I marveled at the roses on my desk.

"I'm glad. I can tell they made your morning."

"How so?" I asked.

"You're smiling aren't you?"

"I am." I said twirling in my chair like a schoolgirl.

"*Dr. Johnson you have a visitor to see you,*" the intercom interrupted.

"Hey, I have to go I have a client coming in." I said before I responded to Ashleigh. "Okay Ashleigh you can send them on back."

I got up and headed to my office door but stopped to fix my hair by the mirror on the way to the door. As I opened the door, there stood Cornell shocking me. "What are you doing here?" I asked.

"I told you I had to see that smile on your face," he said as he kissed me passionately with the phone still pressed to my face.

Once we broke the kiss, I stepped out in the hall and looked both ways to ensure no one saw him come in, with the phone still stuck to my face. I looked at myself like *what the hell* and closed the phone and door.

As soon as I turned around Cornell pressed me up against the door with a passionate kiss. "Hi," he said breaking the kiss.

"Hi." I responded winded.

"I missed you," he said.

"I missed you too." I said in return.

Feeling myself get hot all over again, I moved past him and headed to my desk where the flowers were and got a good whiff of them and played around in the vase. I took the rose food package, opened it, sprinkled it in the water, stirred it around with my letter opener, and replaced the roses back. "These are just beautiful," I said.

"They should be. They're your favorite flowers aren't they," he said.

"They are, I'm surprised you remembered," I said.

"I remember everything about you Symone," he said coming closer to me.

"Really?" I asked picking up the vase and putting it on one of the end tables where my glass globe used to be.

"Yes really. Like how you like how I kiss you long and deeply. And how I kiss that spot on the side of your neck under your jawline." he said behind me moving my hair out of the way exposing my neck that he apparently missed.

"Not here Cornell I'm at work." I begged before he spun me around and sat me on my desk.

"You know what I really missed?" he asked before kissing me again.

"What?" I asked.

"That little thing I do to your clit that makes you squirm," he said with a smile.

"No! I know that look! I'm at work."

But again, before I could say more, his hands were already playing around in my wet oasis. No matter how I turned him down, he seemed to know what I really wanted, and it was what he really wanted as well. And I wound up giving in, despite right and wrong.

****

"Welcome to...." Before Ashleigh could complete her greeting, two bullets pierced her chest...

A full figured woman bearing a khaki trench coat sauntered past the front desk where the receptionist lay clinging to life. Her 4 inch black Christian Louboutin heels pierced the carpeted hallway silently bringing her one step closer to her next victim.

"Oh god," I mumbled.

Cornell caressed my chocolate thighs while he buried his tongue deep into my honey hole beckoning the release of my sugar walls. "Cum in my mouth baby," he summoned.

"Oh god oh god," I moaned.

"Let it go," he stated in between licks. Without missing a beat, Cornell inserts both index and middle finger while not letting go of her my. Moving both fingers in and out in rhythmic motion while not letting go of my clit.

"Oh god yes! I'm cumming I'm cumming." I sprayed a load of juices onto Cornell's face that trickled down to his chest.

"Good girl. Wet Daddy up." before I could release once more, he stood up and inserted his throbbing dick into my saturated pussy. He leans in while slowly stroking my sweet spot, he plants kisses on my swollen belly. "I'm not hurting you am I," he softly asked.

"No," I panted.

"You sure?" he asked again.

"Yes," I moaned.

He then buried his face into my neck. "You feel so good baby. You know I missed this so much," he moans while spreading my ass cheeks apart digging deeper into my wetness. As we get loss in our early morning lovemaking, we are fully unaware of the danger lurking less than 20 feet away...